ABSURD PERSONAS

ABSURD PETUNIAS

AMANDA TAYLOR

© Amanda Taylor, 2021

Published by West End Publications

WEST END
PUBLICATIONS

A CIP catalogue record for this book is available from the British Library.

ISBN 978-0-9955777-7-0 (Paperback)

Book layout and cover design by Clare Brayshaw

Cover image © Juan Moyano | dreamstime.com

Prepared and printed by:

York Publishing Services Ltd
64 Hallfield Road
Layerthorpe
York YO31 7ZQ

Tel: 01904 431213

Website: www.yps-publishing.co.uk

For Robin

'Do you still think the world is vast? That if there is a conflagration in one place it does not have a bearing on another, and that you can sit it out in peace on your veranda admiring your absurd petunias?'

Anna Politkovskaya 1958-2006

CHAPTER ONE

It was 11.45 and a fine spring morning on the small Greek island of Paxos. All the tourists had disappeared after enjoying their obligatory English breakfasts at various tavernas dotted along Loggos' harbour front. One figure remained seated at a table on the crazy paving terrace of a bar close to the village bakery. He appeared to be so near the sea, he could have been floating on it. The darting silver fish in the clear water below were mesmerising. The man wondered if he would draw too much attention to himself if he sat on the wall—took off his brogues, his socks—and paddled his tired feet for a tickling pedicure. Why not? There was no one left to witness such an act of frivolity, only the waiter who kept popping in and out of the building behind on the off chance that further trade might come his way.

The waiter noticed that his sole customer looked as if he was from another era. Despite this being a relaxing holiday destination, the man wore a tie and classic straw trilby. His hat was the only concession to the holiday spirit. He took off his large tortoiseshell spectacles to wipe them clean with a folded handkerchief. Even the way he lifted his coffee cup and sipped was meticulous. The waiter was curious. He could not help thinking there was something familiar about this guy. However hard he pummelled his memory, he could not place him.

'Another Americano, sir?' he asked.

'Ochi efcharistó,' replied the man, shaking his head. His Greek pronunciation was excellent.

'You are English?' tested the waiter.

'Yes,' replied the man abruptly.

What else could he be dressed like that? He was certainly not dressed for the beach. But the waiter, who had a good grasp of English, detected a slight accent, a directness that he could not quite place and a rolling of the 'r's—East European perhaps? Russian even? Neighbouring Corfu was full of Russian tourists. Except this man was suited up more for business than tourism. Maybe his trilling of the 'r's was an English affectation or simply a speech impediment.

'Are you sure you won't have another drink to go with your croissant?' The waiter indicated the man's untouched pastry.

'I am sure.'

'Here for work?' enquired the waiter.

'Yes, something like that,' replied the man dismissively.

The waiter busied himself with wiping down nearby surfaces, half an eye still on his incongruous customer who obviously wanted to be left alone, did not want to engage, did not want him around.

The man took off his straw trilby, revealing thin tufts of grey hair, before carefully placing the hat on the table before him. He looked much older without it. Removing his spectacles again, he began to rub his eyes. Slavic, the waiter could clearly see his facial features were definitely not English now but possibly Slavic. Although the man did not actually smile—indeed did not show any emotion—he appeared to be enjoying himself with the sun on his face in this archetypal Mediterranean port sleeping its way to midday.

The enigmatic customer turned his attention to a young Greek boy, a little way along from the bar, menacing a landed sea cucumber vulnerable on the quay. No doubt the truant with a stick wanted to provoke the cucumber into squirting water or even expelling its own stringy guts through its anus. A manoeuver guaranteed to discourage all predators.

'*Ach*!' screamed the boy, jumping back in delight as the creature spouted water.

The man hoped the boy did not take it that step further. He knew that the act of evisceration was not deadly for this marine animal as the gut regenerated in days. But he had taken a strong dislike to the boy—wished to see him thwarted—children could be immensely cruel.

'My brother's boy.' The waiter nodded proudly to the dumpy boy with cherubic features. Tight dark curls bounced in the breeze round his face as he continued to menace the giant slug.

Just as his customer was contemplating the advantages of being able to disgorge one's guts into the face of an enemy, the waiter started feeding half a loaf of bread to the darting fish. A pleasing act. He looked to see if the man was impressed. The man showed no reaction. Stone-faced he checked his watch instead.

There was an abandoned soap factory at the far end of the harbour. Although it was proving to be useful, the customer was sad to see such a fine building roofless and neglected. Bizarrely, the regal statue of Aphrodite—surveying the scene above an arched doorway—remained intact and in place. It would not have been so long ago that the island farmers from miles around would have brought their olives here for processing. Now the industry was centralised and the really big profits benefiting but a few.

Centralisation, he hated that word. It was the same the world over. His own grandfather and father had been wheat farmers back home. Although their farm had been stolen by the state rather than capitalists, nonetheless, the result was identical: neither grain nor profits reached those producing it. Along with their village neighbours, his grandparents had been brought to the brink of starvation in the early 1930s.

'My uncle's bar,' explained the waiter, eager to elevate his standing.

'Really,' said the man disinterested.

'Pardon, kunnen we bestellen.' The waiter was called away to a young Dutch couple who had chosen to sit inside.

The man's shoulders slumped back with relief into the canvas seat.

A minute or two later, he sat forward, peering into the distance. A small boat appeared on the empty horizon—a punctuation mark where the line of sea merged with sky. Approaching at high speed, on a wave of foam, the boat quickly got bigger. Entering the harbour it finally slowed. It was a super yacht, the *Bettina*.

Staring out of the bar the waiter was intrigued to see it too. Luxury yachts usually chose to anchor in the main port of Gaios. It was unusual for them to visit Loggos but not unknown.

If the waiter was intrigued, his customer outside was fixated by the yacht. A young crewman manned the wheel reversing back to drop anchor. He moved about the side deck professionally unwinding ropes, all action. Beneath his white epauletted shirt his muscles whipped the ropes, ropes themselves, this way and that. Without bothering to deploy the gangplank, a young agile female—again in an all white uniform—jumped off the boat. Despite her short tight skirt, she made a perfect landing on the quayside about thirty metres from where the man sat. The crewman flung her the mooring rope like a lasso.

A light fibreglass gangplank was lowered to allow her back on board and retracted almost immediately.

The watchful customer thought this was a lot to do for two young people but they did it competently, effortlessly, unfazed. It was only a matter of minutes before the swarthy boat owner and his tall blonde companion emerged from below decks in their dressing gowns for breakfast. The lithe young woman now fell into the role of cook and waitress, serving a breakfast she must have previously prepared. The couple completely ignored her. She was merely their hired hand.

Regrettably, an extremely pretty one, noted the man.

He already hated the boat owner. He now regarded the owner's mistress, secretary or whatever else she called herself, with equal distaste. What ignorance to fail to acknowledge the existence of another human being, let alone the provider of food.

It was obvious that they did not intend to disembark. No gangplank, no spreading their wealth in the village bars or shops. No gangplank, no invasion of privacy.

The boy continued playing with the sea cucumber with scant acknowledgement of the luxury vessel pulled alongside.

The man again examined his watch before picking up his iPhone. The waiter could see from inside the bar that he was having a short conversation with someone, could not have been much more than a word or two.

With the waiter distracted by serving the Dutch couple's order, the man took up his bill from the miniature glass tumbler and meticulously counted out the correct change and €1 tip. Lifting up his hat, he dusted it down on his trouser leg.

When the waiter next stepped outside his idiosyncratic customer had gone—his coffee drunk, his croissant left uneaten.

In an instant, the waiter's world—his previous uneventful life—changed. A pulverising sucking sensation hit him. The noise was so great it supressed sound. He covered his ears with his hands and fell in a foetal position under the flimsy vacated table. Glass shattered about him. Peering from his ridiculous, inadequate makeshift shelter, he saw the sea and the harbour front were obliterated from view by water spray and clouds of dust.

Blinking, he stretched his neck backwards trying to focus properly. His neck hurt, his eyes stung, he was deafened.

The Dutch couple—who had preferred to drink inside and protect their fair skins from the harsh sunlight—emerged from the cafe dazed and disorientated. Covered from head to foot in masonry powder, they looked down on him like two zombies. It was as if someone had tipped a bag of flour over them.

The waiter crawled on all fours towards the harbour where his nephew had been playing with the sea cucumber. He only made a yard or two before collapsing. Several minutes passed before the cries and screams for help started.

CHAPTER TWO

Times were lean. The newsroom which had once clattered with typewriters was poorly mimicked by the occasion *click* from a modern day mouse. Flickering screens had replaced strident voices, voices that now whispered confidential messages into individual mobiles. WhatsApp, Skype, FaceTime rules OK. This was more a National Union of Journalists' chapel of deference than dispute. The reporters considered themselves lucky to have a job in an era where papers were struggling to survive.

Like an image from some benevolent fairy, something flashed up from Reuters on the News Editor's computer. Duncan Nelson marched out of his office, an office he hardly ever left unless there was a fire alarm. He sort verification on the big television screen outside his door. He was not alone. A dozen journalists had gathered round. The *London Evening Record* had almost come to a standstill.

Sky was showing video footage of a traditional Greek harbour front, a super yacht speeding in from afar, docking, followed by a terrible explosion and its aftermath. Devastation. The edited footage was being broadcast over and over again. No one moved, transfixed, hypnotised by the repetitive recording. It was 9/11 all over again.

'Jordan, you speak Greek don't you?' Nelson asked a young man with wild hair the colour of bracken.

'I took classical Greek at Oxford, if that's what you mean, Chief.'

'That'll do. Your passport up to date?' Nelson did not wait for an answer. 'Fancy a trip to Greece? You can take Celia Grey with you. Make the perfect holiday couple. I'll have to clear it with Gatsby first of course. Every penny has to be considered nowadays.'

'They can go. This is big. A London based Russian oligarch blown to smithereens on his luxury yacht while docking on a small Ionian Island. Following a phone call from the field, I understand British nationals might be among the dead.' Nelson had not seen the Editor, Gatsby, slipping in behind him.

'Hear that?' A flushed Nelson asked Jordan. 'You can go.'

Old Etonian Erik Jordan was not sure about having Celia Grey foisted on him as a travelling companion. Erik came from a family of girls, sisters and a glamorous mum. He would not have described himself as spoilt but he was. For Erik—renowned for his brief fun flings, fun until the end—Celia Grey might have come from another planet. Intense, socially awkward yet serious about her work, a trouser-suited working-class girl from Oldham or somewhere like that out in the sticks. A frump who would not allow room for anything other than work. Certainly not frivolous bar life flirtations. Still, Erik comforted himself with the thought that he was the senior reporter here and would lead the way. She could follow or go home.

* * * * *

Oh God, there she was struggling up the escalator into the departure lounge. Weighed down with bag and body, barely fitting between the shiny steel static walls, she tumbled onto safe ground from the final moving step. Erik, more used to Naomi Campbell than Bridget Jones, cringed.

'I hate airports. I hate Gatwick most of all,' she puffed.

'You're late,' he told her. 'See, our flight has already been called.'

'This is all so last minute,' she grumbled, adjusting her dark rimmed glasses as she examined the airport's departure board.

Without another word spoken between them, they made their way to the gate for the TUI flight to Corfu. As they stood in line, he looked at her ridiculously large, wheeled carry-on bag in disgust.

'That will take up most of the cabin locker space,' he told her, adjusting the shoulder strap of his business satchel in exasperation.

'It's been measured and weighed. I've had to pay a bit extra,' she giggled, as if this was all a terrific girl guide adventure, before glancing doubtfully down at the canvas rucksack by his foot. 'Something you had at school?' she retorted equally scathingly. 'I hope you've got enough room for clean underwear in there.'

'I wash mine as I go along,' he replied sulkily. 'And, for your information, I have managed a laundered suit and tie in there.'

He had been lucky enough to book a cancelled window seat. Her aisle seat was several rows in front. A relief for Erik, he would not be forced to talk to her. Being early he had had time to pick up a copy of *Teach Yourself Greek* at the airport bookshop. A little revision would suit him far better than having to make inane small talk with Celia.

He could just see her Ariana Grande ponytail bouncing above the headrest as she prattled to a neighbouring passenger. Were all Lancashire lasses impossible like her, he wondered.

He revelled in his window seat, which he had been impolite enough not to offer to Celia. Well, it was every man for himself on this trip. Putting down his book on the tray table, he marvelled at the still snow covered Alps. They must be well on their way. He had refused all food and drink as he wanted to land sharp-witted and hungry. Anyway, aeroplane sandwiches left a lot to be desired for a food connoisseur.

The Scottish pilot introduced himself as Niall Macpherson and his co-pilot some Asian name or other. The sound projection was abysmal. Erik did manage to discern the main man explaining that his subordinate was still under instruction and new to the route.

'That's reassuring,' sniffed the suit next to him, vacating his twin seat for a toilet break.

'I thought you told Nelson you could speak Greek.' Celia's bosom was suddenly hanging over him as she pointed down to his Greek self-help book.

'No, I told him I studied classical Greek at University,' he snapped at the interruption. Celia looked disappointed. 'However I do speak a little everyday Greek, just need to brush up on it.'

'Oh, I see.' She followed his neighbour to the toilet at the back of the plane.

'Nice looking girl that,' said the suit with a silly grin on his face, after squeezing intimately past her in the aisle. 'Pleasant looking.'

'Do you really think so?' retorted Erik. 'She's a colleague.'

In no time at all they were circling what he took to be Corfu Island. Murmurs round him confirmed it. Reluctantly he abandoned his book to the net bag on the seat in front. The island lay off Greece's northwest coast—a jewel in the Ionian Sea—defined by rugged mountains and a resort-studded shoreline. He could see small fishing boats bobbing below and even smaller white waves. From experience he realised this meant the sea was quite rough for the time of year. As they circled lower and lower he could pick out a few colourful umbrellas on the beaches. Perhaps on Paxos they might find time for a little sun worshipping—at least he might find time.

They landed with more than the usual thud. Erik reasoned this was co-pilot practice time.

Celia caught up with him on the tarmac.

'It always amazes me, just over three hours ago we were experiencing a cool spring day in London and now we are here sweating,' she said.

Trust Celia to state the obvious, he thought. Damn it, how many days would he be forced to share her company and crass comments.

'I thought ladies didn't sweat,' he remarked sarcastically.

'I know, they only perspire. Not very original,' replied with matching derision.

Outside the airport Erik waved down a taxi, giving the driver instructions to take them to the offices of the *Enimerosi* newspaper in Corfu Town.

'Can't we go to our hotel room first?' she baulked.

'No, we've come to do a story and that is a priority.'

'Just to wash and brush up.'

'I thought you professed to be a dedicated journalist.

Yes, Seventeen Saint Desylla Street,' he confirmed with taxi driver, ignoring Celia's objection.

'But we are having to cart round all our luggage,' she wailed.

'You mean, your luggage.'

In contrast to Miss Hot and Bothered, Erik was amazed at the relaxed atmosphere in the newsroom of *Enimerosi*. Journalists lounged back in their swivel chairs away from their antiquated computers as if the machines might bite. Adorned by one or two raven-headed beauties in conservative twinsets, all the men wore open necked shirts. Cigarette smoke hung in plumes from desks to ceiling.

'Can I be of assistance,' asked an older guy in English.

'We are looking for a senior reporter, Gorgias Baros,' said Erik, extremely disappointed at the immediate recognition of his nationality.

'Well, you have found him.' Manly shaking of hands with the seated Baros. Celia was disregarded.

'You were expecting us?' asked Erik.

'Big newspaper back home, ya?'

'Yes, big London newspaper.'

'You are unlucky to be here now.'

'How so?'

'Terrible, terrible stink everywhere.' Gorgias ruckled his prominent nose. 'Waste piled this high in the streets.' He indicated to the smoke cloud lingering in the ceiling. The three of them fell silent, horror-struck.

'We didn't notice anything,' said Celia, thinking it was time she made her mark on this blokeish lull.

'I thought the rubbish strike would be over by now,' said Erik. 'It's been going on for ages, years, hasn't it?'

'Yes, but government are threatening to call in riot police if new landfill at Lefkimmi isn't put into operation. Trouble is it was originally judged by EU to be illegal and then given temporary permit.'

'Ah, the EU,' sighed Erik.

'Anyway government insist that 80,000 tonnes of garbage needs to be moved from Temploni site to Lefkimmi.'

'You've spent time in the US?' Erik decided to move the talk away from rubbish.

'How do you know?'

'You have an American accent and your use of the word "garbage".'

Gorgias mocked offence.

'All Greeks have spent time in America. If not America then Australia,' he told them. Adding a conciliatory, 'Occasionally London.'

'What can you tell us about this luxury yacht blown up in Paxos?' asked Erik, eager to get down to the nitty-gritty.

'Why is British paper so interested in this?'

'You must be joking. This is world news,' responded Erik.

'The boat owner had dual Russian and British nationality,' cut in Celia again.

'So?' Greek arms spread.

'So, naturally we are interested,' she replied. 'I believe the two crew members who perished were British as well.'

'You think Russians did this? My sources tell me boat owner was well thought of by Kremlin, an… How you say it?'

'Oligarch,' offered Erik.

'Yes, oligarch, with a direct line to Putin. You English always think it is Russians.'

'Are you surprised after the Novichok incident?' Erik again.

Gorgias dismissed this with a shrug.

'We Greeks like the Russians, plenty of money coming in,' he laughed, rubbing his hands together.

'We try to approach every story with an open mind,' said Erik pointedly.

'Perhaps it was you.'

'We what?'

'You English who blew up boat.' Gorgias began to laugh again. Erik and Celia did not share his sense of humour.

'Not the Germans then,' suggested Erik. 'The Germans can't be behind all this?'

'I don't think …'

'Because to hear you Greeks talk the Germans are behind all your country's problems.'

'We Greeks are like the elephants, we do not forget, Mr Jordan.'

Erik had no answer to that.

'Come.' Gorgias gestured them forward with an appeasing outstretched hand. 'Nice bar round corner, let's eat and drink.'

Erik, whose stomach had begun to grumble, nodded enthusiastically. He had not come here to argue. Until he stood up, Erik had not appreciated how tall Gorgias was. He was an inch or two taller than himself.

The coffee bar was situated off an old narrow backstreet. They sat outside in a courtyard under a green umbrella of vines, their carry-ons parked against a pink plastered wall.

Apart from launching into his cold beer and moussaka, Gorgias spent much of his time on his mobile. He appeared to be arranging for someone called Nicos to meet them.

Celia sniffed in the atmosphere: flowers, cooked beef, cinnamon, ouzo, coffee and above all warmth—a herbal warmth—they could be sitting nowhere else but in Greece.

'Nicos Maragos.' Gorgias proudly introduced a middle-aged, bald-headed man. 'This is my source, my police source,' he whispered into Erik's ear.

'Pleased to meet you.' More manly shaking of hands on Erik's part.

Nicos turned to Celia and kissed her hand.

'Madam, a pleasure,' he told her.

Celia had finally got in on the act big time.

Nicos soon explained he was no longer in the *Elliniki Astynomia* but he had friends in high places. He grinned boastful gold-caped teeth.

After the initial preamble and talk of how Kerkyra was doing in the football league, imperceptibly the mood began to change, tension increased.

Both Gorgias and Nicos seemed intent on a chain-smoking competition. Celia watched in dismay as the small round ashtray filled up with cigarette butts. She could already sense the carcinoma cells forming in her lungs.

Erik too had his eye on the glass roseate ashtray. Far from the laid-back *Enimerosi* newsroom both Greek men looked stressed out here. Nicos particularly kept glancing around, glancing towards the street beyond.

'Of course they have detectives from Athens working the Paxos bombing case,' he told them in lowered tones. 'And, as it seems to be an international incident, I expect Interpol is involved.'

'Do the police have any idea who is responsible?' Erik decided to strike while the iron was hot.

'I shouldn't really be talking to you like this,' replied Nicos. Suddenly apprehension replacing Greek affability.

'I'm sure my paper will make it worth your while,' Erik reassured him.

'Not here.'

'Where then?'

Erik looked round to see a man had slunk into the courtyard and had taken a table by the pink wall near their luggage. He eyeballed him. The man's face disappeared behind a newspaper.

'This is the hotel where we are staying.' Erik tore a page out of his notebook and scribbled the address, sliding it across to Nicos 'Shall we say tonight at eight-thirty?'

Nicos nodded and left.

'What's got into him?' asked Celia.

'Ears everywhere,' whispered Gorgias.

'Is he being followed?' asked Erik, noticing the man by the wall had left too, left his coffee cup half full.

Again a Gorgias shrug.

'We, more especially he, could go to prison talking to a foreign newspaper about this,' he said.

'About this?' asked Erik.

'Greece has no wish to offend our Russian friends at this point in time.'

'Gorgeous Gorgias,' purred Celia, once seated in the back of another taxi—a white Mercedes this time—on their way to the hotel. 'His parents must have named him after the Ancient Greek sophist.'

'You think so?' asked Erik, somewhat taken aback, slightly irritated.

'Think what? Think he was named after Gorgias the Nihilist?'

'No, think he is gorgeous?'

'Yes, I love handsome mature men with slightly greying sideburns.'

'Really? You do surprise me.'

'The moussaka was delicious too but of course you had that vegetarian thingy.'

'*Spanakópita*, spinach pie with feta.'

'Was it tasty?' she asked doubtfully. He nodded.

'I would have thought edgy Nicos was more your type,' he added, apparently as an afterthought.

'Or more your type.'

'What does that imply?'

'Well gay men like bald men, don't they?'

'I'm not gay.' Erik reddened with indignation.

'You could have fooled me and half the female staff in our office.'

'You're kidding,' he huffed.

'I see it now. Look at all that rubbish piled up on the corner there.'

'Stinks,' said Erik, rolling up his window. 'Stinks like this Paxos story.' *Stinks like me closeted with you for a week*, he thought.

CHAPTER THREE

Despite all the financial restraints in the industry, the paper had done them proud. They had reservations in a luxury seafront accommodation with a pool.

'Fancy a swim?' she asked, after they had barely stepped through the hotel entrance. 'I am dying to freshen up with a swim.'

'I'm not sure …'

'Yes or no,' she snapped impatiently.

'No, then.'

Snap. Once his bedroom door was unlocked with his key card, his immediate preoccupation was the mini bar and a Britvic orange juice. Looking round the room he saw that some of the furniture was heavy and old. Indeed there was an elegant tiredness about the whole place which Erik found rather homely and comforting.

After a shower and donning a bathrobe, he stood on his balcony admiring the setting sun over the sea. Hearing energetic splashes, his attention was drawn to the swim pool. Only one swimmer remained, ploughing up and down the tiled lines doing freestyle with tumble turns. So powerful and impressive was this swimmer that Erik was sure it must be male. However it was difficult to pick out a face with obscuring goggles, hat and alternate breathing. Finally, he saw shoulder straps. The swimmer was wearing a female costume. No, it couldn't be, this Olympian couldn't be Celia.

The swimmer stopped at the nearest end, pushed up her goggles and waved. He disappeared back into his room in embarrassment like a voyeur caught on CCTV.

* * * * *

The most beautiful creature hesitated at the top of the sweeping staircase before making a feather-light descent, chestnut hair flowing behind like a mane. He looked at his watch in annoyance as he stood waiting for Celia in the lobby. He hoped she was not going to keep him waiting.

'Been waiting long?' she asked.

'I didn't recognise …' Fooled again.

Gone was the ponytail. Gone the dark rimmed glasses. Her athletic body bulged health in a tight, white Joseph Ribkoff dress.

Sexy did not do her justice. For a fraction of a second his heart missed a beat before resentment kicked back in. How many personas did this woman have?

They chose an indoor table as the nights were cool. Her glasses were soon reinstated from the clutch bag she was carrying. He had to admit that still she did not look half bad—a young Nana Mouskouri perhaps. Celia selected a bottle of the best local red wine on the menu, he a white.

'Do people on the paper really think I'm gay?' he asked her over his zucchini and cheese roulades. He had been festering over the insinuation ever since she had posed it.

'Yes, but that's none of their business.'

'Why do they think I'm gay?'

'A public schoolboy with no steady girlfriend and a white-wine-drinking vegetarian to boot.'

'I've had lots of girlfriends.'

'That's just it. Not one of them sticks.' She tore and dipped a piece of pitta bread into her bowl of taramosalata, taking another swig of her red wine as if there was no tomorrow.

'Salted cod fish roe, are you really enjoying that?' He shuddered, not feeling quite so hungry anymore.

'Had it for the first time in Crete. Takes me back.'

'Crete?' And he had thought this woman had not been anywhere.

'Yes, during my teenage years my parents owned a villa near Sitia. And your parents?'

'A stockbroker in the City.'

'Did you really go through school wearing a stiff collar, buttoned up waistcoat and tailcoat?'

'That was the uniform. Where specifically were you educated?'

'Bolton.'

'And what did you wear at the comprehensive, lipstick and short skirts up to your bum?'

'Are you always this rude?'

'Depends.'

'Obviously Eton didn't teach you any manners.'

'They tried but failed miserably.'

'Actually I went to Bolton School. An independent school with an excellent academic record. We had our own outdoor pursuits place on Ullswater, and an arts and conference centre opened by Diana, Princess of Wales.'

'And a swimming pool, I do not doubt.'

'That too.'

'Figures.'

'Don't you swim?'

'Not well. Though we had a good size school pool.'

'Maybe I could teach you while we're here.'

'I think not.'

'Oh, come on be a sport.'

'I'm not a sport,' said with disdain.

'Do you think Nicos will turn up tonight?' she asked, changing the subject with another deep swig of wine. Erik felt this was for liquid courage to get her through the meal with him. Their antipathy was growing by the minute. He felt trapped in this glass cube of restaurant with a woman he was sure he did not like very much.

'I have my doubts,' he retorted. Bottom lip still pouting over the gay slur and his lack of athletic prowess. He wished Nicos would show up right now to give him a break from this virago. 'I did enjoy fives,' he admitted lamely.

'"Fives"? What sort of game is that?'

'It's similar to hand pelota.'

The waiter sashayed towards their table with the main courses, placing the plates unobtrusively before them. Erik loved the artistry of Mediterranean service. Celia told him she thought it creepy, tucking into her grilled lamb chops with relish.

'That's because you don't appreciate the finer things in life,' he told her, fastidiously examining his potato stew.

'And you're a snob.'

The more they drank the more antagonistic they became. By dessert time, she had started to stress her Lancastrian accent—a deliberate exaggeration it seemed to him—while ordering Míla Psitá me Karýdia.

'Never had that,' he told her.

'Baked apple stuffed with walnuts and raisins, lovely.'

'All the same I'll stick with my yogurt cake.'

Just as they had given up on Nicos, they saw him striding across the room towards them.

'Have you eaten?' Erik asked him.

'No, but it doesn't matter.' Nicos was dressed in the same chinos casual look he had worn that afternoon.

'A coffee then?' insisted Erik.

Reluctantly Nicos acquiesced and took a packet of cigarettes from his breast pocket. He swivelled round in his chair, with one glance taking in the whole restaurant.

Their meal, his coffee and cigarette finished, he asked if they could go to somewhere more private.

'Yes of course, my room,' said Erik.

The three of them clumped over Erik's parquet floor. Slightly drunk, Celia flung herself onto the floral bed. The tight Joseph Ribkoff number left little to the imagination. Nicos asked if he could relieve himself.

'Too much coffee,' he told them.

Erik pointed to the bathroom and raised an eyebrow at Celia.

'I'm tired,' she slurred. 'Must be the swimming.'

'More likely the wine. Listen why don't you go off to bed and let me interview Nicos,' he whispered. 'I'll update you in the morning.'

'No chance.'

'Nice,' said the emerging Nicos. 'A bidet too. Your paper must think this story is worth it.'

'So what have the *Elliniki Astynomia* learnt about the Paxos bombing?' Erik switched his phone to record and placed it on the glass top coffee table.

'No, no phone recording.' Nicos shook his head.

'Can I jot a few things down in my notebook then?'

'No notebook either. No physical copy that can fall into wrong hands.'

'Now come on this all sounds a little paranoid,' objected Erik. Nicos shook his head again.

'Do you want me to tell you what I've heard or not?' he asked.

'Of course. Please go ahead.'

'And payment?'

'I'll write you a cheque.'

'No. Cash, euros only.'

'But it all depends what your information is worth.'

'A thousand euros, shall we say. I'm taking big risk here.'

'Go ahead then,' sighed Erik. He had nothing left to bargain with.

'Is she all right?' Nicos nodded across to Celia on the bed. 'She looks very drunk.'

'I'm not drunk,' objected Celia, opening her sleepy lids. 'Just resting my eyes. A little tipsy, you understand.'

'I am not speaking another word with her in room,' Nicos announced. 'Look at her with her clothing rolled up to the top of her thighs like a tart.'

'Charming.' Celia burst into offended consciousness, attempting to struggle to her feet and pull down her climbing dress. Her nose ruckled peevishly.

'As I suggested earlier you'd better go back to your room and sleep it off,' Erik told her more firmly.

'Just ss ... ho you two can have a cosy boy to boy chat,' she slurred, before slamming the door behind her.

'I'm not sure I like your colleague very much,' said Nicos; watching the door, making sure Celia had gone, never to return. He pulled his chair closer to Erik's until the two men's knees were almost touching. Erik straightened back slightly.

'She's all right when she's sober,' he told Nicos; uncertain why he was defending Celia.

'Women, eh?'

'Yes, women,' agreed Erik.

'The yacht owner was a Russian oligarch called Dmitry Smirnov,' began Nicos in lowered tones. 'But I expect you know this already. He had his thumb in every pie, you understand.'

'Finger,' corrected Erik.

'Sorry?' asked Nicos, looking confused.

'We say he had his *finger* in every pie.'

'You English,' he sneered dismissively.

'Don't be offended. You speak the language well.'

'Better than Gorgias?'

'Better,' placated Erik. Obviously there was some competition between the two men. 'So back to this Smirnov?'

'Do you know what the name Smirnov means?' It was Nicos' turn to be clever.

'No idea.'

'Meek. It means meek. Well, let me tell you, this man did not live up to his surname. He was a friend of Putin's, that is if Putin has any real friends, way back when Putin was KGB officer.'

'Putin didn't become Prime Minister until 1999,' clarified Erik.

'That's right, after Yeltsin.'

'Yes, he was Yeltsin's boy, was he not?'

'But long before this, Putin was a poor boy. He was brought up in a one room apartment in soviet Leningrad, now Saint Petersburg, whereas Smirnov came from a modest business family in Belgorod. Belgorod is the administration centre for Belgorod Oblast. I believe the family began to make a fortune from mining iron ore under Gorbachev.'

'Business-sector entrepreneurs.'

'That's correct. I see you have done your homework, Mr Jordan.'

'So how did the paths of Vladimir and Dmitry cross?'

'I believe they met in Dresden, East Germany. Putin is fluent in German and worked as a translator there while still KGB officer. Smirnov's family business had interests in Dresden, and he was sent there for a few years to oversee operations. Returning from Dresden in early 1990s, Putin then became deputy mayor to Anatoly Sobchak in Saint Petersburg. While in that city, Sobchak made Putin head of Committee for External Relations.'

'Wasn't there a whiff of some sort of financial scandal taking place there?'

'I am impressed.'

'You shouldn't be. The poisonings in Salisbury in March turned English press interest directly East. I always research my area of interest well.'

'Regarding the Saint Petersburg affair, Putin was investigated by city legislative council led by woman called Marina Salye and council member called Yury Gradkov. It was alleged that he had understated prices and permitted export of metals valued at ninety plus million dollars in exchange for foreign food aid that never materialised. Despite the investigators' recommendation that he be fired, he remained head of CFER until 1996. His friend and mentor, Anatoly Sobchak, sacked the city council instead.'

'What happened to Marina Salye and Yury Gradkov?' asked Erik, fearing the worst.

'I believe Gradkov is dead. When Putin became President, Salye claimed she had been threatened and retired deep into Russian countryside, to village near the town of Pskov, with female partner. I believed Salye died naturally of heart attack in 2007. However, she spent final years fearful of Kremlin power.'

'So what has all this to do with the Paxos bombing?'

'Putin has always denied any part in corruptive practices of course.' Nicos ignored the question.

'Are you saying Putin might be directly involved in the murder of Dmitry Smirnov?'

'Never directly.'

'But why? Why would the Russians want Smirnov dead?'

'He was big exporter of iron ore all over world.'

'You mean, he knew too much.'

'Your guess is as good as mine, isn't that what you say?'

'But to kill him on Greek soil?' Erik was incredulous.

'The Skripals were found, in nick of time, poisoned on Salisbury bench. Radioactive Litvinenko died in London hospital bed. All on English soil,' pointed out Nicos.

'And I always thought Greece was hand in glove with Russia.'

Nicos cleared his throat. 'There have been one or two complications of late.'

'Macedonia,' sighed Erik; momentarily forgetting Greek sensitivities. Everything in Greece always reverted to the vexed question of the two Macedonias.

'Yes, Russian meddling in Former Yugoslav Republic of Macedonia is one.'

'In what way are the Russians interested in FYROM?'

'They are terrified of any of their near neighbours applying to join NATO. We on other hand don't like way they are cosying up to Turkey.'

'But what does this have to do with Smirnov and the Paxos bombing?'

'Russians are always changing their alliances and allegiances.'

'But Smirnov was out of the way living and working in London.'

'As you know Mother Russia has long arms. Putin's mentor, Anatoly Sobchak, was sent by him to Kaliningrad to canvass for his election campaign. He died in hotel bedroom, like this one, in uncertain circumstances.'

Erik looked round his room beginning to feel uncomfortable. 'Yes, I heard about that. It was put down to a cardiac arrest.'

'The result of autopsy was inconclusive.'

'You don't believe there is a link in the deaths of Smirnov and Sobchak.'

'No, not link in deaths, rather possible connection with Saint Petersburg and mineral exports.'

'But Gorgias didn't seem to think the Russians were involved with any of this.'

'Gorgias knows nothing.'

Bang. Both men jumped out of their seats. Erik felt the imaginary bullet penetrating through his chest wall. *Bang, bang,* again.

'A car backfiring?' offered Erik.

'No, firecrackers,' laughed Nicos. 'Someone fooling outside in street.'

'You'll keep me informed if you learn more?' Erik began to count out a thousand euros in notes, deciding to bring this interview to an end.

'How much will you tell that girl? I don't trust her.'

'She's a good swimmer though,' grinned Erik.

'Liquor loosens tongues,' said Nicos; ignoring Erik's swimmer comment, considering it some sort of obscure English joke.

CHAPTER FOUR

What a sorry sight greeted Erik at the breakfast table the next morning. Luckily breakfast was served from a choose your own buffet bar.

'Yogurt and fruit, that's all I want,' insisted Celia.

'Can't I interest you in any bacon, eggs and black pudding? What about …?' He teased her until she turned green. 'No morning swim either?'

'Not today, slept in.'

'I'll get you some yogurt and fruit then,' he offered, finally taking pity on her. 'The waiter will bring coffee and tea to the table.'

'Strong coffee,' she murmured, still unable to raise a smile.

When he got back their cups had been filled and the waiter was gone. It was about 9.45 and most of the other guests had already eaten and left. Just one or two Chinese remained, shuffling along the buffet bar holding tightly onto their vacuum flasks in search of hot water. A few of the Greek waiters stood around regarding them with a mixture of bemusement and derision.

'Why do the Chinese do that?' she asked Erik.

'Do what?'

'Carry flasks about with them?'

'It's a cultural thing. They believe warm water helps the digestion while travelling.'

'That's where I've gone wrong.' She laughed for the first time that morning. 'Nonetheless, maybe this flask thing is due to Chinese fears of cholera ever since thousands upon thousands died of the disease during the Taiping Rebellion of 1850.'

'You're a mine of information.'

'I try.'

'I'm very impressed.'

'Have you noticed everything about the Chinese today is designer: designer clothes, designer bags, designer shoes?'

'Even designer flasks and designer masks,' he offered.

'Those too.'

'Last night you found out what my father did for a living. What about yours?' he asked, curiosity building.

'Oh, he's just a reporter like us.' She appeared to brush off the question, asking instead, 'So, what did engaging Nicos have to say?'

He looked around. Their table was like an island surrounded by nothing and no one.

'He engaged,' he spluttered through a mouth stuffed with croissant.

'Come on, he must have told you something.'

'The Russians,' Erik finally admitted.

'He thinks the Russians were responsible for the bombing? And you paid him for that?'

'He's the only lead we've got so far.'

'But we already suspected the Russians ourselves. We didn't need him to tell us that.'

'He's promised to keep us up to date on Greek official thinking.' Erik held his ground, determined not to enlighten her further.

* * * * *

While taking a pee back in his bedroom, Erik felt his phone vibrating. Why did the bloody thing always have to go off at the most inappropriate times.

'Yes,' he screamed, zipping up.

'Jordan?' Duncan Nelson sounded as if he was in the same room. 'You're off to interview the hospitalised bomb victim this morning, are you not?' After a stint on the *New York Times*, Nelson loved using American terminology.

'Yes, our first port of call.'

'How's it all going otherwise?'

'Fine. Everything is fine. I made my first police contact last night.'

'And the hotel?'

'Good, comfortable.'

'And Celia?'

'She's fine too.'

'How are you two getting on?'

'We're OK,' he lied.

'Don't be deceived by Celia. She's an extremely bright girl. Educated at one of the finest schools in the North. She wasn't Oxbridge like you, however she has a master's degree in journalism from the City University, London. And her father was one of the finest columnists in the land. He is now in senior management on *The Guardian*.'

'Is he really.' *Not a humble reporter then*, acknowledged Erik privately. Celia was priceless.

'Yes, Peter Grey, they are extremely rich. A house with a pool in a posh part of Lancashire.'

* * * * *

He met her by the reception desk. She looked very much better than she had over breakfast. Erik had no intention of disclosing his conversation with Nelson at this stage.

'You are very formally dressed,' she said, looking from his tailored, crease-resistant suit and tie to her denim jeans and blue Hilfiger shirt.

'I never dress down when I'm on the job.'

Pretentious bastard, she thought. Flinging her laptop bag across her shoulder.

They hailed a taxi which took them down the coast to Kontokali.

Erik told her he would have rented a hire car if they had been staying here more than a few days. She did not answer but looked longingly out towards the sea and umbrellaed beaches.

In contrast, Corfu General Hospital—built in 1998 according to their driver—was stark and modern. Nothing splish-splash fun about it. The outside structure was faced with magnolia plaster, only interspersing powder blue sections paid homage to the clear sky above.

The driver dropped them off outside the main entrance and wished them well in English.

Inside, the building was functional like any other hospital they had been in back home, cleaner if anything. Erik's voice echoed as he asked for Adras Christakos.

'Ah, yes,' exclaimed a lady receptionist of mature years. 'He is in the intensive treatment unit. Who might you be?'

'We have come all the way from England to interview him,' said Celia.

'Journalists. I doubt his doctors will let you speak with him.'

'Will you try for us?' asked Erik.

The woman reluctantly picked up a mobile and spoke to someone in hushed tones.

'What newspaper did you say you were from?'

'We didn't,' replied Celia.

'The *London Evening Record*,' said Erik.

'You didn't tell me it was by prior arrangement.' She looked disappointed. 'Doctor Fotopoulos is expecting you.'

'London arranges everything,' Erik told her.

The woman looked less than impressed.

'First floor.' She gave a perfunctory nod towards two lifts across the way.

'We'll take the stairs,' snapped Celia.

'The gatehouse keeper. What a harridan,' muttered Erik, with a contemptuous glance back at the receptionist.

They were shocked to see an armed police guard stood on duty outside the door of Intensive Care. Fortunately the name tagged Dr Leonnatos Fotopoulos was available to escort them past.

'The hospital is very quiet, doctor,' observed Erik.

'You are fortunate it is still May. You should see it in the season. It is like a war zone. Blood everywhere from wounded, drunken or drugged English youngsters who have fallen off their mopeds. Even the older tourists …'

'How is the bomb victim?' interrupted Celia.

'Adras is much improved,' Fotopoulos told them, leading them along the seven bedded unit. 'He is a very fortunate young man and I am sure he is eager to tell the world about it.'

In the seventh bed, Adras was pale against the lifted pillow. His face still carried lacerations from the explosion and flying glass.

Celia and Erik introduced themselves.

'I speak a little English,' Adras told them proudly.

'Good, good,' reassured Celia. 'Take your time.'

'In your own words.' Erik pressed his phone's record button.

Dr Fotopoulos, who had been hovering over his patient like a mother hen, left them to it.

'It was a morning like any other working in my Uncle Demos' bar,' began Adras. 'Most of the breakfast customers had gone. One gentleman remained outside. Two Dutch tourists arrived just after him but they chose to sit inside. Then big yacht came in.'

'You saw the boat docking?' enquired Erik.

'I saw her come in.'

'Did you lose consciousness immediately, after the bomb went off?'

'Almost, I think,' nodded Adras. 'I have had memory problems and headaches ever since.'

'Your English is very good, Adras,' flattered Celia.

Adras puffed out his chest which seemed to cause him momentary discomfort.

'Are you OK?' asked Celia.

'As well as I can be. They're burying my nephew today. To think he took that terrible day off school with a cold. One minute he is happily playing near the moored yacht, the next ... Nine years old. What sort of bad luck is that?' Adras sniffed, about to cry.

'Tell me about the gentleman who was seated outside,' cut in Erik, eager to keep Adras focused.

'He was a middle-aged guy, spoke perfect English.'

'So he was English?'

'Well,' hesitated Adras, 'that's just it, his English was too perfect, too precise.'

'What did he look like?'

'He was dressed like a typical English gentleman, like you. Not a tourist, no. Just as if he had stepped out of the film *Tinker, Tailor, Soldier, Spy*.'

'Something out of John le Carré then?'

'Or *The Go-Between*,' offered Adras enthusiastically.

'You like films, Adras?' asked Celia. Adras nodded eagerly.

'I learn English watching *Tinker, Tailor, Soldier, Spy*. I watched both original TV version on DVD with Alec Guinness and more recent film with subtitles. Alec Guinness' English was easier to follow. Nobody played Smiley like him. As matter of fact he was wearing tie just like yours,' he told Erik.

'Who was? Alec Guinness?'

'No, no, man in bar who looked like him,' giggled Adras.

'Like this?' Erik straightened his black tie with diagonal Eton blue stripes.

'Exactly the same.'

'Have you told the police all this?' asked Celia.

'Of course.'

'And the Dutch couple?'

'Just tourists,' shrugged Adras dismissively. 'There was something else I remember about man outside, he kept looking at his watch before making brief phone call. Soon after that he paid and left. The *astynomia* raised eyebrows at this.'

'I bet they did,' said Erik.

'Then boom, the world turned upside down, and I remember little.'

'Strange that this mystery man didn't try to blend in more if he was up to no good,' remarked Erik.

'I've thought about this a lot. Maybe he wanted to appear English,' said Adras, 'when he was something else all together.'

'Do you think he was responsible for the explosion?' asked Celia.

'"Things aren't always what they seem",' quoted a beaming Adras.

'Le Carré's Toby Esterhase,' recognised Erik.

'"He's so conspicuous, he's embarrassing".'

'Again the Circus' eccentric Hungarian anglophile, Toby Esterhase,' acknowledged Erik.

After their acceptance of a *Tinker, Tailor, Soldier, Spy* similarity, the bedridden patient was only too pleased to let them take a few pictures of him. Perhaps he would never enjoy such fame again.

'Tomorrow you will be international news,' Erik told him.

'I am to be returned to Paxos in day or two.'

'Text me when it happens,' said Erik, writing down his number and leaving it on the bedside table.

'I will, I will,' said Adras full of enthusiasm.

On leaving the ward, Erik and Celia took the lift.

'MI6?' suggested Erik.

'No, I am inclined to agree with Adras, the man was altogether too obvious if he was involved at all.' She remained shaking her head until the lift door slid open. 'I mean, I ask you, an Eton tie.'

'Fancy a coffee and a sandwich?' proposed Erik.

'What here?'

'No, I fancy some air. There's a bay and resort just down the road.'

'How do you know?'

'Google Earth, my dear.'

'I would love a toastie.'

'First I need some low denomination notes out of this cash machine. Nelson obviously is ignorant of financial transactions in Greece.'

Real air was good after the hospital's Aircon system. But 'just down the road' turned out to be longer and more complicated. They were glad to rest their legs at the first taverna on reaching the resort. A tall slim waitress brought their ordered coffees to an outside patio table. She scrutinised them from a giraffe perspective. Erik smiled in anticipation of reviving refreshment. He was greeted with blank, down the nose condescension.

'Perhaps a daughter forced into service,' he whispered to Celia.

'Or maybe she just doesn't like the English,' proposed Celia. 'One way or the other, I don't really care.'

Soon the giraffe reappeared wearing exactly the same expression. Wordlessly, she delivered a ham and cheese toastie for Celia and a cheese alone for Erik.

'*Efcharistó polý,*' said Erik.

No response.

They did their best to ignore the now distant giraffe behind the bar and enjoyed the sound of the lapping sea.

'I love the earthy taste of Greek coffee,' said Celia.

'I'm not so sure. Why didn't you tell me your father is Peter Grey?' A sudden unexpected question to disconcert her. He should have known better.

'Why should I? Perhaps for the same reason you don't tell people your father is Sir Timothy Jordan.'

'So we've both done the research,' he smirked.

'What did you really make of Adras' story?'

'You mean about the Eton tie man?'

'Yes, all that *Tinker, Tailor, Soldier, Spy* business.'

'Well, he is either extremely perceptive or delusional.'

'He did suffer from concussion.'

'Hard to tell the truth of it—what he remembers and what he imagines he remembers—but he is one lucky guy. Nelson told me his nephew was blown to pieces, literally.' Erik left her to absorb this information as he went inside the taverna to order a taxi.

Tonight you're mine completely.
You give your love so sweetly.
Tonight the light of love is in your eyes.
But will you love me tomorrow?

When he returned Celia's face had turned to stone. Goffin and King's *Will You Love Me Tomorrow* was still blaring from the sound system.

'Is this a lasting treasure?
Or just a moment's pleasure?
Can I believe the magic of your sighs? Will you still love me tomorrow?'

'A brilliant song,' he said.

'Yes,' she admitted with little enthusiasm.

'Brilliant lyrics.'

'I suppose they are.'

'I saw Carole King perform that song in Hyde Park with her daughter a couple of years ago. Come to think of it, Celia, you are not unlike the younger King when she was with Gerry Goffin. Are you Jewish?'

'No, but does it matter.' Despondent sigh. 'This song makes me feel incredibly sad. I wish they would turn the damn thing down or off.'

'You are an enigma, Celia.'

'I don't want to talk about it.'

'As you wish.' He glared at her, puzzled.

'I'm dying for another swim,' she said, looking longingly at the sea. She was adept at rapid reversals in conversation.

'We'd better make a move then,' he told her. 'I've got to email this story through. You can have a swim back at the hotel.'

But it was not to be. Thwarted in the extreme. A pink flamingo sloshed in the shallow end. A delicate Chinese girl clung to its long plastic neck, riding high out of the water in a traditional flowing silk *hanfu* dress. From nowhere several young Chinese men appeared, to photograph her as she bobbed up and down with excitement.

'She's beautiful. Looks like a model but how on earth is she going to keep that gown dry,' Erik wondered out aloud.

'I'm not going in the pool with that flamingo contraption floating around,' announced Celia sulkily.

'Don't worry, they won't be joining us for dinner. The Chinese don't seem to do dinner, they never appear in the evenings at any rate.'

'Good, I'm off to pack if we are leaving tomorrow,' she said, flouncing off to her room in disgust.

Erik thought Flamingo girl was worth a few photographs of his own. He tried to be surreptitious as he lifted up his iPhone, at first pretending to point the camera lens towards the hotel building before swinging it round to the pool. It was a technique he was working on—one that might prove to be useful in entirely different circumstances.

CHAPTER FIVE

The out-of-season ferries were infrequent. All costs were on the paper, so they hired a fast and more expensive water taxi to take them to Paxos. The bearded captain helped Celia down quite a stretch from the harbour wall to the bobbing boat below. Erik passed their luggage to him and followed unaided. Sometimes he wished he was a woman, cuts down on the risks of broken ankles.

The weather being warm, they chose to sit outside at the back of the boat rather than in the small claustrophobic cabin. Travelling along the east coast of Corfu, with mainland Greece on their left, they enjoyed calm water.

'Look, see, that is the old Venetian fort.' Erik pointed in great excitement to a grey bulwarked structure perched high on a slab of rock.

'Very imposing.' Celia tried to match his fervour.

'We are just passing the Villa of Mon Repos, the Duke of Edinburgh's birth place,' the captain shouted back to them.

Now this really did capture Celia's interest. Erik however was a little disappointed by the modest if architecturally beautiful building. He associated the monarchy with something much more grand and imposing: Buckingham Palace, Windsor Castle and the like.

'But it has a fantastic location looking across the straits to Albania and the Greek mainland,' defended Celia. 'I wouldn't have minded being born there.'

'Instead of Bolton?' He just could not resist it, resist winding her up.

'Unkind,' she retorted.

'Sorry.' He could have bitten off his tongue when he saw how crestfallen he had made her on this beautiful day. And just as they were beginning to get on a little better. He reached for her hand to make amends, she snatched it back.

'How do you really see the North of England?' she asked him.

'Satanic mills, clogs and grey Lowry stick men.'

'You are a spoilt southern prig,' she told him. 'Ignorant too. We have space, wild heather moorland, rivers and some of the most beautiful countryside in England.'

Soon they were out in open sea—an Ionian sea turned rough.

'No playful dolphins today,' shouted the captain, unaware of the discord in the back of his boat.

Celia could taste the salt spray running down her face like tears. She refused to look at Erik for the rest of the journey.

The red jeep they had hired was waiting on the quay at Gaios New Port. The key, they had been told, was under the mat on the driver's side.

'You want to drive?' he asked her. 'We are both insured.'

She shook her head. She had not spoken to him properly since his Bolton comment.

'You'll have to navigate then.' He thrust the provided map and instructions across to her. 'Shouldn't be too difficult. Paxos is only nineteen square kilometres with few roads.'

Hotel rooms were few and far between on Paxos and with their late booking they had been forced to hire a small villa with a big pool—big to him. She was not sure she could tolerate being isolated with this man for any length of time, and isolated they were up a Greek hillside among an olive grove overlooking a blue bay.

'Very secluded,' he said.

'Magical,' she said with little enthusiasm. *It would be magical without you,* she thought.

'Secluded enough for a naked swim?' Asked with a lecherous leer. She made for the villa without replying.

Her mood only improved once she was costumed up and stroking out in the water. After a few lengths she was surprised to see him edging down the pool steps, thankfully in tartan swim shorts. She had seen timid kids at school approaching the water like this, afraid. She had to give him it—he was giving it a try—he went slightly up in her estimation, only slightly. However she did stop training and slid her goggles over her swim hat.

'Do you crawl?' she asked.

'All the time.' His laughter was hollow.

'Try a length of breaststroke then.'

She had never seen anyone so tense in the water. His arms rotated like propeller blades, his legs kicking without rhythm all over the place. He covered the nine metre pool with maximum effort before clinging to the far side gasping for breath. She glided over to him.

'Right,' she said, 'I am going to teach you how to relax in the water.'

With one arm under the small of his back and a hand cradling his head, she asked him to sink back and trust himself to float. Rigid at first, slowly, slowly, his arms and legs fell limp.

'See how the water holds you up. If it supports the Queen Mary it will support you.' Gently she lifted him back onto his feet. 'Now let us try another leisurely length or two together.'

'It's worked,' he told her, sitting on the tiled steps having completed a few sets of one length. 'I'm not as out of breath.'

'Serenity is the key to everything.'

'At this rate I'll soon be challenging Adam Peaty.'

'Not quite. You'll have a lot more work to do on your pecs and biceps.'

Ignoring the lack of physique taunt, he chose to compliment her instead. 'You're a wonderful teacher.'

'For a lass from Bolton?'

'For a lass from anywhere.' Was that awe in his eyes. 'The big question now is do we eat in or out?' he asked her.

'When are we going to visit the site of the bombing?'

'Tomorrow. That can wait until tomorrow.' Following the swim, he felt more relaxed than he had in months.

'I thought the story always had priority.' It was her turn for a jibe.

* * * * *

They found a small beach taverna that specialised in sea food. Celia chose a Greek seafood risotto, *Kritharoto*, and he went for sea bass.

'Not vegan then,' she noted.

'No, I'll risk the occasional salmon.'

They ordered a Cretan white wine that somehow had found its way up to the island of Paxos.

'Why do Greek wines always taste better in Greece?' she asked.

'They don't travel well,' he proffered lightly.

The sun began to set. The mosquito zapper in the awning spluttered and sparked. She looked down on the small deserted beach which must have been cramped in the season. The few drooping umbrellas between each lounger appeared impotent and forlorn.

'I will show you beaches with nobody,' she murmured to herself, suddenly overwhelmed by sadness. Why could she not allow those words to dissolve in the backwaters of memory?

'What's wrong,' he asked, sensing her mood.

'If you are gay, I can understand it.'

'But I'm not. Are you saying you're gay?'

'Aren't many of us given the right circumstances.' She took a gulp of wine. The sourness in the back of her throat suited the moment. 'I was married once, you know.'

'No, I didn't know.' He was not surprised because he had grown to realise that this woman whom he had originally thought a bumbling fool was anything but, indeed in many quarters she would be regarded as something of a catch.

'Briefly,' she told him. 'Didn't work out. Weeks rather than months.'

'Why?' he asked.

'I fell in love with someone else. And you?' she asked quickly.

'Me?'

'Have you ever been married?'

'I think you know the answer to that.'

The waitress lit the candles on their table.

'Fruit, ouzo, retsina,' she offered.

'No, no, we have had enough.' They shook their heads as one. The waitress disappeared into the back of the taverna before reappearing almost immediately with two small bowls of apricots. No, is not an option in Greece.

Erik was not sure why, maybe it was just the romantic location, but he leaned over the table and kissed Celia's cheek before she had time to draw back.

'Don't worry, you know me, no long term attachments,' he reassured her.

'That's just it, I only do attachments.'

'Seriously?'

'Serious attachments, otherwise what's the point.'

They walked back to the jeep in silence.

'Jordan and Grey, we could be solicitors.' He attempted to break the impasse driving back to the villa.

'Yes, let's keep it that way, a working relationship,' she told him coolly.

* * * * *

Erik woke up to the staccato clang of a church bell—bells only sounded like that in the islands—ringing across the softening expanse of Ionian sea. Celia stood at the end of his bed like an apparition.

'Have you forgotten it's Sunday?' she asked him, pulling away his sheet.

'You want to be careful doing that,' he told her. 'Never know what you might find.'

'I've a good idea. Coffee?' she asked. 'Someone has left us a welcome pack: eggs, bread, butter, jam and packet of Loumidis.'

'Breakfast would be lovely.'

'Good, because once you are dressed you are making it. I'm off for a short walk.'

'Kaliméra,' to the old man walking the unmade lane outside their villa. The old man parchment against a blazing backdrop of wild flowers, flowering fennel and thyme. 'Kaliméra,' to the old woman seated against the blue and white church.

Celia looked at her watch on the headland above a sea sparkling with diamonds. Half an hour into her walk, time to turn back.

She was almost home on the cliff path when she called 'Kaliméra' for a third time. No response; no responding 'good morning'; no white and blue church and old lady's indulgent smile; no toothless smile framed in wild flowers; no smile at all from the expressionless face. She rushed back into the Villa Astraea. There was something ominous about the man passing their gate.

'Eggs and toast, ready. Greek Loumidis coffee brewing,' announced Erik, pleased with himself.

There was a knock on the door and a middle-aged woman, introducing herself as Maria, stood there. Maria the owner, or to be precise the mother of Vasilios the villa owner, come to clean.

'*Ekklisia sýntoma*,' announced Maria.

'Church soon,' translated Erik.

'Yes,' agreed Maria hesitantly. '*Epeita, épeita.*'

'You are going to church afterwards.'

'I have just had a strange experience,' Celia told them. 'I greeted a man outside and he blanked me.'

'"Blanked me"?' Maria repeated at a loss.

'Yes, I wished this gentleman "*Kaliméra*" and he made no reply, just stared.' Celia opened her arms to indicate bewilderment.

'Ah, stared,' said Maria, realisation slowly dawning on her.

She grasped the hands of both Erik and Celia, drawing them towards the open doorway, and pointed across the heavily wooded valley.

'Two *Rósoi*, villa over there,' she explained.

'"*Rósoi*"?' It was Celia's turn to be nonplussed.

'Russians,' translated Erik with raised eyebrows. 'She is saying two Russians are staying in a villa over there.'

'Naí, *naí*,' said Maria, nodding enthusiastically.

'Is she saying "no"?' asked Celia.

'No she is saying "yes". Naí is "yes" in Greek, *ochi* is "no".' Erik felt empowered.

'Naí, *Rósoi*, boom!' exclaimed Maria, screwing her face up with disapproval.

She set about the villa with added determination, singing happily with her bucket and mop, as her new guests settled to breakfast on the balcony in thoughtful silence.

'Russians?' Celia was first to speak. 'It seems Maria has made up her mind that these Russians living over the valley are responsible for the bomb.'

Erik watched Celia nervously shattering the shell of her egg. He tried to laugh it off.

'Just conjecture, no proof,' he reassured her.

* * * * *

The jeep bounced down the steep hill to the harbour below. They had unpinned the canvas top, rolled down the windows, and again Celia smelt the pungency of herbs from the hedgerows. It was the same warm smell, although she did not feel very warm at that moment. She pulled her cardigan tighter about her.

The tiny village square was empty.

'This stillness is eerie,' she said.

'Everyone will be in church,' said Erik. 'A good thing because we will be able to examine the scene unhindered.'

'Over there,' she pointed further down the harbour front. 'See, that area cordoned off with scene of crime tape.'

Pretty red and white striped tape billowed in the breeze. It looked more like a festival decoration than a boundary of death. It was arranged so as not to cut off the village square from the main road out. It was draped in segments, ragged and abandoned, the *Elliniki Astynomia* must have gone back to Athens days ago.

Erik took a camera out of his satchel and began snapping at distance down the waterfront. A hole was cut into the quayside exposing construction rubble. 'The yacht must have been moored there.'

They moved forward carefully. A quick check round. There was nobody to see as they ducked beneath the police tape. A yard or two on, down the quay, they found a large oily smudge on the stonework.

'What happened here?' Before the question had left Celia's mouth, she feared she knew the answer.

'This must be the spot where Adras' nephew was caught in the explosion,' confirmed Erik.

'How terrible. Just to leave a stain like this.' A shiver ran the length of Celia's spine.

Adras' uncle's bar, at the far end of the quay, appeared to be wrecked yet the bakery next door looked untouched. They began circling outside the bombed out bar cautiously.

Snap. Snap. Erik's camera began to irritate Celia as if it was some form of intrusion into private grief.

The wall between the bar and the water had been blown out. The tables and chairs had gone on the crazy paved terrace, save one horribly mangled chair. The building was empty inside and looked unstable. However they could see on the vinyl covered bar—now mostly covered in cement—a single empty bottle remained upright and alone.

'Someone must have removed any intact stock days ago,' said Erik.

'No free drinks to be had here.' Celia's laugh echoed hollow.

'It is as if the old crones out of *Zorba the Greek* have come in and stripped the joint clean.'

'I never saw that film.'

'Did you not? It was first released in 1964 starring Anthony Quinn and Alan Bates.'

'Before my time.'

'Before mine too. But that isn't the point, it was a classic.'

They decided to visit the tiny supermarket off the square—the only supermarket open for Sunday trade—but got little out of the taciturn storekeeper.

'Bomb, what bomb?' he spat between open arms.

'The bomb that blew a luxury yacht out of the water over there,' persisted Erik.

'And killed a little boy,' added Celia.

'Who are you wanting to know about bomb?' asked the storekeeper.

'We are from an English newspaper,' explained Erik.

'Puh! Newspapers,' spat the man again.

'We aren't going to get much out of this one,' stage whispered Erik.

They retreated to a cafe, to a table squashed against a wall, and tried to settle their frustrations with another cup of strong Greek coffee.

Church over, confessions discharged, the village was slowly getting back to life. It was amazing to watch how locals on motorcycles, mopeds and cars had become adept at negotiating the damaged road between their table and the sea.

'This is so bizarre, such destruction and carnage in such a beautiful place,' Celia was saying as two yachtsmen arrived and plonked themselves down at a table abutting theirs. Both men still wore their lifejackets. They talked of wives back home and boasted of women coming onto them.

'Did you see the way she leaned over the hand railings in that low cut vest? She really fancied you,' said one of them. He looked as if he had terminal cancer or maybe he was just recovering from seasickness.

'Fancied the boat more than her,' replied his little rotund, bald-headed friend. They both sniggered over their beers like schoolboys.

Erik opened his phone and switched it to mute. He examined the original recording of the anonymous footage of the bombing sent to Reuters.

'Everyone thought this was sent in by a tourist but was it?' queried Erik quietly. 'What if it was sent in by the bomber standing right over there?' He pointed to his left, to what looked like a derelict warehouse at the opposite end of the quay.

'Ah, the old soap factory of Anemogiannis,' Celia informed him.

'Of what?

'The factory was named after Georgios Anemogiannis. He was a hero of Paxos during the Greek War of Independence against the Ottomans.'

'How on earth do you know all this, Celia?'

Was that some sort of appreciation she saw in his eyes? No, she must have imagined it. She took a slim book out of her backpack, shaking it in his face. 'I'm the one with the tourist guide, remember?'

'Come,' he said, wrapping a note in the little glass cup for their coffees. 'Let's go and take a look inside.'

The factory was roofless. Shrubs and all kinds of vegetation had invaded the floor space.

'You are right,' Celia agreed, peeping out of the broken shuttered window. 'All the angles line up. But how could the bomb have been detonated from here?'

Erik lifted up his iPhone. 'Simply, with one of these.'

'But how exactly?'

'Either an improvised explosive had been fixed to the yacht itself previously or someone knew exactly where the yacht would be moored.'

'Are you saying it could have already been attached on the harbour wall waiting for the yacht to come in.'

'From the destruction of the road and wall that is my favoured scenario.'

They examined the floor where they stood. There were a few broken slates from the roof but surprisingly very little litter. One or two beer cans lay strewn about.

'What's that?' asked Celia.

Something glinted silver near Erik's foot. He picked it up from amid a small pile of filter cigarette butts. It was a retro gas lighter embossed with a double eagle emblem. He clicked the flint and there was a burst of butane flame.

'Still in working order,' he muttered in amazement.

They heard a crunch of broken tiles and swung round as one.

'Hello, hello,' someone called out.

Erik quickly pocketed the gas lighter. Celia stared in amazement at the two men confronting them. One she recognised as the indifferent Russian passing their villa earlier that morning.

'Lovely day,' said the other man ridiculously. 'What are you doing in here?' he asked.

'We could ask you the same question. Why are you in here?' countered Erik brusquely.

'We are thinking of buying this place.'

'I see. However I understood it was no longer for sale,' fabricated Erik.

'What is not for sale in Greece today is tomorrow,' piped up the man who had blanked Celia that morning.

'I think it rather dangerous to be standing in here,' said his companion. Whether this was a statement of fact or a threat, Erik was not sure. 'You must come round to villa for drinks,' he continued.

'Yes, yes, we must,' replied Erik without conviction.

'Tomorrow evening,' insisted the Russian, writing down the villa's address on the back of a business card. Then they were gone.

'We aren't going?' Celia was horrified.

'Of course,' Erik asserted calmly, twizzling the business card in his hand. 'We might learn something.'

'What does it say on the card,' she asked.

'It says he represents a property company.'

'Aye, that rings as true as Russia having nothing to do with the Salisbury poisonings.'

'You think they might feed us Novichok in our cocktails?'

'I think they look like two thugs.'

Erik squatted down on the floor, carefully placing the cigarette butts in an envelope and putting them in his trouser pocket together with the lighter. He decided not to push the Russian villa visit with Celia but let it rest for the time being. It was not until they were enjoying two long orange drinks by the pool, back at their own villa, that he remembered the lighter and butts in his pocket.

'That's interesting,' he said, examining the lighter.

'What's interesting?' she asked, yawing wearily.

'This, it's Russian.'

CHAPTER SIX

After a swim and light breakfast the next day, they visited Gaios in late morning. Parking the jeep at the New Port, they walked along the long marina to the centre of the old town. They explored the narrow streets selling everything from flip-flops, sunhats to cotton summer wear. The smell of baked bread and cooking gyros on open spits filled their senses as they crossed a small square bedecked with cafes, tavernas, where Greek orthodoxy seemed to have been pushed to one side in the interest of tourism and commerce.

'That's the Venetian Church of Saint Apostles,' Celia told Erik, after rummaging through the pages of her tourist guide.

'It's tiny.' True to form Erik associated grand architecture with size. However he was not blind to Venetian influence in many of the old Ionian villas they walked past along the seafront road.

'And there he is, Georgios Anemogiannis, in all his glory.' Celia pointed to an impressive green bronze of a young man holding a torch like an Olympian. The statue was set on its own plinth and platform jutting out into the sea.

'Tell me more about him.'

'In 1821, he was a twenty-three year old Paxos captain of a fire ship sent in to burn the Ottoman fleet. Like all the best Greek tragedies he tried but failed, was captured at Nafpaktos by the Turks, before being tortured and killed. I believe they have a statue of Georgios, in a similar pose, on the parapet at the fort at Nafpaktos too. But ultimately he is celebrated as a principal Paxos hero.'

They returned to the main square and sat at a table beneath a huge umbrella. They ordered beers and Celia had a plate of pastitsio while Erik enjoyed vegetable fritters. After lunch they walked back along the snaking marina, passing hundreds of luxury yachts displaying flags from around the world.

A party of Adras' friends and relatives were already gathered in the New Port to meet the ferry from Corfu. The relatives regarded the two English foreigners with scant interest. They had more important family matters to attend to. A small band began tuning up.

'Do you think this is all for him?' asked Celia.

'Undoubtedly so. Another Greek hero.'

After all the other passengers had disembarked from the ferry, a cheerful Adras was wheeled off by two sailors. They placed his gurney on the harbour side with tender care. Loving family members bent to hug and kiss him. When emotions had subsided and there was a lull, Celia and Erik stepped in holding out a copy of the *London Evening Record*. Adras' face smiled down on him from the front page like a mirror image.

'I'm still a handsome guy, aren't I?' he laughed. 'You will both come to my house and visit?'

'Hello again,' said a voice in broken English from behind them. 'How are you both?'

Erik and Celia did not have time to react to the intrusion, as ear-piercing sirens rang out on the road above the New Port. The welcoming party turned to glimpse blue flashing lights through the olive trees. The two Russian men faded into the background.

'Surely the police are not here to welcome me too,' said Adras; beyond caring, just glad to be back home.

'No, they're racing past,' Erik told him. 'Come,' he said tugging at Celia. 'Let's see what's going on.'

'I wouldn't trouble yourself,' one of the Russians shouted after them. 'Probably minor road traffic accident.'

Too late, Erik had already jumped into the jeep and started the engine.

'Don't forget drinks tonight,' shouted the other Russian, as the jeep's tyres screeched on the concrete.

'Bloody Russians,' swore Erik.

'Must say they are persistent. They seem to be stalking us, turning up like that,' muttered Celia.

They did not know it then but those sirens breaking across the peace of Paxos—heralded something else entirely—changed everything about the story they were pursuing.

They saw the blue flashing lights ahead turning right off the main road and bouncing down an unmade track going towards the sea. They followed until a line of police cars blocked their way. Beyond that a line of familiar Greek scene of crime red and white tape cut across the track.

Rubbernecking above vehicle roofs and police heads, what looked like a small pale beached whale was just visible on the sloping pebble beach. But it was not a whale.

'A body,' murmured Erik. 'A man's body, I think.'

'*Poios eísai*?' demanded a policeman on guard. '*Poios eísai*?'

'What's he saying?' asked Celia.

'Who are you,' translated Erik, struggling to get his press card out of his satchel as another uniformed policeman strode towards them from across the beach.

'Can I help?' asked the officer in perfect English. Judging from the pips on his shoulders and the braid on his cap, he was high ranking. He smiled pleasantly, examining Erik's card. 'So, Mr Jordan, what finds you here?'

'*Eímaste dýo dimosiográfoi pou kánoun diakopés,*' replied Erik, refusing to be discouraged from using Greek.

'What are two holidaying journalists doing on Kaki Lagada Beach?' The officer was equally determined to try out his English.

'We were going for a swim,' lied Erik.

'Not today, not from here, as you can see.'

'Who is it?' asked Erik, nodding towards the body.

'He has no identification on him whatsoever. Naked as the day he was born, isn't that how you say it? Pulled out an hour ago by one of your fellow countrymen, who also likes the swimming.'

Celia could see a blond man a little off the half-circle of policemen. He was seated cross-legged on the beach, covered in a blanket, and shivering though the day was hot.

'Can we take a closer look?' asked Erik.

'Why, do you think you might know dead man?'

'Maybe.' Erik tried to sound convincing.

The senior officer beckoned Erik forward, lifting the tape, while signalling for Celia to stay back with his other hand.

'This is no sight for lady,' he told her. This after all was Greece. Celia's chin trembled at the slight.

As Erik and the senior officer approached, the other policemen parted like the Red Sea.

'Terrible, a terrible thing to see on a day like this.' Erik pulled out his handkerchief to cover his mouth and nose fearing he might gag.

There was a smell. Flies had begun to amass round the bloated body. The man, who had long ceased to be a man, rested on his back. There was a livid bruise to the left side of his face. He looked up at the sky through eyeless sockets.

'Well, do you recognise him?'

'Not sure,' prevaricated Erik.

'So, you can't identify this man?'

'It would be difficult to identify anyone in this state. He must have been in the water for weeks.'

'Not necessarily. This is not your North Sea. Waters round Paxos are warm, degrading bodies quicker.'

'He couldn't just be someone caught up in the Loggos incident, collateral damage as it were?'

'I don't believe in collateral damage, Mr Jordan. I only believe in murder or accidental death. Now tell me what are you and your colleague really doing on Paxos? You certainly weren't going swimming, not without towels. And regular tourists don't carry business satchels around with them.'

'We've come to investigate the luxury yacht bombing,' admitted Erik.

'You don't really think these two incidents are connected?'

'His watch has been removed.' Erik pointed to the white band of skin round the dead man's wrist, ignoring the connected question. 'And, see there, that looks like garrotte marks round his throat and neck.'

'Have no worries, team of forensic officers are flying in from Athens as we speak. They are experts, they will get to the bottom of this.'

'Why do you *not* think the two incidents are connected?' Erik threw the question back at him. 'I mean how often do things like this happen on this small quiet island?'

'I'd better escort you back to girlfriend,' shrugged the officer.

'She's not my girlfriend. She is a colleague.'

'Here is my card, Captain Vasilakis at your service.' He even bowed. 'Greek police always wish to be friends with English press. Please call at our station in Gaios in next few days time and we might have more information. If deceased is fellow countryman you might be of use to us.'

Erik thanked him and moved towards the threshold of red and white tape.

'All right mate?' On passing he put a comforting hand on the shoulder of the figure cowering in the blanket.

The blond man just grunted.

'Poor guy is still in shock,' explained Captain Vasilakis.

* * * * *

'I am boREES and he is troFEEM,' announced one of the Russians.

'BoREES and troFEEM,' Celia repeated. Trofim was the ignorant one who had blanked her that morning.

'Yees.' Ingratiating golden tooth smile from Boris.

'Drinks,' offered Trofim; the usually silent straight guy in their double act.

'Ouzo or Vodka?' asked Boris.

Erik could see this was going to be a heavy night.

'Ouzo, with plenty of water for me,' he told Boris.

'Me too,' pealed in Celia.

'With plenty of water?' asked Boris doubtfully. Celia nodded.

'Nice villa,' she told them; wondering for the life of her what she was doing here, how she had ever let Erik talk her into coming.

'Yees.' The ingratiating smile again.

Will you walk into my parlour? said the spider to the fly, foresaw Celia.

'Did you catch police car?' Boris asked Erik, passing him the milky liquid first.

Neither Erik nor Celia ventured a reply.

'Well, I guess some granny lost her goat,' laughed Boris.

'A nanny goat. Good joke, yes?' entreated Trofim.

'Amazing, bumping into you at the New Port like that,' Erik was not laughing.

'We heard *oompah-pah* and wanted to know what was going on,' tight-smiled Boris.

A likely story, thought Celia. The New Port was way off most tourist action.

'Nothing much ever seems to happen in this place.' Boris again.

'Not like Moscow, eh?' Erik could not resist saying.

It was the Russians' turn for reticence. Silence fell for an uncomfortable duration.

'No, nothing like Moscow,' Boris finally conceded. 'But who said anything about Moscow? We both from Novgorod.'

'"Novgorod",' repeated Celia.

'Bet you don't know Novgorod.'

'Yes, I do. It's in western Russia.'

'But you are looking for property here,' Erik sought to confirm.

Boris offered to top Celia's glass up with neat ouzo from the bottle but she declined, covering her hand over the glass.

'I'm driving,' she explained.

'Surely, you OK on these unmade tracks. Hardly ever seen vehicles on them,' persisted Boris.

'Nevertheless, I cannot afford to risk landing in a Greek prison,' she stressed.

'So, are you both still interested in putting down an offer for the old soap factory of Anemogiannis?' Erik changed the subject.

'Nooo, maybe not. Russians like bars, life. Plenty of bars and life on Corfu. Here too quiet,' said Trofim.

'Really?'

'Yees,' said Trofim.

'Even when a luxury yacht, owned by one of your fellow countrymen, has been blown out of the water?' tested Erik.

'What yacht? Where?' Trofim spread his arms askance. He made no effort to sound convincing.

'That was isolated incident,' cut in Boris.

'Now a body has been washed up on Kaki Lagada Beach,' Erik told them.

'Well, well.' Boris appeared surprised.

'Who was he?' asked Trofim.

'I didn't say whether it was a he or she.'

'Usually it is men,' said Boris.

'Not from drowning,' interrupted Celia. 'I've checked the statistics.'

'Back to your original question. They have no idea who *he* was.' Erik studied the faces of both Russians carefully for a reaction.

'Truly?' asked Boris; his face as expressionless as Jo Stalin's death mask.

'Every source of identification was removed from his body.'

'Didn't want anyone to know who he was then.'

'Or that he was murdered,' suggested Erik.

'A professional job perhaps,' proposed Celia.

'Perhaps,' said Boris thoughtfully.

'More ouzo anyone?' asked Trofim. Celia and Erik shook their heads—clear heads were called for in this situation—the atmosphere was growing icy by the minute.

'Tell me, Erik, what you and Celia really doing here on Paxos?' asked Boris.

'We are journalists covering the Loggos bombing.' Erik had decided to come clean. Giving information, in his experience, could lead to gaining information. But then he had never had to deal with Russian G.U. operatives—G.U. an abbreviation for Main (Intelligence) Directorate—which he undoubtedly recognised these two men as being part of.

'Ha! Ha! This makes sense.' Trofim's laughter was hollow.

'And you two? What are you both doing on this small island remote from the main Russian tourist routes?' asked Erik.

'As I said we are exploring property potentials,' explained Boris. No offer of a marble swop here.

'But Trofim just said there isn't enough going on in Paxos for Russian tourists,' persisted Erik.

'That is quite so. But one or two of our clients are actually interested in owning holiday rentals on Paxos.'

'Like the soap factory?' Erik took the Russian double-headed eagle lighter out of his pocket and held it under G.U. noses. Celia exhaled in disbelief. 'Either of you recognise this?'

Boris took the lighter from him and examined it with myopic scrutiny.

'Where did you say you found?' he asked.

'On the floor of the soap factory,' confirmed Erik.

'These retro lighters for sale not just in Russian Federation but in China, Ukraine, everywhere.' Boris waved the lighter about before passing it dismissively across to Trofim for further examination.

'I suspect whoever detonated the bomb on the harbour front could be the last person to use this lighter,' announced Erik, pushing his luck.

'You think we did this terrible thing?' asked Trofim, with all the sincerity of a Yeltsin and Gorbachev kiss.

'I said nothing of the sort,' replied Erik.

'I'm sure Erik didn't mean ...' began Celia.

'No, but that is what he is implying,' interrupted Boris sulkily, sweeping Celia's appeasement aside.

Celia was getting increasingly worried at how this visit was working out. She did not like the way the two Russians were looking at her, particularly Trofim.

'Perhaps Celia would like to stay little longer with us,' suggested Trofim.

'What good would come of that?' demanded Erik.

'Your cooperation,' came Boris' sinister reply.

'She comes home with me,' said Erik.

'If we are bombers, why should we let either of you go?' asked Boris.

'Because we have made sure many people here and in England know where we are tonight. And I am guessing you have no wish to draw that kind of attention on yourselves,' pointed out Erik.

'I think we best call evening at an end,' said Boris. 'Just one thing before you go, Mr Jordan, the murdered owner of yacht was Dmitry Smirnov. Although Mr Smirnov based in London, he worked all over world. He happened to be close friend of President Putin.'

'I know that,' disclosed Erik.

'So you will know we all pursuing same end.' Boris downed his third ouzo in one.

'To find out who committed act of terrorism,' added Trofim.

Nods of understanding all the way round.

'Forgive my curiosity but might I ask how things are in Russia today?' asked Erik.

'Fine, things just fine. People have enough to eat on their tables and churches being built.' Boris' chin jutted pride.

'I thought the average Russian became poorer with the collapse of the USSR. At least during the time of the fifteen republics people were assured of a job, house and a plot of land to grow vegetables,' pressed Erik.

'No, things are good.'

'Good for a few at the top of the feeding chain, that is what I heard.'

'You are mistaken. This dangerous talk.' The threat was there in Boris' voice again. 'Where you hear such things?'

Erik cast him an appeasing glance. 'Must be fake news.'

On that Erik and Celia took their leave—relieved to be allowed to leave.

'Thought we were facing a hostage situation there,' said Erik, on the drive back across the valley.

'Thanks for coming to my aid.'

'Decent of him, though, offering to take you off my hands.'

'You don't really believe anything those two thugs said?' Celia suddenly fell serious.

'Not entirely,' replied Erik. 'But at least we have established one thing.'

'What's that?'

'They're not here simply to buy property.'

CHAPTER SEVEN

Erik slept well that night. His dreams were good. Celia had praised him for their Russian escape with the briefest of goodnight kisses on the cheek.

In the morning they asked Maria if they could extend their stay by a few days.

'No visitors for two week,' she told them, nodding happily to the motion of her broom.

'Do you know where Adras lives?' asked Celia.

'*Boom!*' exclaimed Maria. '*Tromerés, tromerés.*'

'Yes, but do you know where he lives?' Celia repeated the question. No answer.

'*Pou eínai to spíti tou*?' asked Erik.

'Ah!' said Maria. '*To spíti tou eínai káto apó to lófo.*'

'What does she say?' asked Celia.

'Down the hill,' translated Erik. 'I guess we just ask for Adras' house in Loggos village.'

They did just that, calling into the tiny supermarket off the square again. This time, to humour the owner, they decided to fill a basket with a few food provisions first. Then they carefully selected items they were running out of: cloths; soap; washing up liquid and more toilet rolls—the Greek villa owners were very conservative regarding their supplies of bathroom tissues—Celia theorised that they did not like their toilet bins overflowing.

'It's good to get these things now,' said Erik, filling the car boot with plastic bags on the quay. Worries over plastic pollution obviously had not hit the Greek Islands yet. 'Everything closes down at two o'clock for siesta.'

'Sure,' yelled Celia, who was flip-flopping in a dream some metres behind. Once empty handed they both returned back to the shopkeeper.

'*Poú eínai to spíti tou*, Adras, *parakaló*?' Erik asked him in his best Greek.

'*Ekeí*,' said today's more amenable owner, pointing across to a substantial villa with a red pantile roof.

'Greetings,' said Adras from his couch.

A middle-aged woman in black, whom Celia thought she recognised among Adras' welcoming party at Gaios, hovered in the background.

'My mother,' introduced Adras. Pleasant mutterings all the way round.

Mitéra soon disappeared, assured that they were known to her son and intended him no harm.

'You are not the first foreign friends to visit me this morning,' Adras boasted.

'Oh?' Erik flickered interest.

'Yes, two Russian guys called. They said they were renting up the road.'

'What did they want?' asked Erik; a meaningful look passing between him and Celia. Adras did not miss it— Adras who missed nothing.

'They question me about the bombing like you. Who was about before it happened, that sort of thing. I didn't tell them much. I didn't like them very much. I think I've seen those two before but I cannot remember where.'

'The New Port,' offered Celia.

'No, no, before then. My head, my memory has been all messed up,' admitted Adras. 'There is something else I forgot to tell you.'

'Go on,' prompted Erik.

'The man who sat outside the bar and left just before the explosion …'

'Yes?' said Erik.

'I think he could have been Russian too.'

* * * * *

Once back at the villa they resumed Erik's swimming lessons.

'Perfect for de-stressing,' Celia told him.

'Yes, I certainly could do with some of that with all these morose Russians about,' shouted Erik, through his open bedroom door, as he slipped into his swim shorts. 'Creepy.'

'Perhaps murderous,' she shouted back.

'Perhaps,' he frowned.

Celia always insisted they did floatation exercises before swimming. This involved some physical support for him on her part, some bodily closeness that Erik found slightly disconcerting while being perfectly relaxed in every other sense. As she gently lifted him back on his feet from the supine position, he turned and they finished standing face to face on tiptoe in the deep end.

He gently lifted her chin to kiss her. She pushed him roughly away with both hands, and he found himself tumbling back. *Splash*! A wall of water closed round him as he lost his footing. He struggled to breathe, struggled for air.

Realising her charge was in trouble, Celia lifted him back onto his feet again. He felt as if she was toying with him. This was her domain and he was her toy.

'Bloody hell, you nearly drowned me there,' he spluttered. 'What on earth is wrong with you?'

'Never do that again,' she hissed. 'Never try to take advantage of me again.'

'It was just a kiss,' he protested.

'All the same,' she said, 'I'm not just another of your conquests.'

'But Celia I like you.'

She raised both hands, speechless, and stormed out of the pool into the villa.

They did not speak again that day. He took the jeep out that evening, leaving her reading on the balcony. By way of an afterthought he reversed back, rolled down the window, and asked if he could bring her anything. She shook her head.

She heard his tyres slipping on the villa's unmade track, saw the dust flying in a cloud trail as he reached the road. Carefully placing her book on the wicker table, she went to her bedroom to fetch a cardigan. She felt in need of exercise. She had time for a quick walk before total darkness came in.

When Erik returned a few hours later, she was nowhere to be seen. He presumed she must have gone to bed. Knowing her bedroom was out of bounds for him, he was forced to leave it at that.

* * * * *

She did not trust the cliff path at night but took the main metalled road which went down into the village. She had walked only a hundred metres or so when an ominous slate grey car slowed beside her. Her heart began to pound. Was she in danger? There was no one out here to see.

'*Kaló apógevma*,' said the passenger, winding down his window. 'Nice evening for walk.'

Oh, God, she thought. It was Trofim with Boris driving.

'Get in,' said Boris, leaning across.

'Sorry, no, Erik will be expecting me back.' She tried to stop the shake in her voice.

'We saw Erik going into taverna by harbour few minutes ago,' said Trofim.

'Are you stalking me?' Caught out in a lie, she was angry now.

'Not at all. Why you think that?' asked Trofim.

'Stalking, isn't that what persons do in Scotland? Get in,' repeated Boris.

'Get in and we'll take you back to villa. Lady not safe out alone at this time,' said Trofim. He bent backwards, swinging open the back door to block her path.

Flight or fight, she wondered, quickly discounting both options. There were two of them and they were big men. Reluctantly she slid onto the back seat.

'This isn't the way to my villa,' she protested, peering through the tinted windows.

'*Our* villa,' emphasised Trofim.

'Are you kidnapping me?' she asked.

'No, we merely wish to finish other night's conversation,' explained Boris.

Nevertheless, they both closely escorted her into the building leaving no room for escape.

'Ouzo?' offered Boris. She shook her head. She felt sick. 'Coffee, tea then?' Again she declined.

'Boris and I think you too good for Erik, can do much better than Erik,' announced Trofim.

'He is just a colleague.'

'I see things he has written in newspaper,' said Boris. 'Big defender of black people, poor people and gays, is he not?'

'He is a bit of an activist, I'll give you that.'

'Ah, activist,' pondered Boris. 'How activist when he is establishment? When he was educated at Eton?'

'You would have to ask him that,' grumbled Celia, tiring of the cross-examination.

'What do you think he will write about bombing?'

'How do I know?'

'How much do you both know?'

Now we are getting to it, she realised.

'What will *you* write?' cut in Trofim.

'Yes, Celia Grey has quite an audience round world too,' added Boris. 'With special interest in women's rights, is that not so?'

'Something of a lone Pussy Riot,' sneered Trofim.

'Yes, with LGBT sympathies,' concurred Boris.

'You have done your homework on us both.' Celia was becoming increasingly uncomfortable. Where was all this leading?

'Know your enemy, isn't that English saying?' asked Boris.

'Sounds biblical to me,' retorted Celia dismissively. 'And why do you think we are your enemies?'

'We are simply curious. How much have you learnt about bombing? Are you going to write anything detrimental to Russian state?' Boris smoothed down his few strands of hair.

'Why should I if Russia has nothing to do with the bombing?'

'We want to be friends but English press always rubbishing

us.' Celia smiled at Boris' use of the present participle. 'You smile but this is extremely serious matter.'

'No one knows where you are.' Trofim's oblique interruption.

'Is that a threat?' she asked.

'No, just statement of fact,' replied Trofim.

'You should pray that Erik doesn't come looking for me.'

'We never pray. We are communists,' brushed off poker-faced Boris indifferently.

'Do you intend to keep me here against my will?' she asked him.

'No, no, we just want to encourage you towards right path,' he replied.

'And that is?'

'President Putin would never have wanted Smirnov dead.'

'So who did?'

Boris half-smiled. 'If we knew that. That is sixty-thousand dollar question.'

'Could he have upset someone in London?' she asked.

'Maybe. I can tell you Dmitry Smirnov came from upstanding family who had lived for centuries on the Russia and Ukrainian border at Belgorod. No Russians would be involved in bombing.'

* * * * *

'Did you have a good evening?' Erik asked her the next morning over her routine yogurt and fruit.

'Yes, did you?' she replied coldly.

He nodded. 'Had a few drinks in the village and a chickpea burger with tzatziki sauce.'

'What time did you get in?'

'About eleven-thirty.'

'Oh, an hour and a half before me.'

'What do you mean? Where were you?'

'Being held against my will.'

'You *are* joking?' Despite his tan, Erik went pale as she regaled him with her tale of Russian interrogation.

'I'm going up to that bloody villa right now and have it out with them,' he snarled.

'No, don't do that. It will only make matters worse.'

'But they can't take people hostage like that.'

'Listen, I learnt something, they told me that Dmitry Smirnov came from an upstanding family in a place called Belgorod. Did you know that?'

'Belgorod? I heard that name mentioned recently. That's it, I remember now, Nicos did tell me Smirnov originated from there.'

'And you didn't think to tell me?'

'I didn't consider it important.'

'We have to start working together, Erik. This whole investigation will fail unless we do.'

'I agree. Let's shake on it.' He reached out his hand. Despite feeling it to be theatrical, she took it.

'Paxos is one of the most beautiful islands in Greece. But there is something bad going on here. The fact that the bombing took place in paradise makes it all the more poignant,' she said.

'That's very good. Write it down. I will use those very words in my latest communication with London.'

'Look Erik, seriously, I was in fear of my life last night with those two Russians. I am getting really frightened here.'

'What are those birds circling up there?' asked Eric, pointing to the morning sky, turning the conversation.

'Birds of prey,' Celia told him.

'Yes, but what are they called?'

'I think they are Eleonora's Falcons. We used to see a lot of them in eastern Crete.'

'See how they soar using the thermal currents. Amazing birds.'

'Yes, they are amazing. However they have a unique darker side,' she informed him. 'During the breeding season, in late summer, they have been known to harvest small migratory birds. After catching their prey, they pluck out their flight feathers rendering them helpless but keeping them alive. Then they store these captives in their nests or among rock crevices to be harvested a day or two later to feed their young.'

'Just imagine if you are a tiny chiffchaff knowing what fate awaits you.' Erik's face screwed up behind his lifted arm as he continued to watch the falcons swirling above.

'I am beginning to feel like one of those flightless chiffchaffs myself,' Celia told him.

'How do you mean?'

'Contained, controlled, without self-determination until someone decides otherwise.'

'Don't worry, we won't be here much longer. Is it those two bastards across the valley that's upset you?'

'I am not sure exactly by whom but I have this niggling feeling we are being manipulated.'

* * * * *

Erik decided to take the cigarette butts and lighter to Captain Vasilakis that morning. Perhaps there would be a chance to exchange information.

Cigar smoke drifted through the Captain's ajar office door. Erik knocked all the same, instantly coughing on the fug.

'We know who dead man is,' were the first words to greet him out of Vasilakis' Havana clenched teeth. 'Come in and shut the door, Mr Jordan.'

'So, who was he?'

'A Greek officer working for Interpol. They suspected the *Bettina* was either involved with money laundering or drug running.'

'"*Bettina*",' repeated Erik thoughtfully.

'Yes, named after Dmitry Smirnov's wife. Ironically it wasn't his wife who was killed with him aboard boat.'

'Don't tell me, his personal assistant.'

'I expect that was the unfortunate Anna Markova's job description.'

'So are you saying Smirnov was suspected of trading something heavier than iron ore?'

'"Heavier"?—a matter of interpretation. I see you already know about Mr Smirnov's business interests.'

'Obviously, not well enough.'

'Money laundering, drugs etc. are matter of speculation, you understand. Nothing is proven.'

'But that sort of criminal activity could easily be a motive for murder.'

'Indeed.'

'Why are you telling me all this?'

'Whatever I tell you is off record.'

'You know as well as I do nothing is ever off the record.'

'Let us say I am gambling that a leak here and there in world's press might flush more important truths out.'

Erik handed him the envelope with the cigarette butts inside and the Russian lighter. 'We found these on the floor of the Anemogiannis soap factory.'

'I am sure I asked my men to check that place carefully.'

'Do you think that whoever detonated the Loggos bomb might have been standing in those ruins?'

'Could be.' Vasilakis was not about to give anything more away. 'You have beaten us to evidence.'

Erik kept his own counsel. He had no wish to point to Greek police incompetence at this stage.

Vasilakis called for another officer to bag up Erik's exhibits. He instructed the woman to take a cheek swab from Erik too.

'For DNA purposes only. There will have been some cross-contamination.' The Captain's justification fell into Erik's surprised gawping mouth. 'Might as well take your fingerprints as they will be all over lighter along with possible owner's. You can do that on your way out.'

Erik wondered if this marked his abrupt dismissal.

'By the way,' he told Vasilakis, stalling, 'we have some weird Russians staying over the valley from us.'

'Ah! Boris and Trofim. They are harmless. Russian government is as keen to know who killed Dmitry Smirnov as we are.'

'And Anna Markova, and Adras' nephew, not to mention the yacht's two British crew members,' pointed out Erik heatedly.

'We Greeks do not forget them.' Vasilakis looked offended.

'The forgotten ones.'

'No, no, never. Not one of them.'

'Especially not the Greek Interpol officer.'

'No, not him either.'

'His death must be connected with the bombing,' suggested Erik.

'Maybe you are right, but we might never be able to prove it.'

'What was his name?'

'Aleixo.'

'His surname,' persisted Erik.

Vasilakis shook his head decisively.

'You must be good at your job, Mr Jordan, but so am I. Going back to crew members, there were actually three of them but one was taken ill and remained on Corfu just before boat sailed.'

'And who was that?'

'A deckhand, name of Simmons, Jacob Simmons of Shrewsbury. Now this is where I think you could really be helpful to me, Erik. May I call you that?' Vasilakis winked. 'Someone must have tipped bombers off about boat's sailing schedule.'

'Celia and I have already considered that.'

'Will you let me know if you learn anything of interest about Mr Simmons?'

'Where is he now?'

'Without a boat to crew, I expected him to eventually return to England.'

'You've contacted Interpol about him?'

'Yes, and they say he is not in Shrewsbury.'

'He's disappeared?'

'According to your British police.'

'But why would he go missing like this if he's not involved?'

'Shock maybe,' offered Vasilakis. 'You must understand, Mr Jordan, crew of these luxury vessels live on them, some all year round, rent free, food provided, generous wages. Work is hard but there are compensations. Home, where Mr Simmons usually rested his head, has been blown out of water. Other crew members he would have regarded as family have been wiped out.'

'So, do you think this Simmons was involved with the bombing or not?'

'Who knows,' shrugged Vasilakis. 'He has no previous criminal record. Nevertheless, we would like to talk to him.'

Erik left the Captain without mentioning Celia's experience with the Russians the previous night. Apart from keeping his promise not to tell, he feared the *entente cordiale* was still in place between Greece and her eastern neighbour. As they rolled his fingers over the inkpad, he had already decided to tread carefully.

CHAPTER EIGHT

'What's that on your fingers?' Celia was sunning herself by the pool when he got back.

'Ink,' he told her, carefully sinking onto an adjacent lounger. 'The good Captain decided to take my fingerprints.'

'He can't think …'

'No, no, it's a precaution to eliminate my prints on the lighter. Might I use your iPad for a minute or two to check something out?' he asked.

She passed it across. 'Thank goodness for Wi-Fi.'

'Thank goodness for social media too,' he laughed.

'Did you learn anything new from Captain Vasilakis?' she asked.

Erik did not look up as he tapped away at the silent keyboard. Erik, who had never been good at sharing, girded his loins not for battle but for a partnership with this woman who had already rejected him in the most basic sense. He precised his talk with Vasilakis.

'What are you trying to do now exactly?' she asked, lifting her shades.

'I'm trying to locate through various social media platforms this English fellow called Simmons. Simmons was due to sail out as a deckhand on the yacht, *Bettina*, but fell ill only hours before she left her mooring on Corfu.'

'Here, let me try.' Celia snatched her iPad back. 'What is his full name and where is he from?'

'Jacob Simmons and he originates from Shrewsbury.'

'I had a friend who used to live there.'

'I am sure you have friends living all over the place,' acknowledged Erik ruefully.

'Shrewsbury is a long way from the sea but it has a lovely sixteenth century market hall,' she told him, ignoring his throwaway comment. 'In front of the hall there was a pond or bog. Tradition has it that this water was called the Bishop's Pool and was used as the ducking pool for nagging wives and dishonest traders. They didn't trouble to make a distinction between the two. Each time a wife was ducked on the stool her husband had to pay a farthing.'

'And that offends your feminine sensitivities.'

'Certainly does. I have tried LinkedIn first, then Twitter, so far no Jacob Simmons of Shrewsbury. Final resort Facebook.' She tapped on Search: 'There's someone here.' She tapped on About: 'Could this be him?'

'Could be.' Erik remained doubtful.

'Let's try Instagram,' suggested Celia. Again she tapped on Search. There were lots of images of tousled chestnut haired males; cream shorts and muscle bulging matching shirts; luxury decking spanning blue sea and sky. Finally she passed the iPad across to Erik with a lookalike image of one of the young men on Facebook. 'What do you think?'

'Go back to Facebook,' he told her. 'Now we think we know what he looks like, let's see if we can get confirmation.' The Jacob Simmons on Instagram and Facebook was the same. 'So this is the Englishman who failed to crew the boat only hours before she was blown out of the water.'

'Home town, Shrewsbury. Look, here under contact information, he gives both a mobile number and email address.'

'And under work and education—Crew For You Agency. Technically, Mr Simmons is still on the market for hire.'

'I have been thinking, Erik, there is something not right about this business, something we are missing. I've been thinking about the Russians. Why are they so interested in finding out who the bombers are if it was them? They didn't show so much interest over the poisoning of Alexander Litvinenko.'

'You are right, discreet methods of killing is their usual modus operandi.'

'Novichok and Salisbury, a more recent example.'

'Nobody has been named for that yet.'

'They will be,' affirmed Celia. 'But whether they face justice in an English court is another matter.'

'Put some decent clothing on. We are going to the Villa Elina to ask Messrs Boris and Trofim a few more questions.'

'I'm not going back there under any circumstance.' Celia shook her head, horrified at the prospect.

'I'll go alone then,' Erik told her.

* * * * *

The garden of the Elina was magnificent in sunshine. Fresh floral clean lavender and red, pink and purple bougainvillea climbing every available wall. The scent from the flowers was exquisite as they walked up the long path. Celia wondered how something so wonderfully ordinary could mask something possibly so aberrant.

'Well, well, we have unexpected visitors, Trofim,' smiled Boris, beckoning them though the door.

'How niceee,' said Trofim, snapping shut his computer.

'I must say I am pleasantly surprised,' admitted Boris.

'You shouldn't be after abducting and keeping my colleague captive.' Erik nodded across to Celia. Celia shuffled restlessly.

'Please sit down, make yourselves comfortable,' instructed Boris. 'And we didn't hold Miss Grey captive, we just detained her for while.'

'Why?' asked Erik, placing his narrow buttocks carefully next to Celia on the settee.

'We would like to work with you,' said Trofim. 'Why you not like us Russians? You always have us as bad people in films, *McMafia, Killing Eve*, Russians always bad people.'

Erik thought of mentioning the Novichok incident in Salisbury but held his tongue.

'Yees,' said Boris. 'We just want trust of British people.'

'So tell us why you are here?' Celia's dry mouth finally framed the question.

'From top, you understand. We simply want to know who assassinated Dmitry Smirnov,' said Boris.

Erik nodded: this fitted in with what Vasilakis had told him.

'Any ideas?' he asked them.

'No, no ideas but think it might be personal.'

'Why personal,' asked Celia.

'Because,' Boris hesitated. 'Because Smirnov had no business enemies, certainly not in Russia.'

'Might his wife have put a hit on him?' asked Erik.

'Maybe,' shrugged Boris, glancing indulgently across at Celia. 'When you ladies scorned who knows what you are capable of.'

'Not multiple murder, I hope,' she quipped. Her black humour was lost on Boris and Trofim.

'Tell me about Belgorod,' asked Erik.

'City stands on the banks of the Seversky Donets River, about seven hundred kilometres south of Moscow and forty kilometres from the Ukrainian border. It is famous for chalk, wool, wax and *gorilka*,' explained Boris.

'"*Gorilka*"?' asked Erik.

'Type of Vodka,' cut in Trofim, whose flushed complexion rather suggested a partiality for the drink.

'Belgorod has strong construction industry, mechanical engineering, metalworking and electronics,' continued Boris. 'It has changed hands many times. First Germans in April 1918, the same year it then became part of Ukrainian State. In 1941 to 1943, German occupation once more, near destruction until Soviet army won battle.'

'It was once part of Ukraine, you say?' confirmed Erik; his investigative senses twitching.

'Briefly,' replied Boris.

'Though Ukrainians still believe otherwise,' sneered Trofim.

'But why kill Dmitry Smirnov, businessman?' asked Boris. 'No sense.'

Both Erik and Celia had decided to make no mention of fellow English countryman, Jacob Simmons. And, anyway, his involvement was tenuous at best.

'Not to worry, we will soon be out of your hair,' Erik told Boris.

'"Out of hair"?' Boris looked flummoxed.

'Yes, we will be leaving Paxos in a day or two.'

Celia stared at Erik—this was the first she had heard of it.

'Before you leave allow us to show you something,' proposed Boris.

* * * * *

'Why is it always you who decides things?' complained Celia the next morning.

Erik spooning in mouthfuls of cereal and sliced fresh peach made no attempt to reply. Much to her chagrin, he had agreed to the excursion with the Russians. Just as he began telling her how delicious the peach was they heard a honk outside the villa.

'That's prompt, they're here already,' he approved.

'Up market from our battered hire car,' Celia muttered into his ear as they piled onto the backseat of the Dacia Duster SUV.

'Oh, I don't know about that,' he whispered back. 'Our little jeep will be more versatile on narrow unmade roads.'

'And it has a soft top,' she laughed unconvincingly.

'Good to hear guests are happy, yees,' Boris said to Trofim.

After taking a reasonable road out of Gaios, they parked in the small village of Ozias. A plague of cats suddenly appeared from nowhere. Cats ran along the stone walls, ferals came in from across abandoned fields and gardens. Cats do little that is not self-serving.

The Russians gasped, the English stared. A young woman who looked as if she had just stepped out of *Vogue* in a floral gown, a tin of cat food in one hand, a spoon in the other, began feeding her charges.

'I come up here every day to feed these poor creatures,' she told them. 'My name is Carlotta Rizzo.'

'You're not Greek.' Celia was first to regain her composure.

'No, no, I am Italian,' laughed Carlotta. She told them she had a boutique in Gaios. 'Are you going to the Lesianitis Windmill?' she asked.

Boris and Trofim shook their heads but offered no further explanation. As the four of them walked on, Trofim muttered to Boris what Celia guessed to be some lewd comment in Russian.

At least now we have a witness should anything befall us at the hands of these two, she thought.

They walked along a walled mule trail. A pair of butterflies copulated against the warmth of stone. Erik closed in with his iPhone.

'What are you doing?' Celia asked him.

'Nothing,' said Erik. A whirring buzz, swinging the iPhone camera in her direction.

'Thought you were indulging in a little pornography there for a second,' she told him. 'Where are you actually taking us?' Celia turned to the Russians.

'You'll see,' said Boris.

Erik remained unusually quiet. Under any other circumstance this was a beautiful walk.

They abruptly turned left at a signpost and began descending down a narrow rocky track. The track continued towards an arch transcending the sea. A sliver of path bridged the land to the end point. At either side was a twenty metre drop into the crystal blue water.

'Tripitos Arch,' announced Boris. 'Who has good head for heights? Who wants to go across to far edge?'

Erik raised his hand, so did Trofim. Celia shook her head.

'OK. I stay with Celia,' said the gallant Boris. Celia squirmed.

'Don't go,' she appealed to Erik. He shook her off. If not in the pool as a swimmer, here was a chance for him to assert his mountaineering credentials.

Boris and Celia watched the two men descending to the arch. She felt her present geographical position insecure as it was.

Boris took hold of her shoulders from behind to steady her. This did nothing to allay her fear. Maybe he was about to push her over the precipice.

'Long way down,' he said. 'Long way to fall.'

'Will they be long?' she quavered, *long* being the operative word.

'No, no, Erik safe with Trofim.'

'Why have you brought us here?' Her body felt hot, legs like melting jelly, but she managed to make her question sound cool.

'Big tourist spectacle on Paxos.'

'No, the real reason?' she insisted.

'Do you see where Trofim and Erik are now crossing apex? As you English say straight ahead at twelve o'clock.' Boris glowed, pleased at his mastery of the language. She nodded unimpressed. 'We saw man fall to his death from there week ago.'

She stared at him open mouthed.

'How?' she squeaked.

'We watched. He was chased by other men.'

'What were you doing out here?'

'Watching.' Boris squeezed her shoulders harder.

'Who were you watching?'

'Greek Interpol man. Thought he might lead us to bombers.'

'Yes, Erik told me about him. Aleixo something or other.'

'Aleixo Xenakis.'

'But his body was pulled out on Kaki Lagada Beach. It's on the other side of the island.'

'Ionian sea tides run anti-clockwise, then there are wind currents, very unpredictable. However it was surprise to us that his body finished up there.'

'Are you sure you and Trofim didn't push him off?' she dared to ask.

'Yes. No need,' sighed Boris. He seemed to find the question amusing.

'You'd better tell Erik all this when he gets back.'

'Why? I tell you.'

'What time did this happen exactly?'

'About eight in evening.'

'What was this Aleixo Xenakis up to at that time?'

'He also following people.'

'Following whom, where?'

'People recovering treasure from near Lesianitis Windmill. Dig, dig, dig … then they saw Xenakis spying on them and chased him out onto arch. Xenakis not very good spy,' smiled Boris.

'Not like you?'

'That's right.' He smiled gold teeth again. 'Not enough cunning, deception, ruthlessness.'

'And what nationality were these men in pursuit of Xenakis?'

'Not English. Russians, Greeks perhaps. Who knows.'

'And what do you think the buried treasure was?'

'Diamonds, raw diamonds. The *Bettina* was on her way to Israel in the next few days.'

'So uncut diamonds from Russia were being picked up from sites in Greece and transported to Israel by people like Dmitry Smirnov, is that what you are saying?'

'That is what I am saying. However it does not explain bombing. Russia has no wish to interfere with lucrative trade for our motherland and neither do Israelis. It is in both countries' interests to turn blind eye.'

'Are you saying this smuggling operation is state sponsored?'

'I am saying nothing more.'

'You would have me believe that Xenakis was following a criminal gang, and you and Trofim were following all of them out here late in the evening.'

'No, we were only shadowing Xenakis.'

'So you and Trofim just stood back and watched poor Aleixo Xenakis being pushed to his death?'

'No, no, they hit him with shovel first.' Boris was such a dispassionate witness to murder it was almost comical. 'Then they stripped of clothes and pushed him over cliff.'

'And you did nothing?'

'What could we do? They were far away down path. We were totally outnumbered and unarmed.'

'Are you saying these men had guns?'

'Oh yes, always armed, well armed.'

'But how could they have got weapons into Greece?'

'Boat. You can hide anything on boat if you know how.'

'So why are you telling *me* all this now?'

'Kremlin not interest in Xenakis, or smugglers, only who killed Smirnov.'

'How can Erik and I possibly be of any help?' enquired Celia mystified.

'Because you want to know truth as much as we do.'

'Do we really?' Asked without conviction.

'And we think …' Boris paused, collecting his thoughts. 'We think there's English connection.'

'You're not suggesting that because of Salisbury our Intelligence Service blew Mr Putin's friend up?'

'Who knows?' Another Boris' shrug before he fell silent.

'That was fantastic, really hairy looking far down to the sea,' announced Erik, still flushed with adrenaline.

'Made dizzy,' admitted Trofim.

'Good,' said Celia inappropriately.

'What's wrong?' asked Erik, suddenly aware of the two glum faces confronting him on his heroic return.

'I'll explain on the walk back,' Celia told him. Ambling some distance behind Boris and Trofim she did just that.

'Why are you sharing this information with us, two English journalists?' Erik asked the Russians as soon as they climbed into the Duster.

'Russians always painted bad boys in British Press, now Russia victim,' said Trofim.

'Tell world that,' said Boris.

The return journey passed in silence. Celia was relieved once they started bumping down the familiar lane.

'Bye-bye, Englishers,' said Trofim, waving at them out of the passenger window like a child.

'Do you believe their story?' Celia asked Erik as they walked down the path to the Villa Astraea.

'I don't believe anything at this stage. But why would they lie? What possibly could be served by them lying?'

'They could have killed Aleixo Xenakis themselves and are trying to put the blame on imaginary smugglers.'

'True, but why admit they were involved at all? Why acknowledge they were in the vicinity of the Lesianitis

Windmill and Tripitos Arch as a murder was being committed?'

* * * * *

'Do you know what Astraea means in Greek, the Villa Astraea?' Erik asked Celia over a slab of feta cheese, fresh bread, olives, oil and coffee.

'No idea,' admitted Celia; her mouth stuffed with oily bread.

'Astraea is the Greek goddess of justice and innocence who became the constellation Virgo.'

'Is that so?'

'Yes, and that is just what we are going to do. We are going to seek justice and illuminate it.'

'I never realised you could be so poetical.'

'There is a lot you don't know about me,' said Erik, straight-faced and preoccupied.

'Yes, I think perhaps you are right.'

'Waking from our siesta by the pool a thought came to me.'

'Don't tax your brain too hard,' she teased.

'No, I'm serious. Who has most to gain from any disruption of the lucrative, if illegal, diamond trade between Russian and Israel?'

'The Palestinians,' she proposed.

'Bright girl,' he patted her knee under the table. She moved it away. Erik drained his wine glass.

'But hasn't Russia always been sympathetic to the PLO and Hamas in Gaza?'

'Ostensibly, yes. Although in recent years the Russian Federation has moderated its support and tried to portray itself as an honest broker between the Palestinians and Israelis, as the US, under Trump, loses credibility in the area.'

'Do you think we will see Boris and Trofim again?'

'Don't tell me you are growing fond of them?'

She answered in shrieks of laughter.

'I think we should cross back to Corfu tomorrow afternoon. At this time of year we should easily get a seat on the ferry or hydrofoil. But tonight, our last night, I am going to take you somewhere special. Recommended by Maria as somewhere *sik*.'

'"*Sik*"?'

'Posh,' explained Erik.

* * * * *

'Where on earth are you taking me?' asked Celia, as they passed along narrow bending country lanes. They could have been in rural UK, apart from the trees hemming them in were olive trees bearing small white flowers. 'We're not going back to the Tripitos Arch?'

'Thank goodness we hired a small jeep,' was Erik's only comment.

After some further complex manoeuvring down a one way system, they came to some hopeful looking buildings.

'Erimitis,' announced Erik. The restaurant was on cliffs almost overhanging the sea. 'See, there's a viewing platform for customers to get the full experience. The sunsets are renowned for being magnificent from here.'

'No thank you,' replied Celia. 'I have had enough of heights for one day.'

'Sunset and white tablecloths, what more could you wish for,' enthused Erik, doing his best to relax back into the upright chair after the drive from hell.

'This place looks expensive.'

'Incidentals. Don't worry about that.'

Celia needed no further pressing. She requested the appetiser of prawn saganaki on brioch, Erik a Greek garden salad. They ordered the best Cretan wine. On arrival the food was beautifully presented on white plates. White seemed the order of the day at Erimitis.

'Oregano only ever smells this fresh in Greece.' Erik gave his salad a sniff of approval.

'My dish has a splash of mastika liqueur added,' noted Celia, suddenly aware of a peripheral movement, a waving arm. Someone was waving to them from the bar area. 'Don't look now but Boris and Trofim are sitting over there,' she sighed in disbelief.

Before Erik could turn and react, Boris was at their table.

'I haven't seen you two in here before. It's very good. Trofim and I have become regulars. Do come and join us,' he suggested.

'No, no, this is our last night and Celia and I would like a quiet time to absorb the atmosphere,' responded Erik firmly. With surprisingly little offence or fuss, Boris bowed and withdrew.

'Did you tell them you were bringing me here tonight?' Celia demanded.

'No, certainly not.' Erik held out two defensive palms.

The Russians had a guest at their table. He was smoking what Celia took to be a thick Russian cigar. The three men leaned in together in conference. She guessed they were talking about her and Erik. The stranger half turned to wave at them too.

'Who is that at their table?' she whispered to Erik. 'You

don't think he could be the older man at Adras' cafe before the bombing?'

Erik pretended to look back over to the bar, signalling a waiter.

'Stick out as Russians a mile off here, don't they?' he muttered.

'But they wouldn't on Corfu according to Trofim. Why risk such obvious visibility here if they are behind the bombing or killing of Aleixo Xenakis? What does it mean?'

'The new guy is a senior External Intelligence Service agent if ever I saw one,' muttered Erik. 'These SVR guys report directly back to Putin.' Without another word, he got up and left Celia to deal with the waiter and their next orders. He smiled back at her from the viewing platform, iPhone camera at the ready. Then swinging round, he appeared to be focusing on the famous Erimitis' sunset.

'Got what you wanted?' she asked him as he slumped back down into the Van Gogh chair. He nodded.

Their main courses arrived. Vegan Linguini and pork tenderloin flavoured with fresh thyme and seasonal vegetables.

'Looks lovely,' said Erik.

'What's confusing me is Boris said Xenakis was struck by a shovel first. He seemed vague about how he actually died. He said the gang stripped him but didn't seem sure if he was dead before he was thrown from the Tripitos Arch. I wonder what the pathologist found.' Celia tested her honey sauce first.

'That's easy,' Erik told her. 'Xenakis was garrotted, I saw the marks round his throat and neck myself.'

'And you decided to keep that piece of information to yourself as well.' Celia was livid.

'I wasn't a hundred per cent certain.'

'When will you learn to share?'

'When I am sure I can trust you.'

The awkwardness between them lasted way into desserts, way after the Russians had waved and left.

CHAPTER NINE

As they packed next morning and paid off Maria to much tears and hugs, there was a loud knock on the door. A delivery man stood outside with a huge bouquet of spring flowers. Celia gave him a couple of euros tip and detached a small sealed envelope. The note inside read:

> For Celia,
> From Russia with love.

'I can't take these with me. They are beautiful though,' was her first reaction as she pocketed the note.

'Watch out for the Novichok,' warned Erik unkindly.

'What shall I do with them?' Celia stared at him totally disconcerted.

'No idea.' Erik turned away, his expression like thunder.

'*Eísai ziliáris*,' chuntered Maria, pointing and laughing at him.

'What does Maria say?' asked Celia. Erik shook his head. 'What does she say?' insisted Celia.

'She says ...' he hesitated. 'She says I'm jealous.'

'And are you?'

'Don't be ridiculous.'

'Here.' Celia thrust the flowers into Maria's arms. 'These are for you.'

'*Sas efcharistó. Sas efcharistó,*' said Maria, tears of gratitude flooding down her face. '*Aftoí eínai Ómorfoi.*'

'*Gia óla ósa échete kánei,*' Erik told her.

'What's that?' asked Celia.

'I said they are for all she has done.'

They left with Celia's wheeled cabin bag scrunching on the villa's gravel path. They left as the pool man came to clean the one great success they had shared. Celia turned to bid the water a fond farewell. In her experience people fell into two categories—those who loved water, those who did not. She was not sure which category Erik had swum into.

Everything in Gaios was located near either the bus terminal, the Church of Saint Apostles or the seafront. Erik knew the way having already visited Captain Vasilakis' office near the terminal. Both the fronting ferry ticket office and the police station round the back were housed in the same pink-washed building.

Before visiting Vasilakis, they collected their ferry tickets. Luckily, May was a quiet month and they had no difficulty getting seats for the ninety minute crossing to Corfu.

'When the Italians arrive it is always more difficult,' said the female desk clerk in ridiculously high heels.

Captain Vasilakis stretched out a hand to both Erik and Celia as if welcoming old friends.

'Before we leave, we have something of interest to tell you,' said Erik.

'No, no, you cannot be leaving beautiful Paxos so soon,' responded Vasilakis with mock incredulity.

'Yes, we must.'

'Why must? But what is this thing you have to tell me?'

'You say.' Erik appealed to Celia.

'I …' Celia was for once speechless.

'It is about the murder of Aleixo Xenakis,' intervened Erik. Vasilakis raised an eyebrow at hearing the Interpol officer's name. 'We have two eyewitnesses to his murder.'

'Erik, this isn't appropriate,' Celia warned him.

'*Theé mou*,' exploded Vasilakis. '"Appropriate?" We are talking about murder of a Greek police officer here.'

'I'm sorry.' Celia looked to the stained floor. 'It is just that it isn't done for journalists to reveal …'

'Who are these witnesses?' interrupted Vasilakis.

Erik walked round Vasilakis' large desk. He took out his iPhone and showed him some photographs. Vasilakis frowned and paled.

'Those two again,' he muttered.

'Let me see.' Celia snatched the phone out of Erik's hand. 'How did you get these?'

'Remember the copulating butterflies on the mule trail and the sunset at Erimitis? Well, it wasn't just them and it that I snapped.'

'You photographed Boris and Trofim as well,' she sighed.

'And their friend,' added Erik.

'You may well sigh, Miss, but I think it's time you told me what Russians said.' Vasilakis assumed sudden officialdom. 'They are staying at the Villa Elina above Loggos, are they not?'

'Yes,' said Celia.

'Now tell me everything Russians told you about Aleixo Xenakis death.'

'Boris told me Xenakis was pushed over the cliffs near the Tripitos Arch.' Celia nervously stroked a hand across her brow.

'By whom?'

'By diamond smugglers.'

'"Diamond smugglers"?'

'I know it sounds fanciful but that is what he told me.'

Something that both Celia and Erik took to be irony flashed in Vasilakis' eyes.

'Well, I have a piece of news for you both. According to our medical examiner, Aleixo Xenakis did not die from falling from a great height. He did have multiple injuries confirming your story. However, thankfully, he must have been dead before he hit the water.'

'They hit him with a shovel first,' explained Erik. 'The back of his skull must have been caved in.'

'That wasn't mentioned either.'

'The marks round his neck?' queried Erik.

'I can tell you no more. I can say no more until and unless his close relatives get legal representation to access the information.'

Leaving contact details, Erik and Celia made for the New Port. They left the keys of the red jeep under the mat. No one stole on the island, not unless it was minor thefts conducted by visitors.

Celia could not say she was glad to be below decks in her ferry seat leaving Paxos. However both she and Erik were relieved to be quitting a situation they saw as only getting more complicated. An international crisis was developing and it would not be long before Athens was called in big time.

'You shouldn't have made me reveal my sources,' complained Celia.

'I had no choice.'

The *Despina* rolled about in a heavy sea. Celia and Erik fell quiet and slightly sick. Once more their relationship had been pitched into turbulent waters.

* * * * *

They had no pre-booked hotel rooms on Corfu, and this time chose a modest two bedroomed apartment in the Old Town. It had a terrace, partial sea view and free Wi-Fi.

Almost as soon as they had unpacked, Erik rang the mobile of the crewman, Jacob Simmons, who had failed to sail with the *Bettina* on her fatal last voyage. No reply. He tried the given email address, it bounced back immediately.

'I am going to try the Crew For You Agency in London,' he told Celia.

'Yes, we've tried to contact Mr Simmons many times after the accident,' said a very English male voice which was strange to hear. 'He's just not answering his phone. We haven't heard from him in weeks.'

'And you've no idea where he is? If he's returned to England or not?' Erik was beginning to feel a little desperate.

'No, we've no reason to believe he's left Corfu yet.'

On a hunch, the next morning, Erik and Celia took a taxi to the Gouvia Marina were the *Bettina* was last berthed.

'I still have the feeling that someone is tailing us,' said Celia unsettled.

'Even when you're in a taxi?' asked Erik amused.

'Even then.'

'Have you smelt any Russian cigars?' he laughed.

'It's not funny. I *do* have this feeling.'

Celia's fear of being pursued was finally distracted by the passing sight of a good size open air pool, part of a huge marina bar and restaurant complex. No one was swimming—the pool looked empty.

'No,' Erik told her.

'I haven't got my swim things anyway,' she wriggled in frustration.

They asked the taxi driver to stop and paid him off.

There must have been a thousand boats neatly berthed next to each other like sardines in a can in the Gouvia Marina. Erik and Celia looked hopefully for a Union Jack as they walked the pontoons.

Many of the foreign crews seemed to be having breakfast out on deck. They were in the main good willed, spoke excellent English, and wanted to be helpful as Erik asked around about a young crewman called Simmons. But the boating community was a transient one and it seemed an impossible task.

'Yes, we heard what happened to the *Bettina* across there on Paxos. Terrible, a terrible thing.' A German boat owner told them in perfect English, his wife nodding in commiseration.

However, sympathy apart, just as they were giving up all hope of finding the *Bettina's* missing crewman: 'Did I hear you asking about an English man called Simmons?' The German boat owner's near neighbour, sailing under a Swedish flag, shouted across to them.

'Yes, Jacob Simmons. Have you come across him?' asked Erik.

'He asked me only yesterday if I needed an extra hand,' said the Swede. 'We shared a beer or two at the cafe over there. Told me he had a room nearby.'

'Did he give you the address?' asked Erik. The Swede shook his head. Nevertheless, this was the best lead they had.

'Thank you, thank you,' harmonised Erik and Celia. They turned and clumped back along the pontoon towards the cafe bar indicated by the Swede. It was one of many obviously dependent on marina trade.

Blue washed walls, grey cushioned couches, a few yachtsmen enjoying breakfast.

'My stomach is growling,' complained Celia, as they sank side by side on one of the couches.

'Mine too,' agreed Erik 'Do you realise we haven't had anything to eat yet?'

They settled for croissants—Erik insisting on a chocolate one to Celia's disgust—and both enjoyed the best coffee of their whole trip so far. Erik checked his watch 11.30—9.30 UK time. The cafe had a good Wi-Fi and Erik logged in to report back to their newspaper. He mentioned nothing about the murder of the Greek Interpol man, nor anything about Boris and Trofim, that would come later. He did however tell Duncan Nelson that they were trying to locate the *Bettina's* missing crewman.

'Ah, yes, Mr Simmons has rooms two blocks down,' the waiter told them as they paid their bill. 'He was in here enjoying a drink only the other night.'

They pressed for more accurate directions. A minute or two later they were standing in an arched doorway, knocking on a worn wooden door.

'Jacob Simmons?' asked Erik.

A white towel was wrapped round the dark, tousled haired young man's narrow waist as if he had just stepped out of the shower. 'Who's asking?'

Erik flashed his press card.

If this was Simmons, to say he had missed the *Bettina's* final sailing through ill health was something of a surprise.

This fit muscular apparition appeared to be in rude health. Celia could not imagine him suffering from a day's illness. The towel's outline further enhanced his potency—she quickly averted her eyes.

'I knew it would only be a matter of time,' Simmons told them.

'A matter of time for what?' Celia feigned innocence.

'Until the police or you media people caught up with me.'

'Why hide away like this?' asked Erik.

'I've hardly moved from Gouvia Marina.'

'Clever. Who would look for you in the very last place the *Bettina* was berthed?'

'You think so? I was scared, too traumatised to move after hearing of the bombing on Paxos.'

'Why scared?' Celia's eyes flickered interest.

'Will I get paid for this story?'

'Maybe, depends,' said Erik.

'I am stony broke and cannot even afford the fare back to England,' admitted Simmons, making his charity pitch.

'Our newspaper might be able to help you out there. There is a story here, working title: SEAMAN FATED WITH FLU. I can see the headlines,' Erik told him.

'OK! What I haven't told you is that I've been riven with guilt since it happened.'

'"Guilt?" For not sailing with the boat?' asked Celia.

The strong chin began to quiver. Simmons took a deep breath.

'Two of my friends died on that boat.'

'Little has been mentioned of your crewmates so far.' Erik looked to his notebook. 'Anna Parker and Robert Perceval, is that right?'

'They were lovely hardworking people.'

'I'm sure they were,' sympathised Erik.

'It is a shame they got caught up in all this.'

'"A shame",' decried Erik. 'It's a bloody tragedy.'

'Quite so.' Simmons looked taken aback by Erik's outburst.

'And caught up in all what?'

'I just meant … There's something else, something I haven't told anyone.'

'What else?' asked Erik intrigued.

'As I stood, giddy with fever, on the pontoon to wave them off, a man approached me and asked where such a beautiful boat was bound. I told him Loggos on Paxos. I have been wretched about giving away that information ever since, felt responsible for what happened.'

'What was he like this man?'

'Greek, I'd say. He spoke fluent Greek at any rate.'

'Do you?'

'No, no, just a little,' laughed Simmons. 'Enough to get by.'

'So, how did you know this man was fluent?'

'Well … I …' Simmons looked flustered. 'Is this an interrogation?'

'No, just interested. Calm down, mate.'

'He just sounded very Greek. Look, this is all getting a little too much for me.'

'Why do you think anyone might want to harm you now? The mission has been completed,' pointed out Celia.

'I feel out of my depth, don't feel safe anymore.'

'You cannot hide yourself away in this cheap room forever.'

'This room,' Simmons waved to the bare walls, 'is nothing to a man used to living in a shoebox on a luxury yacht.'

'Tell us about Dmitry Smirnov and his personal assistant,' said Erik.

'I have experienced spoilt owners who are tyrannical. I have seen many prostitutes brought on board and cruelly used late at night. I have experienced mistresses who are divas. Some owners bring a hundred bottles of vodka aboard, most of which is gone in a week. Some demand hogs' lard, known as *salo*, to accompany their vodkas when we are a hundred miles out to sea. Some divas throw things at the crew if they think life aboard is less than perfect. They want Cunard service provided by a crew of three on a boat measuring sixteen metres in length by six metres to beam. However there was never anything like that with Smirnov and Anna Markova, just a cool aloofness, a very cool aloofness. You never failed to address him as "sir" and her as "madam", and you always felt you had to be on top of your game or else you might finish overboard.'

'An implicit threat,' helped out Erik.

'Just so,' agreed Simmons.

'So there could have been enemies?'

'Oh yes.'

'Did you ever see any criminal activity aboard?'

'Not as such.'

'How do you mean?'

'Well, it was more after we'd put ashore. I would occasionally run into the boss in bars with some dubious looking company.'

'Did he acknowledge you?'

'No, that's just it, he would invariably turn away.' Simmons rolled a hunched shoulder in demonstration. 'Didn't want to know me.'

'What ports did you sail to?'

'Ports on the Aegean, more often the Med, occasionally the Ionian Sea.'

'Have we got a deal then for your exclusive story?' asked Erik brusquely. Simmons nodded. 'Stay put for the moment.' Erik reached into his satchel. 'Only call me on this.' He handed Simmons a burner phone.

'Do *you* think I am in danger?' Simmons asked him.

'It's a possibility. You might be viewed as knowing too much or could identify the perpetrators.'

'What about the police?'

'All in due course. No talking to anyone. If another paper becomes involved any arrangement with us is off,' insisted Erik.

'I understand.'

'Just one more thing before we go, Mr Simmons, have you ever been to Loggos?'

'Yes, the *Bettina* has anchored there once or twice before. Why?'

'Oh, nothing,' Erik reassured him, gesturing for Celia to exit first.

Simmons gave them a brief wave of farewell from behind his half open door. There was a sadness in his dark eyes, a slight sulkiness about the mouth. Celia liked him.

'So what do you think?' she asked Erik, as they failed to hail the first taxi.

'Don't know, not sure,' he frowned.

'He looks like a clean-cut, straightforward kind of guy to me.'

'So did the psychopath Ted Bundy, so did Andrew Cunanan.'

'Who?'

'Andrew Cunanan. The murderer of fashion designer Giovanni Versace along with a few other young men.'

'You are cynical.'

'That's right, I am.'

CHAPTER TEN

The afternoon saw them swishing in a limousine in and out of squares and alleyways that did not appear to have changed in centuries. The same smells blew through the open car window, smells of the street that were centuries old too.

Sombrely dressed old men huddled in tavernas along the way—only men—playing backgammon or sipping at coffees and beers. A male support system in old age.

Had she been Greek, Celia realised she would be precluded by age and gender from ever being a part of this. *Where are all the women? What support system do they have*?

'No women,' she groaned through the open window.

'Of course not. They are all at home. This is Greece. This is heading east,' responded Erik.

'That's apparent.'

'I sympathise with you though.' Erik dared a wink.

'Do you really?'

'Absolutely.'

Was he teasing her or was he worth slotting up a notch in her estimation? She could never be sure with Erik.

Without fixing a prior appointment, they asked for Gorgias Baros at reception. They were back to the start of their journey—the offices of the *Enimerosi* newspaper.

Gorgias soon appeared and led them off to a private room. 'We will not be troubled in here. So, what have you learnt about our Russian friend's demise?'

'And his personal assistant,' cut in Celia.

'Ah! Yes, Smirnov's "personal assistant". How could I forget her?'

'And the others. One a child,' pointed out Celia.

'Ah! Yes, how could I forget them either?'

'We know little more than when we left Corfu a few days ago,' said Erik, eager to offer the lie, eager to get it over with. Journalists rarely, if ever, share information with other journalists. Gorgias had little time to absorb his disappointment.

'How's Nicos by the way?' enquired Celia coldly.

'Nicos? I haven't met with him since your departure. He seems to have gone under the ground.'

'I hope not,' smiled Erik.

The joke was lost on Gorgias.

'We say "gone to ground",' explained Celia.

'What on earth does that mean?' asked Gorgias.

'"Earth" very good, very funny.' Celia laughed. Gorgias stared back at her vacantly.

'"Under the ground", "earth". When they put you in the ground, they throw earth on your coffin,' explained Erik losing patience.

'No earth, no dirt, in Greece. Occasionally priest will throw sand, but flowers, always flowers in Greece,' announced Gorgias fiercely; none the wiser to the strange nuances of the English language and customs.

'And no Nicos,' acknowledged Celia.

'And no new information from Paxos,' added Gorgias, allowing his disappointment to finally surface. 'But please, I forget my manners. Coffee?' he nodded across to a vending machine.

'This time I couldn't help noticing all the plastic refuse bags piled high on the streets,' announced Celia; slurping on her coffee, the worst coffee she had had since England.

'Terrible! Gets worse every day. Talk, talk, no agreement.'

'Indeed,' said Erik. 'Evidently Corfu has not heard of the Plastic War.'

'Maybe that is where Nicos is,' cackled Gorgias. 'The *Elliniki Astynomia* found out he was giving us too much information and dumped him in trash bag.'

'You're not serious?' said Erik.

Gorgias shrugged and smiled. 'Who knows nowadays.'

'That's not so funny. A Greek Interpol officer investigating the bombing on Paxos was found murdered while we were there.' Erik decided a little disclosure here might be fruitful.

'No! Really?' This was obviously news to Gorgias. 'We've heard nothing, absolutely nothing of this.'

'Well, it's true.' Celia added her weight.

'However I did hear that Athens wasn't too interested in bombing itself as only one Greek national died.'

'Adras Christakos' nephew,' put in Erik.

'Yes, at any other time I would say our authorities were too indolent to bother, all too much trouble on behalf of little island of Paxos. However I think there is a more pressing political reason.'

'And what is that?' asked Erik, all ears.

'As you know the Greek coalition government is led by the radical left-wing party Syriza. We have always enjoyed long historical ties with Russia. That is …' Gorgias paused dramatically. 'That is until recently.'

'Yes, Nicos told me about the growing tensions with Russia over North Macedonia.'

'Did he?' Gorgias looked surprised. 'Ever since FYROM agree with us to call themselves North Macedonia and expressed interest in joining NATO, Russian diplomats—for want of a better description—have been meddling in Greek affairs. Russia has begun to annoy even Syriza.'

'You don't think the trouble over North Macedonia could have anything to do with the Smirnov bombing, the murder of a prominent Russian and friend of Putin's?' Erik asked him.

'Not at the behest of my country. How would the murder of Smirnov benefit us apart from upsetting Russia more? As far as we are concerned the problem of North Macedonia is resolved and they are welcome to join NATO.'

'Who else though would profit from Smirnov's demise?'

'His wife,' laughed Gorgias. 'Then again perhaps he was involved in and knew too much about corruption in higher echelons of state.'

'Such as?'

'Such as Smirnov supplying Palestinians with heavy metals for weapons,' offered Gorgias. 'A year and a half ago, in exchange for Israel skipping a General Assembly vote on war crimes in Syria, Russia's UN Ambassador, Vitaly Chrukin, proposed postponement of United Nations Security Council Resolution 2334 condemning Israel's settlement building on West Bank.'

'So, in light of all this cosying up with the Jews, Russia needed to distance itself from Smirnov's Palestinian business dealings.'

'That's right. Countries' allegiances refashion. At present we Greeks have moved a little away from Russia and closer to Israel. Russia temporarily closer to Israel than Palestinians. Russia is always master of duplicity.'

'And Vitaly Chrukin is dead.'

'Along with five other Russian diplomats in four months, November 2016 to February 2017.' Another Gorgias' shrug. 'New York's Chief Medical Examiner was instructed by State Department not to disclose Chrukin's cause of death that February citing international law.'

'What about Trump?' Celia's question was loaded with disapproval.

'He was only President for one month before Chrukin's death.'

'No, no, I mean regarding the Smirnov's smuggling operation.'

'For once Trump does not enter into this,' chuckled Gorgias. 'No oil or business benefit.'

'We heard the *Bettina* might have been carrying diamonds,' revealed Celia. Erik glared at her.

'Diamonds?' laughed Gorgias. 'That's new one. No, mark my word, Paxos bombing has hallmark of *HaMossad leModi'in uleTafkidim Meyuhadim*—Institute for Intelligence and Special Operations—Mossad to you.'

'Perhaps Kidon specifically,' suggested Erik.

'Ah! Mossad's secret assassin wing.'

It was Erik's turn to shrug, an English shrug, more of a twitch really.

'I am extremely confused as to who is behind the bombing.' Celia told him later. 'First Boris told me Smirnov was involved with diamond smuggling to …'

'Israel. Another connection to that country,' interjected Erik.

'Then Captain Vasilakis suggested to you that Smirnov was trading in drugs and money laundering. Simmons seemed to uphold this possibility with his disclosure that

Smirnov was meeting dodgy characters in every port around the Med. Then again, maybe there is a more plausible motive entirely for the bombing, something we are missing,' suggested Celia.

'Maybe,' replied Erik unconvinced.

* * * * *

Ping! *Ping*! Erik opened his phone to find he had been texted.

British police put in request to visit Paxos.
Vasilakis

'I think we'd better advise Simmons of developments.' Erik flashed his phone screen towards Celia.

No towel, no tousled hair. Simmons was dressed today in a blue shirt and cargo pants. Otherwise he did not look as if he had moved from his room since their last visit.

'If you want to find out who killed your friends, I think it best that you make yourself available to the police back home.'

Simmons gulped over Erik's warning. 'I thought you said "no talking to anyone".'

'The British police are a different matter. You will have to talk to them sooner or later.'

'Think of Anna and Robert,' stressed Celia.

'I think of nothing else,' muttered Simmons.

'Here is a thousand pounds for your story—THE MAN WHO MISSED THE BOAT.' Erik handed him a cheque. 'This will help with your travel expenses back to England. We might call on you in Shrewsbury in a week's time or you can come to our London office if you would prefer.'

'But you don't know where I live in Shrewsbury,' stated Simmons.

Oh, but we do. Flat Four, Tudor Lane.'

'That's amazing. I've only lived there a few years,' remarked Simmons. Celia too marvelled at this revelation. Erik was thorough in his research if nothing else.

'Where did you live before Shrewsbury?' he asked.

'My parents' house in Bayswater, London.'

Celia could see her terrier colleague had instantaneously grasped this piece of information to file it safely away.

'Only use the burner phone if you are in difficulty, or need to contact us urgently,' Erik insisted.

'Thanks.' Simmons gave Celia the James Bond wink.

She blushed. Had he clocked his effect on her during their previous visit? Pulling herself together she regarded him with chaste amusement. Erik scowled.

'How about we all go out for a farewell dinner in Corfu Town tonight?' suggested Simmons.

'That would be …' began Celia.

'Sorry,' Erik cut in. 'We already have a prior engagement before we fly home tomorrow.'

Once outside Simmons' apartment, Celia turned to Erik, 'News to me that we have anything arranged for this evening.'

'Remember you are a professional,' he chided her.

'You are jealous.'

'No I am not.'

'Jacob Simmons is rather dishy though,' she said, enjoying rubbing it in.

* * * * *

They did not have an evening engagement—but once back in their own apartment in the Old Town, Erik's phone immediately bleeped—and then they had.

'Nicos and I would like to take you and Celia to the Bistro Boileau in Kontokali,' said Gorgias.

Erik put Gorgias on speaker.

'So Nicos has risen.'

'Sorry.'

'Never mind. "Kontokali", I've heard of that,' he told his handheld. 'As it happens, I believe we were near there today.'

'The Durrells, it was the home of the Durrells.'

'Ah! The Durrells.'

'Yes, *your* Durrells.'

Erik looked questioningly at Celia. She was nodding eagerly. Again he sought her confirmation to make sure. Again she nodded her head like a demented doll. 'I think you can take it as a definite "yes", Gorgias.'

Gorgias parked his battered old Mercedes in a backstreet just off the Gouvia Marina in the village of Kontokali. Erik and Celia seemed to be drawn to this area like moths to a flame.

'I just hope we don't bump into Simmons,' whispered Celia.

Bistro Boileau's decor was very unassuming bistro. In keeping with the name there was a French feel to the place. However Erik's face fell as he ran down the menu.

'Damn,' said Gorgias, 'you're not a vegetarian?' Erik nodded his guilt. 'Oh dear, this place specialises in steaks.'

'Never mind, I'll settle for Sexy Salad and a good bottle of wine,' reassured Erik.

Gorgias ordered the vintage Boileau Chardonnay for his guests and the vintage Cabernet for himself and Nicos— Nicos who had remained unusually quiet. Gorgias had wrongly assumed Celia would be a white wine woman. She thought it would be graceless to correct the man who was footing the bill.

'*Sofrito.*' Nicos finally half-smiled as he and Gorgias tucked into their rump steaks garnished with parsley, garlic and vinegar sauce.

'Kontokali must have changed enormously since the Durrells lived here.' Celia's comment came through a mouthful of beef. She had opted for the Corfu dish of Regis Fillet cooked in butter with spring onions, cherry tomatoes and sage.

'Alas, yes,' said Gorgias. 'The entire island is getting built up.'

Nicos muttered something in a low voice.

'Sorry?' said Erik hand to ear.

'The Russians are absolutely denying any involvement in the Paxos bombing, or in the death of the Interpol man, Aleixo Xenakis,' he announced; a man who obviously did not go in for small talk.

So Xenakis' name is right out there now, approved Celia.

'Well, they would wouldn't they. The Russians never admit responsibility for anything,' said Erik.

'I don't know. I have a funny feeling about this whole affair.' Nicos cut a further succulent piece off his steak.

'I believe Paxos is now swarming with investigators from Athens,' added Gorgias.

'Only now?' put in Celia.

'About time,' agreed Erik.

'As I've already explained the Athenians take time to react to island events,' said Gorgias, chewing though a mouthful of meat.

'Now that the medical examiner has confirmed that one of their own has been murdered …' Nicos hesitated. 'This is a difficulty not to be ignored.'

'But the bombing?' Celia again.

'Yes, an international act of terrorism in Greek waters,' asserted Eric.

'Until today authorities have been maintaining that it could simply have been accidental explosion, major gasoline leak aboard boat,' said Gorgias.

'I don't understand.' Erik looked nonplussed.

'With additive of ethanol to gasoline, this can degrade older fuel lines much faster than anticipated,' said Nicos. 'This has been message from Athens at any rate.'

'But the *Bettina* wasn't an old boat,' objected Erik.

'Nevertheless that is what they have been saying. As I think I mentioned to you earlier, close Greek and Russian relations have deteriorated over North Macedonia.'

'Ah, Macedonia,' concurred Gorgias.

'Are you telling us because of political sensitivities your government is turning a blind eye to the Paxos bombing?' asked Erik.

'Maybe it is up to you and your newspaper to really put matter before world,' said Gorgias.

'But what about your newspaper?' asked Celia.

'My newspaper is Greek. I am Greek.' Abashed, Gorgias examined the tablecloth.

'Maybe you could go to Athens and make enquiries of top people, people who know,' suggested Nicos.

'Maybe we will but Athens isn't our priority at the moment,' said Erik. 'This story needs more background, more research.'

'You publish then we print,' Gorgias piped up.

'We will say no more,' said Nicos, appraising the empty tables, the out of season bistro.

And they didn't. Everyone tucked into their apple pies and chocolate mousses and said nothing. Nothing was forgotten either.

CHAPTER ELEVEN

As Erik and Celia waited in Corfu airport digesting more than their previous night's meal, Erik got a text from Simmons saying he had already booked today's flight back to Birmingham. Celia watched Erik fiddling with his iPhone for several minutes.

'That's strange,' he suddenly announced. 'There isn't a flight from or to Birmingham today.'

'Are you absolutely sure you've checked properly?' asked Celia.

'Certain. See here, look.'

A dark presentiment about Jacob Simmons clouded their return to England. When a few days later they failed to contact him in Shrewsbury, it was not a surprise to either of them. Nevertheless, Duncan Nelson decided to run the story—THE MAN WHO MISSED THE BOAT.

'Give this Simmons lad a little more time. Then go to Shrewsbury and follow up. I sense there is a story within a story here. But first you are off to Holland tomorrow,' he told them.

'"Holland"?' A collective shriek.

'But we've only just got back from Greece,' complained Erik.

'Amsterdam, to be precise. I want you to interview the married witnesses from the Loggos bar.' Nelson consulted his iPad. 'Josi and Marten Beekhof. I understand they have recently been repatriated. You're booked on the first flight from Heathrow to Schiphol.'

'I suppose we should be grateful it's not Gatwick,' moaned Erik.

Celia did nothing to back him up. Erik wrongly presumed she was too travel weary to say anything.

* * * * *

'You're very quiet this morning,' he told her. Celia had not said a word since they had hooked up at Heathrow.

'This trip is difficult for me,' she replied.

'Difficult, how?'

Celia smiled glumly. Erik decided not to push things as they took their seats on the plane, not for the moment anyway.

I will show you beaches with nobody on them. Someone, who she had thought was the love of her life, had told her that a long time ago. The complication of the past had been with a student attending a World Council of Churches conference in London. They were both very young, both married. Celia would never have believed that such a thing could happen, such a magnet could have drawn her from the true course. The complication of the present was that the student had been Dutch, and ever since she had avoided any reference to the Netherlands like the plague. All memories to do with that particular part of the world were deep and bittersweet—Shakespearian almost.

Now she was flying over the North Sea with someone else whom, against all expectations, she was attracted to.

'Do you think your first love is ever a reality or always a dream?' she asked Erik, looking down on a sea of cresting white horses though a cloudless sky.

'Are we talking about your ex-husband or the affair?' he asked.

'You have a good memory.'

'For some things.'

'I am referring to the latter.'

'An affair is often perfection because it's normally over before it falls into imperfection.'

'Is that why you have had so many of them?'

'Could be.' He smiled. 'Then again maybe I have never liked anyone enough to suffer their shortcomings.'

She returned to the cresting white horses below. Things had changed. For once Erik had insisted she took the window seat on the plane.

Without words—She wondered about her Dutch lover. At first Celia had held off writing once they had returned to their homeland. She had no wish to rock the marriage boat, then passionate pain in my heart letters of longing began to flow across the North Sea, this same sea she was crossing now. She had been haunted for years by the question of whether the relationship had been a holiday attachment or something far deeper.

Some days Celia was sure it must have been just a fling. Then again, running and rerunning the scenario of their relationship, she was not so sure: *we are rich*. But they were not rich—their relationship was doomed, never to be tested by toilet mornings.

Robin had wanted to stay in England once the summer came to an end. It was Celia who had insisted it was best to return to Holland and work things out there first. Then after a while there had been references to 'new friends' and even the 'pain in my heart letters' began to dry up.

She was never to see Robin again. When the end came, it was cold, clinical, a scalpel blade of severance—the pain had been devastating.

In her dreams Robin was always distant, there was a remoteness to the image. Maybe their relationship had been insubstantial from the word go.

'The trouble is when love goes wrong our ego is reluctant to admit we made a mistake,' she said, turning back to Erik. 'We go on enjoying the fantasy. But with Robin it didn't have time to go wrong because it was cut short by circumstances and distance.'

'Robin,' he repeated.

'Yes, Robin de Vries.'

'And what did Robin do for a living?'

'Training for the priesthood.'

'He was going to be a priest?' Erik raised an eyebrow at this.

She nodded, impressed with Erik's persistence if not his perception. 'I didn't say Robin was a *he*.'

'But a woman cannot be a priest.'

'They can in The Old Catholic Church of the Netherlands since 1998. They also have married male priests and even divorcees.'

'So this affair was with another woman?'

'Yes. Although "this affair" might be too grand a title.'

'But not for you?'

'I never do flings.'

'So I've come to realise. Although you appear to bumble along through life, Celia, you actually plough a straight course.'

'A straight course, I like that.'

'So does that mean you are predominantly gay?' He could not conceal his disappointment.

'I'm not predominantly anything. It depends on whom you meet, how much you like them, how much you fall in love with them.'

'Tonight with words unspoken, you say that I'm the only one, but will my heart be broken, when the night meets the morning sun? I'd like to know that your love, is love I can be sure of, so tell me now, and I won't ask again, will you still love me tomorrow?' Eric's whispered rendition was word perfect.

'Shut up!' She told him louder than she had intended.

'So tell me now, and I won't ask again, will you still love me tomorrow? Will you still love me tomorrow? Will you still love me tomorrow?' he teased—or was it tortured?—until she stuck her elbow into his side. 'The song—makes sense now.'

'It was playing on my car radio … the night … the night we …'

'The night you consummated your relationship,' filled in Erik.

She didn't reply.

'Robin, a nice unisex name.'

'Robin was often impenetrable. A dark forest. Often a dark forest of cool sad discontent.'

'I'm sorry,' he said.

'She was distracted by something heavy I could not get hold of.'

'I detected a hesitancy from the word go regarding this trip.'

'With reason, Robin originally came from Utrecht but was living in Amsterdam the last I heard.'

'Let it go. You don't have to justify your relationship to anyone or to yourself.'

'I know that. My real regret is that I never fully appreciated her religious calling.'

'But she gave you reason to believe she loved you?'

'Yes, but I am not sure even the *Oud-Katholieke Kerk van Nederland* would accept a gay priest. It was a hard ending and it is still painful.'

'How old are you, Celia? Early thirties?'

'Thirty-two.'

'Well don't let this woman mar the rest of your life.'

'I'll try not to. Speaking of names, I noticed you spell your name with a k. Erik, quite an old fashioned name.'

He smiled at her customary abrupt subject change. 'My father majored in Icelandic sagas.'

'"Majored", how American.'

'That's because he was. He came to Oxford on a Rhodes Scholarship and stayed.'

'How did he get from Icelandic sagas to stockbroking?'

'That's another story.'

'So he named you after Erik Bloodaxe?'

'No, Erik the Red actually. But what about you? Celia isn't exactly a modern name.'

'Oh, that's easy, I was named after my mother's sister, Celia Fosdyke, the famous novelist.'

'Fos ... dyke,' sniggered Erik. 'I like that.'

'That's not funny, verging on homophobic.'

'Writing is in the genes then?' Shamed, Erik changed tack.

'Yes, if you believe in all that.'

'I do.'

'Where does that leave Erik the Red?'

'It makes me a warrior for truth.'

'And justice?'

'Certainly for justice,' he confirmed.

Celia felt her ears popping, they must be descending.

Why do you always think with your heart rather than your head? Another taunt from the historical past. Perhaps that had been the trouble, Robin was set on being a priest. She was both spiritual and analytical, whereas Celia was … Yes, an artist of sorts who always followed her heart, would have followed her heart to the ends of the earth. The whole episode had knocked her off balance. Now she was minutes away from stepping foot onto soil she had vowed to avoid.

'Robin was an existentialist embarking on one of the most orthodox careers. She was complicated, a mix. I met her when I was a rookie journalist covering a seminar on the problems of pastoral care in de-Christianised communities. On the final night of the conference dinner, I found my secular self surrounded by ecclesiastical students. Then they seemed to suddenly evaporate but Robin remained sitting next to me. She asked if I would like to get some air out in the quadrangle. That is when she kicked off her shoes and walked barefooted. The Robin I knew didn't particularly seem to believe in rules, laws or tradition. Perhaps joining a breakaway church suited her. She believed in making her own morality as she went along.'

'Could be dangerous,' remarked Erik under his breath. 'Dangerous for society.'

'Society?' Celia hooted. 'Society is made up of a host of cruelties and hypocrisies. It is never wrong to love. But ultimately it was I who was left to walk barefoot with two fingers up to society.'

'I could never see you making such a crude gesture, but rather moving easily and unchallenged between the sexes.'

On a flow, released, Celia chose to ignore his eloquent analysis. 'No doubt she was afraid of the consequences of our relationship.'

'"Afraid" being the operative word.' Erik made no attempt to hide his scepticism.

'Do you know what *fon* means?' she asked him.

'Fon, aren't they people from West Africa?'

'No, I mean the Middle English word *fon* as in *fond.*'

'No idea.'

'It means a fool, an idiot. If someone is *fond* they are foolishly infatuated, deluded. Anyway a *fon*, that's me.'

'I don't think that is you at all,' Erik told her. 'Indeed I have developed a growing *fondness* for you myself.'

To Celia's amazement he took her hand and kissed it.

'My orientation doesn't bother you then?'

'I think I half-knew all along.' His smile could be charming.

Almost there, an intake of breath. Over the coast, over the flat lands, over small neat fields.

'Everything is so neat and clean here.' She could not stop herself examining all the faces in the street—following every flaxen head—just in case.

'I have never seen so many bicycles.'

'Or bridges and canals. And the houses along the canals look unreal, as if they've been sculptured out of sugar for a cake.'

'A cultural shock from Corfu Town.'

'But I liked the disorganisation of Corfu Town.'

'Even the stink from piled up rubbish bags?'

'Well no, not exactly that.'

* * * * *

'Josi and Marten Beekhof?' asked Erik. Two early morning faces appeared, jammed one on top of the other, in the doorway of the modern boxlike apartment block in Haarlemmerbuurt.

The couple, who were obviously nervous, did not answer at first. Marten hovered above Josi protectively. He was a giant of a man, must have been six foot six, a mythological Lange Wapper.

'Marten Beekhof?' Erik again addressed his question up at the giant. He knew the Dutch were famous for being tall but this was ridiculous.

'Who wants to know?'

'We're Erik Jordan and Celia Grey from the *London Evening Record*. We've recently returned from Paxos where we've been covering the story of the bombing.'

'How is the waiter doing?' was Marten's first question. 'Is he OK?'

Erik nodded, Celia nodded, they all finished up nodding.

'I'll never forget him. He tried to crawl away like a crab,' svelte, blonde-haired Josi tells them.

'He wasn't crawling away, darling, he was trying to reach his nephew,' put in Marten.

'His nephew who didn't make it,' added Celia.

'How horrible,' said Josi. 'I thought at first it was just the boat.'

'What? Didn't the Greek police tell you how many casualties there were?'

'No, no, they asked a lot of questions but told us little,' explained Marten. 'We learnt more of what had happened from the Dutch newspapers.'

'You'd better come in,' suggested Josi.

They squeezed after her through a narrow hallway and into a colourless sitting room. Celia was reminded of the cream and beige decoration of a hotel she had once stayed in on Orkney. Yes bland, but bland had eventually grown on her.

'Please, sit,' said Marten, pointing to a functional two seater sofa upholstered in grey fabric.

'We made statements at the police station. I hope we don't have to go back, I never want to go back there.' Josi glowered.

'I am sure that won't be necessary. But can you tell us what precisely you saw just before the explosion?' Celia asked her gently.

'We chose to have our coffee indoors. Marten's face had got badly sunburnt the day before,' explained the girl. 'There was an old guy sat outside at a waterfront table. He looked odd, not dressed like a tourist at all, that's why I remember him. He was dressed old fashioned English.'

'Yes, agreed her partner. 'Can you believe it, he was wearing a tie in Greece?'

'Like this?' asked Erik, flicking out his own tie—the giveaway tie.

'I cannot say it was exactly like yours but if it wasn't the same it was close,' replied Marten.

'I noticed the tie too,' agreed Josi. 'I wondered how anyone could bear to wear a tie when it was so hot.'

'We wouldn't have been able to recall any of this, if we hadn't had to go over the horror of it so many times for the police and in our own minds,' said Marten.

To the best of Erik's memory only Adras had mentioned the old man sat on the waterfront wearing a similar tie. He struggled to recall if he was wearing his Eton tie during any of his interviews with Captain Vasilakis. If he had been wearing the tie, it would have been on their last meeting at Gaios police headquarters before he and Celia caught the ferry to Corfu. Vasilakis had made no reference to it.

'The tie could be an important clue,' he muttered.

'Well, I am almost a hundred per cent certain it was exactly the same as yours,' said Josi.

'Did anything else strike either of you as unusual that morning?' asked Erik.

'Only that it was particularly quiet. All the tourists must have gone to the beach. Until …' The glower again.

'We are being rude. Can I offer you both a coffee?' interrupted Marten.

'That would be lovely,' responded Celia.

'There is just one more thing that might interest you, that interested the police, just before the bomb went off I took a video of Loggos outside the cafe with my iPhone. The police downloaded it but it's still on here.' Josi handed Erik and Celia her phone. They peered hard at the small screen.

The old man seated outside had his head turned away towards the sea. It would be impossible to identify him. But Josi had caught a flash of light across the water. Something was reflecting from a broken window in the soap factory. This was not the same footage of the bombing sent to Reuters, this had been taken just before the explosion from an entirely different perspective.

'See that,' said Erik in great excitement. 'We were right. Someone *was* standing in the old soap factory just before the bomb went off.'

'We wondered about that.' Marten returned with a tray of four coffees and took another look at Josi's iPhone. 'What could it be shining from there?'

'A cigarette lighter, a gun or a phone. I suspect it might have been a cell phone, something like a Nokia 105. It would have been specially adapted to give a signal to detonate the explosives once the yacht docked.' Erik rubbed at his five o' clock shadow.

'But how can we prove anything?' asked Celia.

'We can't but it is looking more than likely that the assassin was waiting concealed inside that factory well out of the way.'

'And the old man wearing a tie?' asked Josi.

'Maybe the mastermind of the whole operation,' proposed Erik.

The Dutch couple looked shocked. No one spoke, trying to process the information.

'Good coffee this.' Celia was first to speak the prosaic.

'Yes, we have just bought a new machine,' said Marten. 'A De'Longhi PrimaDonna.'

'Sounds expensive.'

'It is. Very,' he admitted.

'Josi,' Erik addressed the young woman directly. 'Would you send that video to my iPhone, it could be useful?'

'Of course.'

'And maybe your newspaper might help us with our compensation claim,' suggested Marten.

'What, for injuries sustained in the explosion?' asked Erik, concerned.

'No, no,' laughed Marten, 'for our lost holiday.'

* * * * *

'Fancy seeing some of the sights,' asked Erik, once out on the street again.

'Yes, I'd love to go to the Van Gogh gallery, or the Rijksmuseum.'

'They are a little further away. What about the Allard Pierson Archaeological Museum attached to the university,' he suggested, hailing a taxi.

What they didn't know was that the museum was closed on Mondays. However Celia soon recognised they were near Amsterdam's red light district and coffee shops. Cannabis wafted onto the street out of every doorway.

'Fancy sampling Amsterdam's coffee culture?' asked Erik.

'I'm dying for another coffee, only a coffee,' she qualified.

The coffee shop owner seemed surprised when coffee was all they required.

'Don't smoke,' explained Erik.

Nevertheless they both emerged from the shop, heady on hash fumes.

They found themselves standing in front of a window display, displaying wares of flesh—to be accurate one woman's flesh for sale, after all it was still morning. The prostitute looked to be Malaysian. Celia found she was locked onto the woman's hard hostile stare. Who would blink first? How different their lives were, had been.

'Do you approve of this?' she asked Erik, moving uncomfortably away.

'The Dutch maintain it serves a purpose.'

'A purpose for whom? Not for the women. It must destroy them.'

'I have to agree with you there.'

Walking from the disturbing scene, over one of the picturesque bridges, as it so often does tragedy and humour collided. They collapsed in gales of laughter. Suddenly struck by the ludicrousness of their position. Who else but a couple of Brits would visit the red light district at 11a.m. in the morning because the Archaeological Museum was closed.

'Time is marching on. We'd better get a taxi back to the airport hotel and collect our bags,' suggested Erik, glancing at his wristwatch.

Van Gogh's yellow sunflowers would have to wait, regretted Celia. She was suddenly struck by the memory of the colourful flowers in the garden of the Villa Elina—an awkward memory at that.

'I liked Amsterdam very much,' she told Erik, brightening over a light salmon lunch at the airport hotel. 'And I thought Marten and Josi were lovely.'

'Me too, particularly Josi.' Erik winked, crunching into his nachos and salad.

They spent the meal trying to piece together all they had learnt, trying to make sense of everything.

'It was worth coming for the video alone,' said Celia.

'Absolutely.'

'What do you really make of this tie business?'

'It worries me.'

'Why?'

'Because a tie like this is something typically worn by an MI5 or MI6 officer.' Erik caressed the silk.

'I'm never really sure of the difference.

'MI6 concentrates on international intelligence, while MI5 concerns itself with domestic affairs.'

'Why only MI5 and MI6? What happened to all the other MIs?'

'MI1, British *Military Intelligence*, also Cryptography, was set up in World War One; MI2 was responsible for Russia and Scandinavia; MI3 was responsible for Germany and Eastern Europe, whereas MI4 was involved with aerial reconnaissance. Those obsolete departments evolved into other larger agencies between the Great Wars.'

'You *are* well informed.'

'It pays to be well informed,' concluded Erik.

'Do you think our Secret Intelligence Service is mixed up in the Paxos bombing then?'

'Or is someone trying to implicate SIS?' offered Eric. 'I ask you, an Eton tie for God's sake.'

'You wear yours.'

'I'm not on special operations,' he pointed out.

'No, but you might as well be.'

'How do you mean?'

'Well, it looks as if we are doing all the digging whereas the Greek and English authorities aren't exactly proactive. Unless they are engaged in some sort of cover up,' she suggested.

'How true.' Erik smiled. 'I think we should separate for the time being. You go back to London and visit the parents of the two dead crew members. I will fly on to Corfu if I can get a last minute ticket. I still have some troubling business on Paxos to settle. Then perhaps we can both go to Shrewsbury to interview Simmons in greater depth.'

'That is if he has ever arrived in Shrewsbury.'

'We will soon find out.'

'Be careful, Erik.'

'I always am.'

And that is what they did. Erik, luckily, got a spare seat on the afternoon flight to Corfu. Celia allowed him a farewell brotherly kiss, before waiting in front of a huge central gas fire in the hotel lounge. She saw on the monitor that her KLM flight to London had been delayed, but she was happy enough reading Frederick Forsyth's *The Outsider: My Life in Intrigue* which she had picked up from a second-hand stall on Amsterdam's open air book market. When she eventually boarded her own aircraft, she felt lonely without Erik to argue with over the window seat. She was going home without him. Momentarily, she felt bereft but she had survived Holland. She had survived Robin. *Without words—* she had survived the memory of their lovemaking.

CHAPTER TWELVE

The situation had changed—Gorgias had not lied—Paxos was a hive of buzzing Hellenic Police. They were swarming in and out of Gaios town. Erik took a taxi to Loggos, they were swarming there too in a biomass of blue. Nothing was to be gained from being mixed up in this demonstration of strength. He decided to look up the two Russians at the Villa Elina. Leaving his taxi ticking over in the lane outside, he walked into the grounds. He felt like a trespasser but there was nobody about to see. Brushing the dusty window with his hand, he saw the villa's interior had an empty neglected look too. Boris and Trofim looked to be weeks gone.

However Captain Vasilakis, and a cloud of cigar smoke, were situated exactly as before in his office.

He sat bolt upright as Erik walked into the room.

'Are you ghost?' he asked. 'I never thought I would see you again.'

'Is that what you were hoping?'

'No, no, I quite like you despite you being newspaper man.'

'I see the *Elliniki Astynomia* are here in force.'

'There has been added complication.'

'In what way?'

'Smirnov's personal assistant, Anna Markova, had dual Russian and American nationality.'

'You're joking.' Erik's laugh was gleeful. 'So now Uncle Sam is involved.'

'US special agents arrived two days ago.'

'They are known as field rats in the trade.'

'Very good, because they are scuttling everywhere.'

'Believe me, there will be little hope of placating your Russian friends if the Americans find them responsible.'

'I know,' said Vasilakis, sucking deeply on his cheroot. 'It is all in hand.'

'Is it, is it really?' Erik made no attempt to hide his incredulity. 'And what about the old man sat outside the bar wearing a tie like mine?'

'What about him?'

'An Eton tie. He left just before the bomb exploded.'

'There again, we don't want to upset you English if old man was innocent.'

Erik thrust his phone in Vasilakis' face. 'Have you seen this video taken by Josi Beekhof, one of the Dutch tourists?'

The Captain stared at the small screen. 'No, believe me, I've never seen this in my life.'

'Then someone is deliberately withholding information from you. See there, something is clearly flashing in the soap factory.'

'Athens,' sighed Vasilakis. 'Athens has taken over.'

'Ah, yes, they have been putting forth the theory that the additive ethanol in gasoline corroded the *Bettina's* fuel pipes, that it was an accidental explosion.'

'That could be so.' Vasilakis looked hopeful.

'The *Bettina* was a new boat, her fuel pipes would hardly have been used.'

'I am no expert in these matters.'

'And what about the murder of Aleixo Xenakis?' Erik had not come all this way to mince around.

'We have already discussed him.'

'And you told me very little. Did you ever interview the two Russians at the Villa Elina?'

'Mr Boris and Mr Trofim have gone.'

'Of course they have, the Americans are here. And you've not even enquired Boris' and Trofim's surnames, their given names.' Erik shook his head in disbelief.

'Neither of two Russians smoked by the way. I offered them cigarettes when I chanced upon them in Loggos taverna.'

'And you consider that conclusive evidence that they were not involved?'

'No, but I did have foresight to collect cups after they had enjoyed coffee at my expense. DNA results, back from Athens, did not match cigarette butts left in soap factory with coffee cups. However we did find their fingerprints on lighter with yours.'

'I could have saved you a job there. They both examined it soon after I had found it in the soap factory. Could Athens identify the DNA on the butts to any known person? Were there any other fingerprints on the lighter?'

'Mr Jordan, I am local policeman doing the best I can. I want truth as much as you do. Six people have been killed on my island in suspicious circumstance. However higher Hellenic authority have closed us down, will tell us nothing, apart from telling us to say nothing further.'

'I'm sorry …' began Erik.

Vasilakis scribbled a quick note. 'See, I have a friend, a high up friend at foreign embassy in Athens. You will find him sympathetic. He is connected to opposition party in coalition government. Take this to him and he will see you.'

Erik picked up the note pushed across the table to him. 'I'm sorry, sorry again for losing my temper. I know you are under constraint.' He made for the door. 'Take care, Captain Vasilakis.'

'You also, my friend. I have strange feeling you will find answers in Athens and London more than here.'

'And the Americans?'

'The Americans know nothing *yet*.'

* * * * *

The Hellenic Ministry of Foreign Affairs government building was classical architecturally yet dwarfed by a towering new build. It sported both the Greek and European flags above its portico. Erik showed his press card and was immediately escorted to the door of a Mr Kyrillos. He was obviously expected. Vasilakis must have rung ahead and forewarned him. Michalis Kyrillos' office was surprisingly pokey and shabby inside. Erik wondered if this was a sign that his politics were out of favour.

Good. An out of favour diplomat was more likely to be cooperative, dish the dirt, than a government man.

The opposition party in coalition with left-wing Syriza was the right-wing populist Independent Greeks Party. Unlikely bedfellows and from recent media speculation so it was proving to be.

'Vasilakis says, here, you are a journalist from the *London Evening Record*.' Kyrillos shook the Captain's note like a hooked fish. 'A left-wing newspaper am I not right in thinking?'

'The *London Evening Record* is an independent paper, always has been and always will be.' Erik stood his ground.

'Please, sit, Mr Jordan.' The Independent Greeks Party man held out his bony hand across the worn table.

Erik took it. Although from the word go he was not too sure he liked Vasilakis' right-wing diplomatic friend very much, but he needed information.

'How can I help?' Kyrillos rubbed his dry hands together—dry even though the room was stuffy—even though he wore a tie as if to distinguish himself from Syriza.

Erik cleared his throat. 'My newspaper is interested in the bombing of the *Bettina* on Paxos. As you will know two British nationals, Anna Parker and Robert Perceval, lost their lives in the explosion.'

'You use the word "bombing" when we are not sure that is the case.'

Not the ethanol gasoline excuse again. Erik winced to himself.

'And the murder of your Interpol agent, Aleixo Xenakis, around the same time?' he queried, smiling slyly.

'Who said he was murdered?'

'According to the medical examiner he was strangled, garrotted,' elaborated Erik.

Kyrillos looked nonplussed. 'Who told you that? Not Vasilakis I hope.'

'I found out,' Erik told him vaguely. Adding, 'Some Russian investigators befriended us on Paxos.'

'Did they really?' Kyrillos' interest seemed to be piqued by this. 'Russians, you say?'

'Yes, I was fairly sure they were G.U. or SVR agents.'

'Are you telling me that Russian intelligence operatives were working on Greek soil without our knowledge?'

'Without *your* knowledge, without *your* party's knowledge perhaps.' *Divide and rule*, Erik struggled to hide another smile as Kyrillos struggled to catch his breath.

'You do realise, Mr Jordan, that Greek and Russian relations are rather delicate at the moment over the proposed Republic of North Macedonia?'

'Yes, I have heard that.'

'So you will also have heard that people are saying we are heading towards an ice age between our two countries over it.'

'Indeed. And is the Independent Greeks Party in concordance with Syriza over the Former Yugoslav Republic of Macedonia changing its name?'

Kyrillos tried to shrug this off, would not be drawn at first, before finally admitting, 'We do not think it is beneficial to fall out with Russia.'

And there it was—the confusion of European politics, the mess over the Balkans—when the far right was happy to get into bed with the far left.

'So are you saying that if Russia was involved with the bombing and murder of an Interpol officer, Greece would turn a blind eye?'

'I will be honest with you, Mr Jordan, the two incidents you mention are unofficially no longer considered to be unconnected. But our party categorically believes Russia wasn't involved. However ...' He took a deep sigh. 'Our partners in coalition wish to officially maintain that the sinking of the *Bettina* could still have been an accident.'

'"Categorically" no Russian involvement?'

'That is what I said. Look at it this way, Mr Jordan, why would Russia want to kill Dmitry Smirnov, Putin's friend? What would they gain from his death?'

'Nevertheless, you believe Smirnov was the target?'

'Who else?' Kyrillos made an open arm appeal.

'So who wanted him dead?'

'Isn't that what we are all trying to establish?'

* * * * *

It didn't take Celia long to find out that the crewman, Robert Perceval, was brought up in an orphanage near Birmingham. Unfortunately he had no one, no living relative left to grieve.

Next she rang the parents of Anna Parker in nearby Bush Hill Park. She told them she was a journalist on the *London Evening Record* and had just returned from covering the story in Paxos. This seemed to impress them. They, in turn, told her that the Greeks were refusing to release their daughter's body. Could she help with Anna's repatriation? Celia told them she could make no promises, but a story about their daughter would help keep her name in the public eye.

'Can I come round?'

'Please do,' said Mr Parker.

'This morning?'

'We'll be in.' *Click*, he was gone.

'Although Anna had chosen to sail the world …' began Mr Parker an hour or so later.

'She was our world,' sobbed Mrs Parker.

Celia did a quick visual over the small suburban lounge which looked more 1950s than twenty-first century. The couple were obviously fans of bisque porcelain figurines.

'I am so sorry for your loss.' Celia heard herself sounding too much like Joe Kenda, the Colorado Springs TV detective.

More sobbing from Mrs Parker and now Mr Parker had tears welling in his eyes. The couple sat on the couch opposite—locked together for support—gelatinous and inseparable in their suffering. Celia fell quiet, contrite, suddenly overwhelmed with the ramifications of this unspeakable act. Not a lot of attention had been given to Anna Parker and Robert Perceval. Two young people's lives obliterated in a puff of smoke. But for the Parkers they had lost their main reason for living.

Whatever else Celia knew she had to pull herself together, remain professional in this tragic situation. 'Tell me a little more about Anna? Where did she go to school? Did she go to university or college? Was she good at sport? That sort of thing.'

'Anna simply loved the sea,' said Mrs Parker. 'From a young age she wanted nothing more than to sail round the world.'

'Shortly after leaving school she saw the job with Crew For You advertised in our local paper,' added Mr Parker. 'And that was that. We saw little of her since she took to ocean cruising.'

'Are the agency being helpful?' asked Celia.

'I think they are doing their best,' sighed Mr Parker. 'We've been in touch with the Foreign and Commonwealth Office of course. It's just the Greeks who are proving difficult.'

'I am sure you will have Anna back with you soon,' reassured Celia. *What is left of her*—the elephant in that suburban sitting room.

'Just recently Anna wrote us a rather disturbing letter,' admitted Mr Parker.

'The police say it must have been her last letter,' added Mrs Parker, sobbing again. 'I cannot believe she is dead.'

'She didn't like the owners very much, wrote that they were the most arrogant people she had ever worked for. But what worried Mother and I more was she expressed serious misgivings about a fellow crew member.'

'Which crew member?'

'That's just it, she didn't give a name.'

Celia mulled over this piece of information before opening her mouth again. 'It would have to be Robert Perceval or Jacob Simmons.'

'Yes, she did mention those two names in previous correspondence. But in that final letter she wrote that one of her male colleagues wasn't pulling his weight, didn't mix anymore, didn't seem to be taking the job seriously.'

'But you've no idea to whom she was referring?'

Mr Parker shook his head. 'No idea, sorry.'

'It's strange but I don't really feel she's gone from us forever.' His wife began to weep again.

When Celia emerged from the Parkers' semi-detached house, she saw the same youth she had noticed on arrival still watching her from across the road. He leant casually against a red pillar box. If he was trying to look incognito, he looked anything but, indeed he looked ridiculous wearing his grandfather's flat cap with a fag dangling from the corner of his mouth. Nonetheless the bizarre can quickly turn dangerous. Things can happen even in the leafy suburbs of the London Borough of Enfield, people can get stabbed, murdered here too.

Fight or flight—she crossed the road to confront Peaky Blinder.

'Are you watching me?'

'No, not you exactly.'

'Then who?'

'The house.'

'Why?'

'What's it to you?'

'Because unless you explain yourself or move on, I am about to go back into that house and get them to call the police.'

'I'm committing no crime.'

'How about loitering with intent?' *Worth a try.*

The youth reached into his trench coat pocket. Celia took a step back. Was he pulling out a weapon?

'Thomas Barrow, *Enfield Post*.' He flashed his press card.

'What's your game, Thomas Barrow?'

'The same game as you I expect. Except my paper wasn't granted a private interview with Anna Parker's parents.'

'And why was that?'

Barrow chewed on his cigarette thoughtfully. 'The *Enfield Post* is too small, not important enough. Hasn't got the same financial clout to pay for stories like the nationals.'

Celia, who had questioned the morality of having Simmons on the payroll, was furious. 'I'll say this once, Mr Barrow, my paper hasn't paid a penny to those poor people. They are a decent couple grieving the loss of their daughter. All they want is to be left alone.'

'Why did they agree to speak to you then?' He was becoming petulant. Celia shook her head, would not be drawn. 'And not to me?' he persisted.

'Maybe you didn't ask them nicely enough.' With that she walked away.

'Stuck up bitch!' She heard him mutter in her wake.

Once back at the office she thought it best to inform Nelson of her conversation with young Barrow.

'Damn,' he said. 'Soon they'll all be round there knocking on the Parkers' door, grinding them down. Can't be helped, we don't have exclusive rights to everyone involved with this story. The important thing is to be the first, to get the first interview. Write what the Parkers have had to say about the loss of their daughter and we'll publish tonight.'

Celia got as much pathos as she could into her article, THE GIRL WHO LOVED THE SEA, holding back only on Anna's libellous dislike of the owners and suspicion about one of her crewmates.

Then again in English law you could not defame the dead. However one of the principals—Jacob Simmons—was still alive and in their pay. She had to be careful.

CHAPTER THIRTEEN

'The two extremes of the big **C** are coming together,' explained Erik, returned and refreshed over a cool beer in the newspaper's local watering hole.

Celia stared at him bemused. 'I'm afraid I don't know what you mean.'

'Russia and the far right are joining forces over the Balkans, certainly in Greece, over the future of the Former Yugoslav Republic of Macedonia. The big **C** is about to form the big **O** for Oh no, leaving the liberal West nowhere.'

'But *is* the West liberal?'

'I believe most people in the West are basically liberal. But liberalism isn't regarded as exciting, sexy enough. So extremism is in danger of filling the middle ground. I fear the Balkans is just the start of it. The whole of Europe could be next.'

'That's frightening.'

'Yes, it is. Particularly in light of Europe's historical past.'

'Did you find out anything to add to our story during this latest trip?'

'Smirnov's mistress had dual Russian and American nationality. US special agents are crawling all over Paxos and, of course, Boris and Trofim are gone.'

'What about British Intelligence?'

'Nowhere to be seen. Low key.'

'But isn't that what they do best?' asked Celia.

'You could be right. However two British nationals have lost their lives.'

Pondering the mystery, Celia took a gentle sip out of her newfangled cherry flavoured gin. 'Good choice, this is lovely.'

'I'm getting to know your tastes.'

Still cradling her glass, she scrutinised his face. 'Possibly.'

'There is one thing that struck me after my latest visit, the Greeks are adamant that the Russians are not responsible for the bombing.'

'If not them, then who?'

Erik noticed Celia had turned her attention to a man in a mackintosh in the far corner. The man was not directly in Erik's view but he could see him clearly reflected in a mirror. He was holding a whisky glass and kept glancing at his tabloid newspaper. From its layout, Erik guessed it was the *Evening Standard*.

'You're not still paranoid about being followed?' he asked her.

'I almost set about a young guy camped out opposite Anna Parker's parents' house two days ago. He looked like something out of Peaky Blinders. He was merely a reporter on the local rag.'

'Did you get much out of the Parkers?'

'Not that I could use but something which may be of interest to us in the future,' said Celia lowering her voice. Erik supped at his ale, all ears. 'They told me that Anna did not like Smirnov or his mistress, but more significantly she was apprehensive about one of her crewmates.'

'Which one?'

Celia leaned in closer. 'Regrettably she did not name him.'

'Don't worry about that gentleman in the corner unless he can lip-read.'

'Maybe he can.'

'You have a point there,' agreed Erik. 'If he is an agent, I'd be surprised if he couldn't.'

Just as he finished the sentence, the man in the corner seat got up and a swish of mackintosh passed them by.

* * * * *

Celia was seated before her computer screen the next morning searching for a story of interest to follow. The government had just approved a controversial plan for a third runway at Heathrow. She felt hot, bothered and indifferent. The Met Office had confirmed that May had been the warmest since records began in 1910, and was also likely to be the sunniest since 1929. June was proving to be no better. England did not know how to deal with heat, not like warmer parts of the world, not like Greece.

Greece, Paxos, she could not get them out of her head.

She almost jumped out of her skin as a sweat glistening face appeared looming above her screen.

'Seen this?' asked Erik, passing her a rival newspaper.

'You frightened me to death there.'

'Today's news. Scooped by the opposition,' he explained.

An agreement has been reached between the Greek prime minister, Alexis Tsipras, and his Macedonian counter part, Zoran Zaev, whereby the name 'Republic of North Macedonia' will be adopted.

'Fancy a little fresh air?' Erik asked her. 'Come on, I'm driving us to Shrewsbury to interview Simmons. It will take three hours via the A40, M40, M6. I've fixed it with Nelson.'

'But do we know that Simmons will be there?'

'Whether he is there or not will not stop us investigating him.'

Celia was terrified. Erik's driving was far faster and much more cavalier in his own car than the hire car in Paxos. Celia would have argued about their chosen route but Erik switched on his Sat Nav to counter any risk of dispute. However she had to allow that the black Audi R8 reached Swan Hill in just over three hours.

After one or two premature turnings they found Flat 4, Tudor Lane, and Erik hammered on the door. 'Anyone at home?'

'Can I help you, luv?' A grey female head eventually appeared above next-door's hedge.

'We are looking for Jacob Simmons,' Erik told her.

'Ah, Mr Simmons. His flat has stood empty for months.'

'And you are?' asked Celia.

'Why I am Mrs Baker, luv, his landlady. My son and I own the property.'

'Can we take a peep?'

'Might you be interested in renting?'

'Yes, we could be,' interrupted Erik. Celia glared at him. How easily lies rolled off his tongue.

'Are you a couple? The flat might be a little small for two.'

'No, we are brother and sister,' Erik told her.

'Yes, I see the resemblance now.'

'It's just my sister who might want to rent.' Erik kissed Celia's forehead. She flinched. 'Isn't that right, sis?'

'Of course, my dears, you can take a look although there's little to see. Mr Simmons stripped the place bare of all his belongings before he left. I'll be letting it on an unfurnished basis.'

The landlady disappeared into her own house to get the keys.

'Why did you have to tell her that?' Celia hissed at Erik.

'What?'

'That I was your bloody sister.'

'I liked the idea.'

'You're impossible.'

Flat 4, Tudor Lane, was indeed bare: clean white decorations but empty and soulless.

'It's been left very clean,' observed Celia. 'Or did you clean it, Mrs Baker, after Jacob Simmons left.'

'No, I didn't touch a thing.' Mrs Baker shook her shaggy crinkly hair. 'Mr Simmons was scrupulous, exacting in his habits.'

'So did he settle his final payment for the flat?' asked Erik.

'Yes, Mr Simmons always paid his rent on time too.' Mrs Baker began to look suspicious.

'We're from a newspaper, Mrs Baker,' confessed Celia. 'We're both journalists. My colleague was teasing you about me being his sister.'

Mrs Baker's lips fell adrift. 'Why?'

'Because he is a clown.' Celia got huge enjoyment from saying this.

'I do apologise, Mrs Baker. My colleague's right, I do have a weird sense of humour.' Erik frowned his apology, his expression turning even more serious. 'Now allow me to be absolutely honest with you, your previous tenant was involved in an incident over in Paxos, Greece.'

'Not that terrible bombing we've all been reading about?'

'Yes, as a matter of fact …'

'I didn't see his name mentioned anywhere.'

'Actually, I've just written a piece featuring him,' Erik told her. 'You obviously aren't a *London Evening Record* reader, Mrs Baker.'

'We just buy the local paper once a week. Is he alright, Mr Simmons?'

'He is OK as far as we know. He wasn't on the boat that got blown up. But we are trying to locate him,' explained Celia more kindly.

'I must admit I thought at first you were in trouble, luv. Particularly when your friend here said he was your brother.'

'No, no.' Celia scowled across at Erik again.

'With looks like that I wouldn't have put anything past Mr Simmons.'

'He isn't my type though, Mrs Baker.'

'No, certainly not her type,' put in Erik maliciously

'Good thing too. The things these young lasses get up to these days.' Mrs Baker's mouth tightened into blue rinse disapproval.

'Did he have many girlfriends?' asked Celia.

'Not that I ever saw. He did have one or two foreign gentlemen visitors and, yes, I do remember there was one young lady whom he introduced me to as Alexandra. Funnily enough, he too told me she was his sister.'

'"The things these young lasses get up to these days",' mimicked Erik, once they were back in the Audi.

'You're not very funny. You nearly messed up that whole interview. Drive,' Celia told him.

* * * * *

151

They made the *London Evening Record* office just before five.

'Shrewsbury any good?' asked Duncan Nelson.

'He wasn't there,' replied Celia. 'Cleared his flat out.'

'No, but we got an interview with his landlady, a Mrs Baker,' said Erik with more enthusiasm. 'She won't have realised it but she has given us something to work on.'

Celia regarded him doubtfully. 'Really?'

'Well, for me to work on.'

True enough Celia was recognised as having the common touch during interviews, while Erik was known as a brilliant researcher. Indeed, not for the first time, Nelson wondered if Erik could be some sort of genius on the autism spectrum.

'Anyway you two have a visitor waiting in Gatsby's office. He's been here an hour. We've had to feed him with tea and biscuits.' Nelson escorted them to the Editor's office, maintaining his raised eyebrows, before leaving them to it.

Celia was relieved to see that Gatsby was not there either but her mouth fell open on seeing who was.

'Do I know you?' she asked.

'I don't think so,' replied the man.

'Too hot for your mackintosh?'

'Ahh, a lady with good powers of observation.'

'You were spying on us in the pub.'

'"Spying", now that is a word we never like to use.'

'Who are "we"?'

'That, my dear, will eventually become apparent.'

'What do you want?' asked Erik, tiring of the vacillation.

'We want your cooperation.'

'Or else?'

'We will close you down.'

'Close the newspaper down?' asked an incredulous Celia.

'That would be the final act. No, we would simply close the story down.'

'What story?'

'The Paxos explosion story of course.'

'And how do you propose to close it down when it is already out there?' Erik again.

'I suppose you have heard of a DSMA-Notice System?'

'Of course a Defence and Security Media Advisory Notice,' interpreted Erik.

'But we can avoid all this unpleasantness if you simply work with us.'

'Exchange information, you mean.'

'That's right and your Editor agrees.'

'So you have us boxed in a corner.'

'We don't want you to think of it like that, more as your patriotic duty.'

'I've never heard of a DSMA-Notice System,' interrupted Celia.

'It's the old D-Notice,' explained Erik.

'So we can't pursue this story, leaving our competitors free to do so.' Celia glowered.

'Certainly you can. All you have to do is run the important stuff through us before you publish.' The intelligence officer handed Celia a card with a mobile number on it. 'Only use this number if either of you get in extreme difficulties. Otherwise you'll find me sitting on a bench in Kensington Gardens at ten a.m. every Sunday come rain or shine, across from Round Pond facing the Palace.'

'Reading *The Sunday Times* of course,' interjected Erik.

'Of course, like all the best films.'

'This is all rather clandestine, isn't it?' muttered Celia.

'Nonetheless, as I am sure you are both aware the safest contacts, especially in this day and age, are face to face.'

'And Nelson and Gatsby have really agreed to this?' Eric scowled. Mackintosh Man nodded and smiled.

'This means a one way exchange of information,' Erik told Celia when he had gone.

'I'm surprised at Nelson and Gatsby going along with it.'

'They had no choice with the threat of a DSMA-Notice hanging over them. And Gatsby has been after a gong for as long as I've know him.' Erik smiled slyly. 'However Intelligence has left us some leeway, "important stuff" is a matter of interpretation.'

'But if we can't publish.'

'No, but we can find the truth. And didn't we say that revealing who is responsible for this terrible act is our main objective. Perhaps then SIS might let us publish first.'

'You've been in this situation before, Erik.'

'Once,' was his cagey reply.

'Have I just been recruited too?'

'I think you have.'

Celia flipped Mackintosh Man's card over in her hand. 'Can you believe this? Only the British Intelligence Service could come up with this: David Williams, Structural Engineer, Cardiff.'

'That's part of his wallet litter. What is called a backstop company. Both MI5 and MI6 create a whole life legend for these guys.'

* * * * *

After their trips to Greece and Holland the everyday took over, everyday dramas happening to regular people. An

English couple, Charlie Rowley and Dawn Sturgess, were critically ill in hospital after picking up a perfume bottle in Amesbury, Wiltshire. Amesbury lies just seven miles from Salisbury. The perfume bottle was believed to be contaminated with Novichok.

While Charlie remained in a stable condition, on Sunday, 8th July doctors were forced to turn off Dawn's life support machine at Salisbury District Hospital—Dawn, a totally innocent victim of tit for tat global espionage. Celia saw it at home on the morning breakfast programme. She did not know either Charlie or Dawn but was inexplicably struck by a feeling of sadness. Something like this could happen to anyone. Something like this could have happened to her already.

The trouble that Michalis Kyrillos had intimated to Erik came to fruition in early July too. The Greek Government expelled two Russian diplomats and barred the entry of two more accusing them of undermining the national security of Greece. The move was made public, which was seen by experts as unprecedented in the two countries' relationship. Amid the subsequent acrimonious exchanges, Greece accused the Russian Foreign Ministry of 'disrespect for a third country and a lack of understanding of today's world, in which states, regardless of their size, are independent and can exercise an independent, multidimensional and democratic foreign policy.'

'Russia cannot bear to have North Macedonia as a NATO ally on her borders,' explained Erik to Celia during their coffee break. 'By the way I've bought you this.' He pushed a cylindrical shaped object, wrapped in happy birthday gift paper, across the table to her.

'It's not my birthday.'

'Never mind, open it.'

She carefully stripped away the wrapping paper. Inside was a pink plastic thing that at first, to her intense disgust, she thought was some sort of tacky sex toy.

'A hot pink pepper spray for your added security,' explained Erik.

Celia held up the pepper spray with a bemused expression and began to laugh.

'What's wrong?' he asked innocently.

'Do you think I'll really need this?'

'I hope not but you will feel better carrying it around in your pocket or purse.'

Back at her desk, a tower fan oscillated a gentle breeze as she worked her way through this and that story. She broke off to glance across at Erik. He was glowering over his screen as if still struggling with the mystery of Simmons' whereabouts.

Then one morning, towards the end of this searing month, horror flashed across her screen melting the Teflon exterior of a story hardened journalist.

Erik saw her face. Erik—who was becoming fixed and focused on her every change of expression—walked over to her desk.

'You OK?' he asked.

She did not answer. Her attention glued to the news video. There had been terrible wildfires on the coastal resorts of Attica. The village of Mati, just eighteen miles east of Athens, was severely damaged. There was an apocalyptical Reuter's picture of hundreds of people wading into the sea amid choking smoke. The elderly sat on rescued chairs on the shoreline—their feet paddling in the water—to avoid being burnt to death. Many people were feared dead.

She felt as if all her life blood was draining to her own feet. She felt faint. Without realising it she had grown imperceptibly attached to Greece. Celia released her fingers on shift, command and key three. The shutter sound of a screenshot.

'We don't need man's intervention on the violent front, nature can cause mayhem and destruction all by itself,' sighed Eric, nodding at her screen.

He was not the only one to have observed Celia.

'Oh good, you've seen it,' said Nelson walking towards them.

'Oh no!' exclaimed Erik.

'Don't be like that young Jordan. How about some more practice with your conversational Greek? How about another little jaunt, this time nearer to Athens?'

'I've just returned from Athens,' complained Erik.

'Well, you can go again. You can both go again. You get on so well together.'

Celia and Erik both pulled a face.

'Seventy-four people believed dead so far. However we want human interest stories not statistics. Remember, it is individual experiences that carry the most impact. Right up your street, Celia. Did I tell you, I loved that piece you did on the young English lass that died on the boat?' Nelson physically patted her on the head.

'Anna Parker,' sighed Celia.

'That's right, Anna Parker,' confirmed Nelson.

'We'll go,' Erik told him. 'But only if you book us into a hotel with a pool.'

'That's rather insensitive, Erik,' interrupted Celia, pointing to the Reuter's image frozen on her screen. 'These people have lost everything.'

'Then we must report on the story,' said Erik. Adding with a wink across at her, 'But a hotel with a pool won't hurt.'

Celia's day did not end there. Escorted by a member of staff, she had two visitors.

'Came by taxi,' explained Mr Parker. 'Don't drive into London anymore.'

'You will be popular with the mayor,' quipped Celia. Then immediately regretted it on seeing their serious faces. She glanced towards the Editor's and News Editor's occupied offices before turning back to her guests. 'Both of you come with me, we'll be more comfortable in our reception area downstairs.'

The Parkers accepted the offer of tea—obviously it had been challenging coming into town.

'This arrived a few weeks ago.' Mrs Parker handed Celia what looked to be a ring box. 'Anna must have sent it just before she set sail to …' Her voice cut out.

'Paxos,' sighed her husband.

Tea arrived as Celia snapped open the tiny box. 'A thimble, the most exquisite thimble.'

'Anna knew I liked to sew,' sniffed Mrs Parker.

Celia rolled the thimble in her hand. 'This isn't just any thimble. It looks very expensive.'

'I agree,' said Mrs Parker.

'There was a short note with it from Anna. It said the thimble was given to her by someone on the boat,' explained Mr Parker. 'We showed it to the police but they didn't seem very interested.'

'No, well they wouldn't be.' Celia did not hide her sarcasm. 'Do you mind if I show this to a colleague?'

'You mean keep it?' asked Mrs Parker doubtfully.

Celia took out her phone. 'No, no, I'll ring him to come down now.'

Eric smiled round at the gathering as he began to examine the thimble like a jewellery expert on the Antiques Roadshow. 'I am no expert,' he eventually admitted, 'but my grandmother used to collect these. It looks very old and made of gold.'

'I love the waffle top. And aren't those rubies set into the clover leaf decoration?' asked Celia. Celia who had never lifted a needle in her life but saw the beauty in this exquisite object.

'See, there, I can just make out the maker's mark **КБ**,' squinted Erik. 'Do you mind, Mr and Mrs Parker, if I keep this for a week or two and have it identified by a professional?'

The Parkers nodded their agreement, happy that someone at last was taking an interest.

'It has just struck me that there were two Annas aboard the *Bettina*. Did your Anna ever say why exactly she didn't get on with Anna Markova, the owner's assistant?' asked Celia.

The couple shook their heads.

'I don't think Anna had much to do with her,' said Mrs Parker. 'Too high and mighty, that was my impression.'

'But they were the only two women aboard,' pointed out Celia.

'Why, do you think she could have given our Anna the thimble?'

'We might never know.'

'I still can't believe she's gone,' said Mrs Parker.

It did not take Erik too long to establish from a friend at Sotheby's that the thimble was Russian. The maker was Karl

Bock (**КБ**). Bock who was an Imperial Court Jeweller in the early 20th century. He had shops in Saint Petersburg and Moscow. It was indeed worth a lot of money.

'Another Russian link,' he told Celia.

'Do you think Anna Markova would have given Anna such an expensive thimble?'

'The value of things to those people isn't the same as ours.' Erik's brow furrowed. 'Then again Anna Parker could have stolen it. Such a small item to stow away.'

'Oh no, I don't want to believe that.'

'A lovely present for her poor mummy back home,' suggested Erik, sceptical as always.

'The Parkers aren't exactly poor.'

'No, but they were compared to Smirnov and his girlfriend.'

CHAPTER FOURTEEN

So it was back to Greece and a seafront spa hotel at Markopoulo Mesogaias on the Attica peninsula.

'No expense spared,' muttered Erik, looking down on his reflection in the highly polished reception floor as they booked in. 'Nelson has really surpassed himself this time.'

'Are you surprised with the horrific story he has given us to cover?' Key card in hand, Celia made for her bedroom.

Erik followed on like an obedient dog. His room was conveniently next to hers. However harrowing the Mati story facing them tomorrow, he was determined to enjoy the evening in five star indulgence.

'Fancy a swim before dinner?' he asked Celia. 'The Chinese tourists appear to have fled back home taking their pink flamingos with them.'

Missing out last time on big pool swimming, he was eager to try this lavish irregular shaped pool. The water was surprisingly much warmer than that of the villa's small pool. But then they had swum at the villa in May, now a July sun was beating down on them. Today he knew what it felt like to be a small fish in a vast pond. Even with Celia in support next to him, he felt vulnerable.

However recalled confidence kicked in and he managed four lengths.

'Let's try some front crawl,' she suggested.

Although Celia had never given him reason to hope on the romantic front, he was eager to comply and please to the point of drowning.

His arms windmilling and his legs splashing out all over the place, he spluttered and struggled to breathe before his feet found reassurance on the bottom.

'Don't worry about breathing at this stage,' she told him, unmoved by his effort. 'Try a few strokes without breathing. Breathing will come naturally. Sooner or later you will learn to breath in the trough behind your head, the trough made by your head. The position of your head in front crawl is all important.'

He tried and tried again. Rolling to his right side, he eventually managed a few gulps of air.

'Good, good, you are getting the hang of it,' she encouraged.

'How about dinner now?' He felt exhausted.

There were several restaurants to choose from. The night was humid and close and they decided on an outside restaurant with a fan whirling in the roof above. As on their visit to the glass cube restaurant on Corfu, she chose the local red, he the white.

'The Secret Restaurant eh? We could have done with this on Paxos,' laughed Erik.

They laughed, and laughed more, and the tables around them took on a tipsy swirl. They did not know it then but their lives were about to change dramatically. They were like ingenuous soldiers on the brink of war.

* * * * *

Over breakfast, by the pool, Celia showed Eric one of the more tragic individual screenshots she had taken from Reuters, which had already been used by the *Irish Times*. It showed an old lady in the sea at Mati. Grief stricken, she was falling forward from a wooden chair. Her bewildered middle-aged daughter stood guard over her. Beyond them people paddled in the water as if out on a day trip. But this was no day trip, this was Hell. The old lady's grey hair, the choking grey fug of smoke clinging to the water, the water itself grey. They were almost indistinguishable, one from the other.

Eric passed the iPhone back to Celia without a word.

'Apart from the people burnt to death, many have drowned too,' she told him.

Again Eric did not respond. He was remembering what it felt like not being able to breathe doing front crawl, his head underwater.

'Terrible,' he finally muttered. 'Too terrible to contemplate.'

'Fuelled by gale-force winds the wildfire trapped hundreds of people on beaches, roads and in homes east of Athens. It raged through Kallitechnoupoli, through Neos Voutzas and Rafina, reaching Mati where it finally stopped at the coast. The death toll is rising daily.'

A television flickered above their table as they spooned in yogurt and berries and gulped down coffee. Just as Celia was about to attack her custard *bougasta*, something caught her eye on the TV. It was a photograph of two beautiful twin girls superimposed over a devastated Mati. She raised a finger to her lips to silence Erik, and they both tuned into the dull monotone.

It appeared a father was making an emotional appeal for information about his missing nine year old daughters.

'What is he saying precisely?' Celia asked Erik.

'Something about them last being seen with their grandfather debarking from a rescuing fishing boat.'

'Come on, get your things,' she told him. 'This could be our human interest story.'

'I've not shaved yet,' he objected.

'Forget about that. You'll look like modern man, like David Beckham.'

'Without the tattoos,' he pointed out.

'Who cares what you look like in this situation.'

'Obviously not you.'

Approaching Rafina, along the Attica eastern seaboard, they began to see evidence of the fire out of their taxi window. But the village of Mati had suffered most—Mati turned out to be another world up the road—a torched war zone.

Erik ran nervous fingers over his bristled chin. 'I covered Aleppo a short while back. It looked very much like this.'

Hundreds of burnt out cars littered the streets, pavements were carpeted in ash, blackened trees lined paths that had once led to people's homes, homes that were now nothing more than charred frames. The acrid smell of smoke still lingered in the air.

They had arranged to meet their old Corfu friend, Gorgias, along the Poseidonos Avenue. As their driver reluctantly trundled through the still smouldering demolition site, chuntering dissatisfaction all the while, they were relieved to see a large hand waving them down. Gorgias had offered to guide them for the day, and they jumped into his hired vehicle without further ado.

'Like Dante's Inferno, no?' he asked, turning to his backseat passengers. They nodded stunned. 'We get occasional fire on islands in summer, but nothing like this.'

'Maybe global warming is responsible,' proposed Celia. Erik shrank, surely now was not the time for her to air a climate change agenda.

'Maybe,' retorted Gorgias dismissively.

'Would it not be better to walk and get people's impressions at ground level as it were?' suggested Erik. 'Celia and I will record everything.'

'If you would like,' replied Gorgias, obediently parking up. Going to the back of the vehicle, he started unloading some serious camera equipment from the boot. 'What pictures I take today, we will share.'

They stopped to speak to a woman, who was wearing a mask, amid the ruins of her life. She was engaged in the hopeless task of salvaging anything she could from permanent obliteration.

'All gone.' She appealed to them with open arms as if they could magically make it right. 'All gone but me.'

'*Boró na páro ti fotografía sou*?' asked Gorgias.

'*Naí*,' replied the robotic woman in surprise.

'*Pós epivíoses*?' asked Gorgias. 'How did you survive?'

'How? The sea,' she replied again in English. 'Nothing till smell of smoke and then fire coming down hill, pine cones exploding round ears, fire burning my back as I running.'

'But you lived,' said Gorgias.

'Yes, I did. My husband is still missing. He stayed to save house.' She turned to Celia. 'Will you help me to find?'

'The authorities will help you find him,' intervened Gorgias, a comforting hand on her shoulder.

'Puh! The authorities. Police closed roads. Many people died in cars unable to escape. Not one fire engine come.'

'We are so sorry,' said Erik, looking round powerless.

Little more was to be gained and Gorgias moved them off further down the street.

Another woman—her left arm bandaged, her right hand to her mouth—stood confused amid a lot of dead cars. Gorgias lifted up his camera without asking.

An old lady screamed down on them from her damaged apartment. Gorgias translated: 'Mati is finished. Why has God deserted us?'

They next addressed a fellow in overalls, who looked like a workman but was probably a householder, tugging at metal sheeting before giving up hands on hips. Could he tell them about his experience of this tragedy?

Click! Recorders on again. Gorgias' camera shutter snapped together again.

'It happened so fast,' translated Gorgias once more. 'The fire was in distance, then sparks reached us. Then fire was all around us. Hot wind before it was indescribable. Wind that sucked air, oxygen out of lungs.'

'How terrifying,' sympathised Celia.

'*Polý travmatikó*. Very traumatic,' Erik told the man.

'Called firestorm,' said the man in broken English.

They left the man dejected, outfaced, his hands fused back on his hips.

'I woke up from siesta just before six p.m. By eight p.m. the fire had destroyed Mati. I spent seven hours in sea. Water up to here,' another man told them in very good English, gesturing to his neck. 'Many children and old people drowned around me. I will never get over that night.'

'I think we have seen enough,' Erik told Gorgias; his voice was breaking, his hands shaking.

'Where are you staying?' Gorgias asked him.

'Poria, on the coast near Markopoulo Mesogaias,' replied Erik.

'Then I can drop you off on my way to airport. But, please, I have one more thing to show you at Kokkino Limanaki.'

No one spoke as they travelled back down the coast. Even Gorgias for once was subdued.

'Twenty-six men, women and children fled burning Mati in convoy of cars. Finding main route gridlocked, they turned down here,' he told them, detouring down a metalled trail still lined with wrecked burnt out cars. 'Unable to drive further they search on foot to find path down to sea.' Gorgias pulled over and stopped, they all got out of the car. Silently he led them to a small glade of charred trees only fifteen metres from the edge of a high cliff. 'Exactly here, trapped between fire and fall, this party of families and close friends huddled together in threes and fours to protect selves and children against heat. Here they were found entwined in death.'

Celia looked to Erik for elucidation on how such a thing could have happened. Tears welled in his eyes—the same tears began to roll down his cheeks. She was astonished. Touched and embarrassed, she turned to Gorgias.

'It really is time to go,' she told him. 'By the way has anything further been heard about the two missing nine year old twin girls?'

Gorgias pointed to the scorched earth. 'Found huddled in a four with grandparents.'

'Oh no,' said Celia.

'Hopefully they died of smoke before fire reached them.'

Click! Whorl! Erik took a few iPhone stills and a video recording. Celia was relieved, service as usual. He had not forgotten he was a journalist after all.

Gorgias whistled as he turned off Vravronos Avenue and drew into a parking space in their luxury hotel. 'This must be costing your people a packet. They must have been keen for you to come over here to cover wildfires.'

'We are becoming our paper's Greek correspondents,' Erik responded dryly.

'And the bombing on Paxos, is that still of interest?'

'Oh yes. Celia has already done an impact story on the parents of the dead female crew member. And I did a small piece on the deckhand who missed the sailing. There are so many anomalies. I am still trying to follow things up.'

'Difficult to fathom, yes?'

'Exactly.'

'Greek government still maintaining it could have been accident.'

'Are they really?' asked Celia.

'They have tourist industry to consider. And what with bombing and now wildfires, it is not looking good for Greece.'

'No, not good at all,' agreed Erik.

'However, I have a piece of information for you off record.'

'As you well know, as a fellow journalist, nothing is ever off the record,' Erik told Gorgias as he had Captain Vasilakis.

Gorgias only laughed. 'After seeing what we've seen today, I don't really care.'

'I'm with you there,' agreed Celia.

'So are you ready for private information which is no longer private?' asked Gorgias. They both nodded. 'One of marine engineers, a Corfu man who examined remnants of the *Bettina*, told me he could find nothing wrong with fuel lines. They were in perfect condition despite bomb.'

Erik's eyes lit up for the first time that day. 'That really is interesting.'

'I'll send you some photos if you send me video recording you took at Kokkino Limanaki. As you English say, publish and be damned. Till next time.' Gorgias smiled his gold teeth adieu.

'What will he do with the video recording?' A perplexed Celia asked Erik as they walked into the hotel.

'Sell it of course. I suspect Gorgias is the type of bloke who has his finger in every media pie.'

'Is he to be completely trusted though?'

Erik shrugged cynically. 'Is anyone?'

The receptionist handed them their respective card keys.

'Only fancy a sandwich from the pool bar tonight,' Erik told Celia as they reached their bedrooms. 'Couldn't face a full meal, not after what we've seen today.'

'How about a peaceful evening stroll first, to the Sanctuary of Artemis at nearby Brauron?' she suggested.

'The what?'

'It's famous, one of the earliest and most revered sanctuaries of Attica. An important settlement was established at the inner end of the bay of Brauron during the Neolithic period. It flourished particularly from Middle Helladic to early Mycenaean times. The temple itself is in the Doric style and dates from the 6th century BC.'

'I see you have done your homework again.'

'Let me have a quick wash, change my shoes and we'll get going.'

Meeting up in the corridor, a minute or two later, Celia handed him the temple guide for safekeeping.

'Tells us all we want to know,' she assured him.

'Lead on Lucy Worsley.'

The mile walk took them along a rugged coastline and then on a track through scrubland. Of course when they reached the museum and temple site, they were closed. But they were journalists and had had a hell of a day. They started circumnavigating the perimeter fence.

'We should be alright. Greece is so financially challenged at the moment they cannot afford to guard every archaeological site,' reasoned Erik.

'I hope you are right. I don't fancy spending the night in a prison cell.'

'Here,' pointed out Erik. 'The wire is lifted and broken. I'll hold it up higher and you crawl through.'

'Not a very elegant entrance to the Sanctuary of Artemis, crawling through on all fours,' groaned Celia.

'Oh, I don't know,' came the retort from above as Erik appraised her backside. 'Now you do the same for me.'

They sat on a warm ancient stone beneath a tree. The sun was still powerful. They gazed upwards, following columns of antiquity scratching the blue sky as they always had done.

Celia reached into Erik's deep jacket pocket for her guide and began to read. 'The Brauronian Artemis was worshipped as the goddess of vegetation and hunting, but also as the protector of women in child-birth and of infants. As priestess of Artemis, Iphigeneia dies and is buried in Brauron where she too is honoured as a goddess of child-birth. The sanctuary of Artemis was rural in character and was renowned for its festival, held every four years, when a procession was made from the Brauronion of Athens to the sanctuary at Brauron.'

'Quite a walk,' said Erik.

'What, our walk just now?'

'No, the walk from Athens, silly.'

'But what an amazing place.'

'It is so calming here. I'm in need of a bit of sanctuary after the day we've had,' he told her. Celia noticed his hands were shaking again.

'Did Mati bring back memories of Aleppo?' she asked.

'Suffering is the same the world over, whatever the cause, but it's the children who hit you worst of all. Adras' nephew blown to bits on Paxos, the two twin girls burnt to death at Kokkino Limanaki, what did they ever do to deserve such fates? There was one little Syrian girl in Aleppo, there is always one, and I can't get the image of her out of my mind. She was perfect but dead, a mass of dark curls round a sleeping pallor, a thermobaric bomb had sucked the young life out of her.'

Celia was alarmed to see Erik was crying again as he had done earlier over the death of the two Greek twins. This time they were alone and she gently ran her hand across his tears. She felt an overwhelming softening towards him. He pulled her towards him like a child seeking comfort, his head resting on her chest in the embrace. They stayed locked together for a minute or two, and then he kissed her like a man not a child.

'Not here,' she told him.

'Why not here?'

'Someone might come.'

'But we could pay homage to Iphigeneia, the goddess of childbirth.'

'You are joking.' Celia pulled back.

Although a man who believed in seizing the moment, Erik could see that if not the risk of physical interruption the temple was surrounded by hills and they could be being observed.

'Where then?'

'Back at the hotel of course.'

An hour later the world stopped in Celia's room, at least it went away for a while.

'Strange to fall in love with the most unexpected person in the most inauspicious circumstances,' she told Erik, as they sat up in bed chewing on ordered sandwiches.

'Is that what this is, "love"?' he asked slightly bewildered.

'What do you think it is?'

'Love,' he conceded.

* * * * *

'I have never felt so relaxed,' he told her the next morning.

'I can tell from the way you're swimming. You've managed almost a length of front crawl.'

'Yes, I feel I've really achieved something. Meaning in the pool of course,' he laughed.

'I'll be taking you for a wild water swim soon.'

'A what?'

'Wild water open swimming. I know a beautiful spot to swim in above Coniston Water, then there is Coniston Water itself. You can swim across to Peel Island and back.'

'Peel Island? Wasn't that the basis for Wild Cat Island in Ransome's *Swallows and Amazons*?' he asked. Celia nodded. 'One day I would love to swim that. And thank you,' he told her.

'For the lesson?'

'No, for being uncomplicated you.'

'Have you thought over what Gorgias said about the *Bettina's* fuel lines being in perfect condition?' she asked, as they climbed up the pool steps to dry off.

'I didn't for one moment expect anything else.'

'Nor did I,' she agreed.

CHAPTER FIFTEEN

They soon found themselves back in the sweltering environment of the London office. Erik got a surprising email from Michalis Kyrillos of the Independent Greeks Party. He said he had just read the *London Evening Record*'s emotionally charged article on the wildfires near Rafina and the terrible human loss. He gave Erik and his co-writer the thumbs up. Unknowingly he gave Gorgias' photograph of the bandaged woman amid the dead cars a double thumbs up too. The text went on to say, in appreciation of your empathy with the Greek people, I have some further information regarding the Paxos bombing. I believe you gave Captain Vasilakis a lighter found near the scene of the bombing. Our forensic science department, here in Athens, has concluded that the lighter, though Russian, was among a batch widely exported across Eastern Europe.

So Boris had been right about that too, acknowledged Erik quietly to himself.

This is additional confirmation that Russia cannot be held accountable for the bombing, concluded Kyrillos' email.

Erik went over to Celia's desk were she was beavering away at some society scandal. He wanted to kiss her hair. She looked up askance before morphing into appropriate office civility. He handed her his phone and the email instead.

'Distributed widely across Eastern Europe, do you buy into this?' she asked him. 'It seems a strong assumption to make about Russia's lack of involvement on such flimsy evidence.'

'I'm really not sure. The Independent Greeks Party does not like Syriza caving in over North Macedonia. Neither do the Russians. Michalis Kyrillos might be furthering his own agenda. Then again it is an interesting piece of information.'

'We are being used as pawns here in a propaganda game.'

'Maybe,' agreed Erik thoughtfully. 'Then maybe not.'

He fell very quiet for the next few days. It was his turn to be glued to his computer screen. Kyrillos' text seemed to have been a light bulb moment.

'Are you holding something back from me?' Celia eventually asked.

'Phew!' Erik blew. 'I can't conceal anything from you.'

'Conceal what?'

'I'm a little further down the road on my research regarding Jacob Simmons.'

'Really?' Celia's pupils dilated. 'Do you know where he is?'

'No, but I know who he is and where he came from.'

'I'm all ears.'

'Jacob's real name is Yakiv Balanchuk—Yakiv is Jacob in Ukrainian.'

'"Ukrainian"? That's a surprise. He hadn't a trace of an accent.'

'Do you remember he told us that his parents lived in Bayswater, London? I checked the county court records. I had an inkling that as immigrants they might have changed their names by deed poll. And, yes, I found that a Yegor Balanchuk had changed his entire family's surname to Simmons. Next I checked the 2011 census for that area. I found that both Jacob's mother, Yulia, and father, Yegor, originated from the Kharkiv region. They had four children including Jacob and an Alexandra. To make absolutely sure I then checked the electoral register for the same address. Husband and wife were still documented but now as George and Julia but there was no Yakiv or Jacob. Alexandra and the two younger brothers were still registered with the same Christian names.

'You have been busy. Have you mentioned your meticulous research to Mackintosh Man?'

Erik shook his head. 'Like the alliteration by the way.'

'It's a gift.'

'Do you remember Simmons' landlady in Shrewsbury told us she had been introduced to his sister Alexandra?'

'And two foreign gentlemen,' added Celia still puzzled. 'Could they have been his two brothers? Could this be a Ukrainian family affair? A cell even? But why?'

'That we have to find out. The world seems to have forgotten but this conflict in eastern Ukraine is still going on,' muttered Erik.

Every time Celia visited his desk, Erik seemed be viewing graphic videos and photographs of fighting in the Donetsk region of Ukraine.

'Wasn't that Malaysian plane shot down near Donetsk?' she asked him.

'That's right, flight MH17 from Amsterdam to Kuala Lumpur was shot down in July 2014. A total of two hundred and eighty-three passengers, including eighty children, and fifteen crew members were killed.'

'And Russia denied involvement.'

'Of course. But they will have a little more difficulty denying this set of images showing three Ukrainian POW paratroopers being horribly abused by the Russian backed Donetsk People's Republic rebel forces in Shakhtarsk. The photographs are believed to have been taken by a Russian photojournalist, Andrei Stenin.'

'I don't know how you can bear to look at this stuff,' she told him. 'Stenin has caught the anguish in those young lads' eyes appealing for mercy. Injured, beaten in battle, tortured by bullies purporting to be soldiers.'

'Stenin paid the price for his art too. He went missing shortly afterwards and was found dead in a burnt out car in a field with two other men. There is gossip among journalists that it might have been a revenge killing by Ukrainian paratroopers with the 79th Airborne Brigade.'

'All this is like another world.'

'Unfortunately, it *is* part of our world. Our world isn't all society weddings. If you had been on the foreign desk as long as I have you would know that. Here the DPR are making one prisoner pull a comrade's body across the road and dig his grave. I don't give much for the chances of any of those poor bastards' survival.'

'It makes me feel sick,' Celia told him.

'I just try to understand the situation.'

'I can accept terrible death in accidental wildfires, but all this deliberate cruelty and carnage in Ukraine is beyond me.'

'Maybe I'm addicted to man's inhumanity.'

'I thought you had had enough after Aleppo.'

Stung by Erik's society wedding put down, Celia began a little Ukrainian research herself and came across the name Irina Dovgan. Irina was from eastern Ukraine and helped her country's army in Yasynuvata, until the town fell under the control of pro-Russian separatist rebels. For supplying

Ukrainian soldiers with clothing and food, the rebels accused her of being a spy, tortured and beat her with rifle butts. They then subjected her to public humiliation by tying her to a post in Donetsk city centre. Irina was draped in a Ukrainian flag and made to hold a sign reading *Ukrainian agent and baby-killer*. Passers-by would beat her and take photos of it. A Brazilian photographer, Mauricio Lima, happened to be walking past and took a telling photograph of Irina, her eyes tightly closed, as a blonde ponytailed woman kicked out at her.

Celia beckoned Erik over to see Lima's iconic photograph of Irina and her abuser.

'See, when society breaks down how quickly people revert into brutal hysterical chimpanzees,' he spat out in disgust. This was the real Erik. The Erik who so often used either flippancy or anger or both to hide his sensitivity. This was the Erik she loved.

Celia showed him another photograph, perhaps even more shocking, of a bearded young thug in a macho pose with his hand on the head of beaten Irina on her post.

'What happened to Irina? Did they kill her?' he asked.

'The wheel turns—the photograph was splashed over the world's most widely read newspapers. *The New York Times* started a campaign for her release.'

'Umm, one telling image and good journalism can change the course of history.'

'It changed Irina's, it saved her life. Two foreign journalists pleaded with the pro-Russian Vostok battalion leader, Aleksandr Khodakovsky, to release her. I believe she and her husband have moved to Kiev.'

'For once a happy ending.'

'Yes, a happy ending. We must keep going.' Celia briefly ran her fingers down Erik's arm.

'How do you mean?' he asked.

'We must find out who is responsible for the Paxos bombing.'

* * * * *

'Hi, I'm Erik Jordan and this is my assistant Celia Grey.' Erik did his best to ignore his 'assistant's' scowls.

'Yes, so?' An elderly man, whom they took to be George Simmons, looked them up and down suspiciously on his doorstep. The Simmonses, aka the Balanchuks, lived unbelievably in a street off Bayswater's Moscow Road.

'Mr George Simmons?' asked Erik. 'Can we have a word?'

'He's not here.'

'Who's not here?'

'My son, Jacob, people come looking for him.'

'What people?'

'Better come in than standing outside for world to see.' After a quick scrutiny up and down the street, George hustled Erik and Celia into the hallway. 'Police?' he asked.

'Press,' Celia explained.

If anything George looked relieved.

'Come in, come in, please,' a plump squat woman appeared and beckoned them into a back sitting room. At a guess George was in his early eighties, Julia looked to be half his age.

A second marriage, wondered Celia.

'My wife Julia.' George did the formalities.

'Tea? Please.' Julia was obviously eager to *please* whoever they were.

Celia was reminded of her visit to the Parkers, although their sitting room had been suburban English whereas this was definitely not. The colour scheme was teal and beige. One painting of a snow-clad mountain hung on the wall. Artificial flowers graced the top of a heavy mahogany dresser along with a photograph of the Simmons' children. Celia walked over to the photograph to observe it closer. One of the lads, still a teenager then, she recognised as Jacob.

'My eldest, my Jacob,' pointed out Julia proudly, before going on to indicate with her finger further members of her brood.

'Are any of them here now?' Celia glanced at the door as if Julia's children might materialise at any moment.

'All gone now,' said Julia.

'Grown, flown nest,' affirmed George.

'Do you know where Jacob is at the moment?' Erik asked them.

'Might we enquire who exactly wants to know?' responded George, guarded.

'We work for the *London Evening Record*. We had the pleasure of meeting Jacob in Corfu and, as we were writing an article on the bombing of the *Bettina*, he offered to liaise with us back in the UK.'

'Jacob, he know nothing of bombing.' George was clearly on the defensive now.

'We went to see him in Shrewsbury but his landlady told us he'd gone,' said Celia. 'Packed up and gone.'

Julia looked uncomfortable. George huffed and puffed.

'We know nothing. We cannot help,' he finally came up with.

'So nobody knows anything,' said Erik. 'Disappointing.'

'Sorry to disappoint,' said Julia, wringing her hands in frustration, seemingly on the point of tears. 'Jacob not bad boy, good boy.'

'I am sure he is,' empathised Celia.

'Yes, we just want to talk to him as arranged,' added Erik. *As paid for*, he thought less charitably.

Julia's face wrinkled with worry. Her hands shook holding the pot as she poured tea into glass holders. Celia remembered the recent images of horror she had seen in the Ukraine and wondered what this couple had fled from.

'Sugar?' asked Julia. Erik and Celia shook their heads. 'No sugar?' She stared at them in disbelief.

'I take mine black,' said Erik.

'"Black"?' Julia looked even more confused.

'Erik, Ukrainians don't have milk in their tea,' explained Celia, smiling with embarrassment across at their hosts.

'I get milk,' announced Julia.

'No, its OK,' Celia told her.

They watched in amazement as Julia spooned three heaped teaspoons of sugar into George's glass. Later, sipping at their own drinks, they knew why. The tea was incredibly strong. Nevertheless, the warm tea seemed to bring a warmer feeling between the four of them.

'So, who else has been looking for Jacob?' Erik asked George.

'Police, I think. No uniform but police.'

'I'm really sorry about this,' said Celia. 'You've come to this country to escape trouble and it has followed you here.'

'Oh, trouble. Trouble all life,' complained Julia.

'My father was young man, just married, during the Holodomor.' George took a deep glug at his sweet tea. 'Do you know Holodomor?' Celia and Erik shook their heads. 'Was systematic starvation of Ukrainian people by Stalin. Millions of Ukrainians died over eighteen months period between 1932-33, on the most fertile lands in Europe.' George sniffed at the absurdity. 'Third of all Ukrainian children perished.'

'Please, George.' Julia let out a small wail. 'Young people no want to know about this. Russians died too of famine in Volga and Caucasus.'

'My father saw Russian soldier force my grandfather, a proud Kulak, to snuffle in dirt for grain. "See he is pig," they laughed as old man tried to get to feet, pushing him down to ground again with boots,' continued George, undaunted by his wife's opposition. 'Old man died two weeks later of shame.'

'And your father?' asked Erik.

'Ah, my father, shot a month later for disobedience.'

'"Disobedience"?' asked Erik.

'Yes, he refused to go to collective. My mother left pregnant with me. Only women left.'

'Did you know the name of the man who murdered your father?' asked Celia.

'Oh yes, he was well known to us. He was commandant of area.'

'His name,' asked Erik, tapping on his phone's Notes icon.

Silence fell in the teal and beige room. Storm clouds gathered outside and the room fell poetically dark.

'Agavva Bychkov.' George gave a short restless cough—this was obviously not a name easily mentioned.

'How did Jacob feel about this?' asked Erik.

'Before his time,' shrugged George.

'But the conflict is still going on in Donbass region between Ukrainian nationalists and pro-Russian separatists.'

'Oh, I know, I know, thirteen thousand killed. Always trouble in Ukraine,' shrugged George again. 'If you like to know more about Holodomor, try Association of Ukrainians in Great Britain. Pen, paper, Julia,' he instructed his wife.

Julia scuttled over to a writing bureau, returning to George who proceeded to write them out an address in Holland Park Avenue.

'Thanks for this,' Erik told him, standing up and pocketing the note.

'And thank you for the tea.' Celia pointedly addressed Julia.

Erik was not finished yet. He had one parting shot to fire over Ukrainian bows. 'Though Jacob told us he was coming back to England, our immigration and passport service has no record of him entering the country.'

Despite Julia paling at the word 'immigration', the Simmonses did not look particularly staggered over the failure of their prodigal son to return. It was Celia who stared at Erik in amazement—this was news to her.

'Did you know Jacob had girl on boat?' asked Julia.

'A crew member?' Celia suppressed her astonishment. Then why should she be astonished, Jacob was an attractive enough stud.

'Believe so.'

'Anna Parker?'

'Never told much but could have been Anna.'

'Is that true about Jacob not entering the country?' Celia asked Erik, once they were back in the car.

'Yes, after our Shrewsbury trip I decided to do a little digging through our friends in high places.'

'Mackintosh Man?'

'The same. Thought I'd put him to some use.'

'Interesting, about the girlfriend.'

'Maybe it wasn't Anna Parker. Just suppose it was Anna Markova—now that would have made for happy sailing.'

CHAPTER SIXTEEN

'How's the Paxos story coming along?' asked Nelson; an aside with a hint of impatience.

'Getting murkier by the minute,' replied Erik, following an editorial meeting in the Chief's office. 'I've just received this over the wire from one of our contacts in Greece.'

'"Over the wire", a rather out-dated expression if I might say so,' said Nelson.

'I'm just an old fashioned boy.'

'Come on. Is it something from Gorgias?' encouraged Celia. Erik nodded. Nelson crossed his legs and waited.

'I quote,' said Erik. 'Following Russia's retaliatory move early this month, Greece intends to recall its ambassador. The Greek Foreign Ministry statement of 10 August 2018 says: "Since Russia began fighting as comrade in arms with Turkey, providing it with a number of facilitations in the security sector, it appears to be steadily distancing itself from positions befitting the level of friendship and cooperation that has characterized Greek-Russian relations for the past hundred and ninety years. It appears not to understand that Greece has its own interests and criteria in international politics." The statement goes on to accuse Russia of "attempts to a) bribe state officials, b) undermine its foreign policy, and c) interfere in its internal affairs".'

'Good lord,' said Nelson. 'Do you think this will affect the way the Greeks investigate the Paxos bombing?'

'Possibly. I am not sure how Michalis Kyrillos will take it though,' Erik told him.

'Who on earth is Michalis Kyrillos?'

'He is a member of the Independent Greeks Party, a conservative nationalist party who are in coalition with Syriza.'

'That must be a marriage made in hell.'

'Very much so,' agreed Erik. 'But strangely enough the Independent Greeks are at one with the Russians against North Macedonia being known as such.'

'They are frightened that North Macedonia will appropriate Alexander the Great as one of their own, can you believe,' filled in Celia.

'War can start over such small things,' exhaled Nelson. There was a knock on his door.

'Sorry to bother you, sir, but this is marked URGENT for Ms Grey and Mr Jordan.' The young secretary hovered in the doorway holding a nondescript, heavily wrapped parcel.

'Put it down there,' said Nelson, indicating his desk. 'Strange to be addressed to you both.' He began examining the brown paper parcel suspiciously, moving it this way and that with a pencil. 'Greek stamps and a Greek postmark. Were you expecting anything from Greece?' Erik and Celia shook their heads. 'It says it is only to be opened by the two of you. Bulky, too much wrapping, no return address. I don't like the look of this. I have experienced something similar once before.' His bonhomie expression suddenly evaporated. 'Get out! Just go!' he yelled. He had pressed the emergency button under his table before Erik and Celia had time to react and quit the room. Following quickly behind them, they could just hear Nelson's mobile ringing above the alarm. 'Suspicious parcel at the *London Evening Record*,' he told the 999 operator. 'Evacuate the building,' he screamed to all the other journalists on the floor. 'Now!'

Police sirens approached as the newsroom emptied. The newspaper offices, being in a central London location, were soon cordoned off. And it was not long before all the workers—journalists, secretaries, advertisers, printers, standing outside on the pavement—experienced the excitement of seeing the British Army's bomb disposal team moving in with their equipment.

'Well spotted, sir. You've saved life and limbs today,' a senior army officer told Nelson an hour later. 'It was a particularly vicious device with a tricky detonator. The intended victims of this weren't meant to walk away alive.'

Erik and Celia were stood next to Nelson as the officer delivered his message. Celia felt as if her legs were giving way under her. Erik put an arm round her to steady her, an arm that was shaking too.

* * * * *

'Enough is enough.' Nelson told them the next morning as he oversaw the replacement of his ruined desk. 'Let the Paxos story go. It's becoming too dangerous.'

'We can't,' said Erik. 'This shit makes us even more determined.'

'"Us"?' repeated Nelson, flashing a query at Celia.

'"Us",' ratified Celia.

'Even your minder is getting cold feet,' Nelson told them.

'What, in this weather?' joked Erik. 'He should wear warmer socks.'

'Look, when Thames House or Vauxhall Cross—or wherever he's from—has cause for concern, so should you.'

'I have. However I have an appointment in Notting Hill Gate with the Association of Ukrainians in Great Britain. See if I can learn more about what is involved here.'

'I thought George Simmons had given you an address for them in Holland Park Avenue,' said Celia.

'Nothing in life is straightforward, my love. George got it wrong. The AUGB main headquarters and archives are in Notting Hill Gate.'

'And you?' Nelson asked Celia. 'What are you doing with your day?'

She nodded across to her desk. 'Within safe sight for the moment.'

The AUGB central office building appeared to be Georgian, clad in London stone, with an immaculate pillared portico. A smiling lady—whom Erik took to be an archivist—met him at the door to escort him through the complexities of Ukrainian history.

'Holodomor is based on two Ukrainian words: *holod* meaning hunger, starvation, famine, and *moryty* meaning to induce suffering, to kill,' she explained patiently.

'Do you mind if I record this information?' interrupted Erik.

'Of course I don't mind. The terrible extent of the Holodomor has been denied for so long. The number of those who died during those eighteen months between 1932 and 1933 is almost unimaginable, but it's equivalent to the number of students in the UK, or Wembley stadium filled almost eighty times over. The famine was the largest and most secret of Stalin's purges. It was covered up and denied at the time and for many decades afterwards. Only since the fall of the Soviet Union have documents become available which tell the full story of this most tragic page in 20th century history. Survivors of the famine are now able to talk openly about the Holodomor. Many of those survivors have had to live with the trauma of seeing their mothers, fathers, sisters and brothers die a cruel and needless death from starvation, for some the memories are still too painful to recall.'

'I met one such man only the other day,' Erik told her.

'Everything possible was done by Stalin to cover up the true horror of the famine in Ukraine. There are many eyewitness accounts from journalists and others which describe, often in harrowing terms, the widespread misery of starvation and death in a land of plenty.'

'The denial itself must have caused terrific resentment.'

'The denial of truth always does,' she agreed, opening out a book on her desk. 'Relatively few photographs of the period are available, but there is a body of authenticated photographs taken by an Austrian, Alexander Wienerberger, who stayed in Kharkiv during the summer of 1933 …'

'"Kharkiv",' repeated Erik.

'Yes. And again we have photographic evidence from Dr Fritz Dittloff, former Director of the German Government's Agricultural Concession, Drusag, in the North Caucasus, which the Soviet government shut down in 1933.'

'Well, they would wouldn't they.'

'Most of these photographs, many of which are reproduced here, were originally published in books in 1935 and 1936 by Dr Ewald Ammende, a Baltic German politician, who among other things was Secretary-General of the European Nationalities Congress.'

'May I?' Erik slowly began to examine the photographs.

'In the last few years, international bodies, faith leaders and countries around the world have begun to acknowledge the full horror of the Holodomor. Ukraine passed legislation in 2006, declaring the Holodomor an act of genocide against the Ukrainian people. President Yushchenko made international recognition of the Holodomor a personal campaign, and called on Ukrainians all over the world to work towards raising awareness of the Holodomor, particularly in 2008 which was the 75th anniversary of the Holodomor.'

Erik was hardly listening as he stared down on black and white depictions of horror. If anything these images were worse than recent pictures of the conflict in eastern Ukraine, certainly in scale. 1932—33 Ukraine was a world inhabited by Auschwitz ghosts to come. Helpless dying horses littered fields, emaciated corpses lined the streets of Kharkiv. One haunting photograph was of a poor one-legged man lying naked in a corn field. His rib cage merely that—a fleshless uncovered cage—his wizened penis hanging limp and useless from a cave of groin.

'The call to action has been taken up in every country where Ukrainians and those of Ukrainian descent live, through commemorative events and awareness-raising initiatives …' The archivist stopped, seeing the impact of the terrible images written across Erik's face. She squeezed his arm before pressing on. 'The Ukrainian community in Great Britain is also playing its part to raise awareness. During 2008, the community across the country participated in the International Torch of Remembrance rally and a major national commemoration was held in Westminster Central Hall and the Abbey. Our ultimate aim is to persuade the UK government to follow the lead of countries like Australia, Canada and the USA in acknowledging the Holodomor as genocide.'

'Have we not?' asked Erik surprised.

'No, the British government recoiled over the word *genocide*. This is not about politics, reparations or blame, but about basic human morality and respect for life. We urge everyone to join the campaign for recognition to honour the memory of the millions who died so needlessly and to prevent such atrocities from ever happening again.'

'But surely collective memories of the events of 1932—33 must be fuelling the cruelties and hatreds going on in Donetsk and Luhansk today.'

'Alas ...' The archivist looked to the floor. 'I fear it is more the repression of our history that fuels the fire.'

'I will do my best to help publish your message. I cannot promise good news on every front though,' warned Erik.

'Is there ever good news on every front?' laughed his host.

'Tell me, if I wish to trace a Russian's family tree, how would I go about it?'

'I am hardly the best one to advise on that. However you will find there are a few East European and Russian genealogy sites that have sprung up recently.

'Thank you so much for your time, forbearance and help.' Erik reached down and kissed the lovely lady's hand.

* * * * *

'You're not suggesting there is a connection between the Holodomor and the Paxos bombing.' Celia turned off her computer to regard Erik with incredulity.

'What do you know about the Holodomor?'

'I have been doing my own research with you out of the way.'

'So tell me about it.'

'The Holodomor, as Julia intimated, was a famine that affected the Northern Caucasus, Volga Region, Kazakhstan, the South Urals and even West Siberia as well as the Simmons' homeland.'

'Although, regrettably, Stalin seemed to favour diverting Ukrainian grain to feed greater Russia rather than those poor peasants working Ukrainian fields.' The photographs of Ukrainian starvation were fresh in his mind. The photograph of a muffled peasant woman, a younger and older boy standing at either side of her, and on a stool in front of them the severed head of another child for sale—this image would be burnt into his brain forever.

'Did you know that Mikhail Gorbachev himself lost an aunt and two paternal uncles in the village of Privolnoye, Southern Russian, during the years of 1932—33?' she asked.

'No, I didn't.'

'That surprises me, I thought you knew everything.'

'I do know that two and a half thousand people were convicted of cannibalism during this period.' Finally came his angry response. 'And undoubtedly many more were reduced to the same. God damn, they were selling human body parts in the markets.'

'Things got that bad?'

'That bad,' he confirmed. 'So give me the reasons for the Holodomor.'

'Stalin was terrified of Ukrainian nationalism. A shortage of grain—due to drought, disease and a policy of forced collectivisation—helped put the nationalists down without the cost of war.'

'Now we are getting closer to the truth,' snapped Erik.

'An additional cause for the famine was blamed on the decrease in the agricultural workforce and an increase in industrialisation.'

'That's rubbish! They shipped all the land owning Kulaks off to concentration camps.'

'Sounds familiar. But industrialisation could still have played a part.'

'Yes, but mill and factory mechanisation happened in eighteenth and nineteenth century England without such dire consequences to our rural peasantry,' tested Erik.

'I don't know. People were very poor in the cities.'

'Nothing like I've seen happened in Kharkiv,' objected Erik.

'Well, our rural folk weren't seeking independence and Uncle Joe wasn't their PM.' Celia attempted to lighten the topic.

'I learnt something else really interesting at Notting Hill Gate this morning. Like you our government refuses to accept the starvation of millions of Ukrainians as genocide.'

'That's unfair. I admit it does sound like the denial of the Irish Potato Famine all over again.'

'We are in agreement then?'

'Totally.'

'Don't forget all those terrible Indian famines under British rule either. I expect our politicians are afraid of the pointing finger.' Erik, always one to be outraged by injustice, flushed and turned away.

* * * * *

Same setting, another time, another day.

'I found myself in Kensington Gardens yesterday morning,' announced Erik, standing before a plate glass window of grey London clouds.

'Really.' Celia remained fixed on her keyboard. 'You didn't think to ask me to come with you.'

'I got the impression you weren't too keen on our mackintosh friend.'

'What did you tell him?'

'That Jacob Simmons' real name was Yakiv Balanchuk.'

'Was Williams surprised?'

'No, he knew already.'

'Does he know where Jacob is at present?'

'He has no idea. However I showed him the photographs of Boris and Trofim and he recognised them as Russian agents straight away. He was a lot more circumspect about the older guy with the cigar at Erimitis.'

'That's interesting. Why?'

'Not sure. Maybe he just didn't know who he was, then again maybe he did. You never know with these people.'

'Would you like to come round tonight and I'll cook us a Thai red curry with pickled cucumber?'

'I'll bring some wine.'

'Red or white?' she frowned.

'Both,' he laughed.

'I think you will be staying the night then.'

'Can I?'

'This curry is delicious. I love the taste of coconut.' Erik was telling her ten hours later in the fading light of her expensive though minimalist Maida Vale flat. Though Maida Vale prices were sky high this was not the centre of her world, he could see that. The flat was obviously somewhere to eat and sleep occasionally, possibly purchased for her by rich parents. 'Celia, I have something rather important to tell you. I didn't want to bring it up in the office.' He took an extra mouthful of white wine for courage.

'Yes?' She was all ears.

'Our recruitment into British Intelligence hasn't turned out to be a one way exchange of information after all.'

'Oh?'

'No, Williams told me that the female crew member killed on the *Bettina* wasn't Anna Parker.'

Celia's mouth fell open.

'What?' she asked in disbelief.

'No. A DNA comparison, taken in this country, confirmed the dead girl wasn't Anna Parker.'

'Who was she then?'

'Vauxhall Cross presumes, yet to be proved, that Anna must have swopped places at the last moment with this unknown person. No doubt under the pretext of having to stay to look after the sick Jacob.'

'Do the Parkers know?' asked Celia.

'Yes, they have been informed.'

'What about my feature article on Anna?'

'We will have to publish a retraction. There is no blame attached to you, you weren't to know.'

'Have you told Nelson?'

'I didn't have to, he already knew.'

'So he has British Intelligence Service accreditation too?' Erik nodded.

'Why aren't I surprised?' scoffed Celia.

'I am just the messenger.' He attempted a reassuring smile. This whole business was beginning to get on his nerves, spoiling his evening. He just wished it would all go away.

'I will go round to the Parkers tomorrow,' Celia told him.

'Is that wise?'

'Under the guise of returning the Bock thimble to them.'

'Oh, God, I'd forgotten that. Where is it?'

'It is in my safekeeping. I have a strongbox in the wall of the guest bedroom behind a photograph of Anna Politkovskaya.'

'Ah, Anna Politkovskaya, the assassinated Russian journalist.'

'Well, although Anna was a Russian national, her parents were Ukrainian.'

'Very appropriate.'

'Yes, and you'll be sleeping with her tonight.'

CHAPTER SEVENTEEN

Erik returned to the office the next morning feeling he had been unfairly treated. They had not slept together once since Markopoulo Mesogaias. He found his own double bed in St John's Wood a spacious and lonely place these days. He was not having much luck with the Russian genealogy sites either. They were sporadic and less than comprehensive.

Meanwhile Celia made her way back to the Parkers' home in North London. She could not justify, even to herself, her behaviour towards Erik. She felt angry about everything.

In contrast it was a beaming Mrs Parker who opened the door. Celia was completely thrown.

'Come in, come in, dear. It's lovely to see you again.'

'I wanted to return this.' Celia held out the thimble in the palm of her hand.

'Terence isn't in at the moment,' explained Mrs Parker, examining the thimble closely. 'She's alive you know. Our Anna is alive. I have felt it all along.'

'Yes, I have heard and I feel terrible for doubting your instincts.'

'But she is still missing, dear, and this is the only recent gift or word we've had from her.' Mrs Parker held up the thimble again. 'This is the only proof of life left to us. Tea, dear?'

Celia nodded. The same bisque porcelain figurines were in place but somehow they looked brighter in the knowledge that Anna might be coming home after all.

'The *London Evening Record* will amend my article, THE GIRL WHO LOVED THE SEA, with an up-to-date explanation that your daughter wasn't on the *Bettina*.'

'It was a lovely article though, dear,' objected Mrs Parker. 'You captured our Anna perfectly.'

'But it wasn't entirely true.'

'I have dug out the most recent photograph I could find of Anna. Couldn't bear to look at it until now. Would it be of any use, dear?'

After tea and biscuits and hugs on the doorstep, Celia looked up and down the suburban street expecting to see Peaky Blinder still camped out. No doubt most people were at work and the street was empty. The reporter from the *Enfield Post* had abandoned his post. Pity, because the fact that Enfield girl Anna Parker's remains had not been found on the boat, and yet she was still missing, only added greater mystery to the story.

'How did it go?' asked Erik coolly, as Celia settled back in her office chair.

'Mrs Parker was charming and grateful for the return of her Russian thimble. She is just relieved that there is a possibility of Anna being alive.'

'I hope you didn't build up her expectations.'

'Of course not. How could I when I know nothing. Do you think she still could be alive? And have they any idea who the dead girl on the boat was?'

'By "they", I presume you mean Vauxhall Cross.'

'Well, I don't mean the police. They won't tell us anything.'

'You are firing all these questions at me when I know as much or as little as you do. If you want answers then you must visit Kensington Gardens next Sunday morning,' he told her somewhat dismissively.

'Are you sulking because of last night?'

'Not at all. I got a good night's sleep beneath Anna Politkovskaya.'

'You were honoured. She was a beautiful and intelligent journalist.'

'I knew you were upset about the Anna Parker article.'

'If only I had half of Politkovskaya's bravery and determination to get to the truth,' sighed Celia.

'Oh, you have. I think you have.'

* * * * *

Sunday morning came in muggy and warm although the leaves had begun to wither and brown towards autumn on the trees. She decided to walk to Kensington Gardens from her flat. But as soon as she stepped outside her door, she got the feeling that she was being followed again. Erik would say she was being stupid, especially when she was going to meet the man who, in all likelihood, would be the one detailed to follow her.

All the same she decided to take the precaution of diving into her small local cafe, where she often stopped for a breakfast bagel and coffee. As she flew past the counter she gave a quick wave of acknowledgement to an amazed Chaviv, the owner.

'Nothing today', she shouted to him, as she made for the rear exit and the yard. Paranoia vanished once in the comfort of a backstreet where any potential assassins would be visible. All the same she kept a hand in her pocket round her Mace pepper spray.

Just as arranged, Williams was reading *The Sunday Times* on a park bench between two lifebuoys. He was totally isolated as the mist that had been hanging over Round Pond moved towards him.

'Your newspaper is out of date,' she told him.

'What?' His head jerked up in surprise. 'Miss Grey, fancy seeing you here. Do please join me. By the way,' he whispered, shuffling along the bench, 'I wouldn't be so naive as to be holding up anything other than this morning's newspaper.'

'I'm sure you wouldn't,' she responded acerbically.

'Anyway it is very interesting.'

'Expect it is.'

'You don't like me very much, do you Miss Grey?'

'Celia please. I don't like what you stand for.'

'And what is that, Celia?'

'The Establishment undoubtedly.'

'Unlike your father, Sir Peter Grey.'

'My father was a well-respected journalist on *The Guardian* for years. A newspaper that upholds liberal values.'

'True, but now he is on the board of the Guardian Media Group.'

'That makes him part of the Establishment, does it?'

'No, but helping me makes you part of a firm that works to protect and support British interests.'

'Like Anna Parker?'

'Yes, like Anna,' sighed Williams.

'And what about Jacob Simmons? His family were from the Ukraine.'

'He still is a British citizen missing abroad.'

'And you have no idea where he is?'

'No idea.'

'His parents seemed a decent couple.'

'I take it you have interviewed the Balanchuks then.'

Celia nodded. She was intrigued that Williams did not use the Balanchuks adopted English surname.

'Don't pretend. You know every move we make,' she told him.

'I think you overestimate the resources at our disposal, Miss Grey.'

Ignoring his return to a more formal method of address, she asked, 'Tell me, I am curious to know how much involvement did MI6 have in the murder of Putin's friend, Dmitry Smirnov?'

'Why? Why would MI6 wish to kill a man who was bringing money into this country?'

'The Salisbury poisonings,' suggested Celia, off the cuff.

'Oh, you mean a revenge killing. This might be something of a surprise to you but we don't go in for that sort of thing in this country.'

'There was a man sitting at a Paxos bar, wearing an Eton tie, just before the *Bettina* was blown up.'

'Ah Eton, that could have just as likely been your colleague, Mr Jordan.'

'The man was middle-aged. Indeed you yourself fit the description.'

'Nice try, Miss Grey, but like holding up an out of date newspaper none of our agents would be foolish enough to sport an Eton tie. Certainly not the man you see before you. And operations in foreign lands do not fall under my remit at present.'

Celia fell silent. Williams was a proficient counter puncher.

'What is the real reason for you seeking me out?' he asked her.

'Have you any idea where Anna Parker might be? Or who replaced her on the boat?'

'To the first question the answer is "no". To the second …' Williams hesitated. 'The answer as to who was Anna's replacement on the *Bettina* is a little more complicated.'

'Why?'

'Athens sent us the young woman's remains eventually. She was in bits actually. We had one of the most eminent Home Office registered pathologists examine them.' Williams gave her the long hard stare as if weighing up whether or not to reveal any more information.

'And?' demanded Celia. The suspense was killing.

'The DNA analysis of various body parts came back as predominantly Irish.'

'Irish! How predominantly?'

'Ninety-seven per cent. They also discovered that she had a mutation in the pigment gene MC1R like many Neanderthals.'

Celia stared at him at a loss. '"Neanderthals"?'

Williams looked pre-eminent. 'We are looking to identify a missing Irish girl with fair skin and reddish hair.'

'Could she be considered a strawberry blonde then?' asked Celia.

Williams nodded. 'She could. Why, have you come across somebody like that?'

Celia shook her head. 'Did Crew For You have anyone like that on their books?'

'No, the London police have already checked.'

'I wonder how Anna Parker feels about Deirdre Doe taking her place on that ill-fated boat.'

'We'll only know that when we find her.'

'The Greeks will not accept that the Russians are behind the bombing.'

'As I am sure you are aware, Greek and Russian relations are delicate at the moment.'

'So what do you think?'

'From the photographs that Erik showed me of the Russian officers on Paxos, from their status alone, the Kremlin is taking the bombing very seriously. It must be, to say the least, extremely embarrassing for the Greeks to have a friend of Putin murdered on their soil.'

'Do you know the journalist Gorgias Baros?' asked Celia, riding in on a wave of perception. Williams nodded. 'And Nicos Maragos?' The nod again. 'I thought so.'

'Tell me, Miss Grey, who do you and Mr Jordan think could be responsible for the bombing?'

'We really have no idea yet.'

'You know our American friends are now taking an interest because of Anna Markova's dual nationality.'

'So I've heard.'

'However, the real reason might be that the CIA would love to lay the blame for the bombing at Russia's door.'

* * * * *

Celia was sweating over a wok of stir-fry that evening when the landline began ringing. This was unusual, rare, she hardly used her home phone.

'Yes,' she answered a little annoyed. It was Sunday night for God's sake.

'Miss Grey?'

'Yes.'

'We know where you live, Miss Grey. We know who you are working for. We advise you to lay off so called investigative journalism into Paxos bombing.' Spoken with a foreign accent. There was a strange, muffled tinny echo to the voice.

'And who might "we" be?' She struggled to control the shake in her own voice.

'It doesn't matter who we are. It matters that you heed warning for your own wellbeing.'

'My wellbeing?' Celia was incredulous.

'Yes, until now you have enjoyed excellent state of health.' With that implicit threat the caller rang off.

She checked 1471. The caller had been on Withheld of course. Looking cautiously round her curtains down onto the street below, she rang Erik from her mobile.

'Shall I come round?' He immediately offered.

'No, I think I'll be all right.' She had to see this through herself. She did not want to be reliant on Erik. She did not want to be reliant on anyone.

'I'll get in touch with Williams in the morning. There could be a leak in MI5 or MI6.'

'I did tell you I felt as if someone was watching me, following me. Maybe you will believe me now.'

'I neither believe nor disbelieve you,' said Erik. 'I just didn't see the point of upsetting you more without proof.'

'You don't know what it's like to feel you are being stalked.'

'Don't I?'

'Not you too?'

'Maybe,' replied Erik cautiously.

204

Although she had told Erik she thought she would be OK on her own during the night, he could tell from her white face the next morning that she had not been. She looked as if she had hardly slept a wink.

CHAPTER EIGHTEEN

Another Sunday—a week later—with some trust restored between them in their rocky relationship, Celia invited Erik for a swim in the Serpentine Lido.

'A taste of open water swimming in London,' she told him. 'It's open until mid-September. It'll be one of our last chances to test the waters. See you outside at ten a.m.'

She took the underground via the Bakerloo line to Piccadilly Circus and then the Piccadilly line to Knightsbridge, both of which were thankfully quiet. Erik was already waiting for her outside the Lido, trunks and towel in hand. As he paid the £4.80 entry fee for both of them, he wondered what he was letting himself in for. It was overcast but not raining.

'They have a swimming club that meets at eight a.m. every Saturday morning throughout the year. I was thinking of joining,' she enthused.

'Really?' he responded with distinct apathy.

The communal changing room had old fashioned box cubicles. By the time they emerged there were only a few lockers available in which to put their clothes. They decided to share a locker and Erik tied the key inside his trunks. Gone were the tartan swim shorts, in were the Speedos.

Despite a NO DIVING notice, before she could stop him, Erik, in his agitation, had jumped in off the jetty instead of a slower acclimatisation down the steps. The cold water hit him like a wall. He gulped for air. Thankfully she was immediately in the water next to him, reassuring him to breathe slower and easily.

'I've never felt so cold,' he shivered.

'Just float, keeping your head above water, until the thermoreceptors in your skin adjust.'

'The what …? I won't get used to this in a million years.'

'Yes, you will. Now let's swim a few strokes.'

They set off doing breaststroke along the line of white pillow floats marking out the Lido from the rest of the lake. At first Erik swam faster than he had ever done before to keep warm.

'How am I doing?' he spluttered, settling to a more even pace.

'Just great. Fancy trying a few strokes of freestyle?'

'I can't see the bottom,' he complained, lifting out of his front crawl stroke. 'It's like swimming through cabbage soup.'

'Well, this isn't the Ionian sea.'

Suddenly, to his amazement, he began to feel hot. 'I have this burning sensation all over my body.'

'Good, we'll do a few more breaststroke laps and then get out.'

'But I'm not ready to quit yet. I'm beginning to really enjoy this.'

'No, this is your first immersion. One or two times up and down the floats and that's it.'

'Celia,' he protested.

'I don't want you getting hypothermia on your first visit. It will put you off for life.'

True enough, by the time Erik climbed up onto the pontoon he was shivering and his speech was slightly slurred.

'I feel tipsy now,' he said; grinning like a drunk, grinning at this achievement.

'Never mind, your core temperature will soon pick up again.'

They were greeted by slow hand clapping as they attempted to wash off under the outdoor shower trickle.

'Bravo,' a grey-haired woman shouted across to them.

'Are you a swimmer?' Celia politely asked the woman on passing. Erik had rushed ahead, too cold to stop.

'No, not me,' replied the cut-glass accent. 'Not likely.'

To Celia's amazement, the woman, with a neat pixie haircut, followed them into the empty changing area. Erik's cubicle door was already shut.

'Veronica Bruce.' The woman held out a well-manicured hand to Celia. 'Friend of David Williams.'

Oh, Celia should have known, should have recognised the uniform earlier: the Harris tweed jacket worn before colder weather properly kicked in; the vintage silver thistle lapel brooch.

'How did you know we would be here?' she asked. Veronica Bruce gave a dismissive shrug.

'I told her,' came an utterance from behind the closed cubicle door.

'Get dressed and I'll buy you both a warming cup of tea in the Lido Cafe. Would you like anything to eat?'

'No,' said Celia. 'We already have breakfast arranged.'

Veronica had tea waiting for them at a discreet corner table indoors. Erik would have felt too cold to sit outside anyway.

'You're both braver than me,' she told them, giving an artificial shudder.

'Or more foolhardy,' suggested Erik.

'Now,' she turned to Celia. 'David told me about the threatening phone call you had the other night. We, in the department, are getting more and more concerned about your welfare. How many people know your landline number?'

'Hardly anyone. My mother.'

'Quite so. I don't want to alarm you but it could be possible that someone entered your flat.'

Celia shook her head. 'I'd have known. I wasn't aware of anything being out of place and the door was locked.'

Veronica's smile was condescending. 'Hmm, that's the whole point, it's called a black bag operation. A locked door is nothing to a professional and if they were just after your phone number why disturb anything else.'

'You're frightening me.'

'That is not my intention. We are here to protect you. If you are agreeable we would like to put surveillance cameras in your flat and once you step outside assign an agent to follow you.'

'So it wasn't you?'

'What wasn't us?'

'I had this feeling ever since Greece, ever since we were covering the Paxos bombing, that someone has been following me.'

Veronica paled at this. 'You should have told David straight away.'

'At first I thought it must be David,' explained Celia, adding, 'But what about Erik, isn't he in as much danger?'

'I think you both could be at risk. Forgive me in these days of equality but some foreign nationals would see a woman as an easier target. Also Erik has a track record of resilience, so why expend energy on a tougher nut?'

'The parcel bomb was addressed to the two of us.'

'True enough. A cowardly act. And all the more reason to take these extra precautions.'

'I expect so.' Celia sounded unconvinced.

'You do know we have identified the two Russian "tourists" responsible for the Salisbury poisonings. They are a trained military doctor called Mishkin and a veteran Colonel Chepiga. However we suspect a third man might be involved,' Veronica sniffed complacency.

Having little more to say after that, she finished her tea, got up and with a 'cheerio and toodle-oo' vanished through the door.

'Does anyone really still use "toodle-oo" in this modern era?' Celia was incredulous.

'Veronica does. Don't underestimate her though,' warned Erik. 'She is an extremely clever woman.'

* * * * *

After their swim, their rather upsetting meeting with Veronica Bruce, Celia took Erik to Chaviv's for a breakfast bagel. She felt she must compensate Chaviv for her previous rude behaviour. After her profuse apology, the cafe owner gave her his customary toothy smile as if nothing had happened. He made no enquiry, showed no curiosity, as to why she had dashed through his cafe and out of the backdoor the previous weekend.

'You do know who Veronica Bruce is?' asked Erik, clattering their tray of food onto a street view table. 'She'll be way above the rank of Williams.'

'No, why should I? I detected a slight Scottish accent, and then there's her surname, and the tweed jacket and thistle brooch was a slight give away.'

'What a coup for her, helping to identify the Salisbury poisoners,' cut in Erik. 'She's about to become a departmental head. If she's involved then Vauxhall Cross must be worried about us.'

'We are well and truly tied into this mess, aren't we?'

'More worryingly we've been burned.'

'What do you mean?'

'Our identity has been compromised as freelance agents working for SIS.'

'We couldn't withdraw if we wanted to now, could we?'

'I fear we've become an essential part of the investigation.'

'Are you happy with that?'

'I have to be.'

'I suspect I'm the main bait to catch the bombers.'

'That too,' admitted Erik. 'You know you are always welcome to stay with me in St John's Wood if things get too heavy.'

'I wouldn't be lone bait anymore,' she pointed out.

'And you wouldn't be at risk of sleeping with me either,' he complained bitterly.

'Is that all you can think about at a time like this?'

'Was that thing between us in Greece a holiday relationship? Merely a one night stand?' He decided to come right out with it.

'No, of course not.'

'I think you've never got over that Romeo and Juliet thing.'

'You like your Shakespearian references, don't you?'

'Or should I say that Juliet and Juliet thing?'

'You're so funny,' she sneered.

'And you enjoy seeing yourself as a victim of a blighted love affair.'

'If I didn't know better, I'd say you were jealous.'

'You cling to that Juliet and Juliet thing as a protection against real involvement.'

'I don't like to be possessed.'

'God forbid you're ever that.'

'Just because I was too tired and upset to sleep with you the other night. Is that what this is all about?'

'I might have been a comfort.'

'Look, Jordan, I'm not just one of your sexual playmates to be dumped when you've had enough. I want a relationship that is more than sex.'

Erik sunk his teeth into his cucumber and cream cheese bagel. Celia pushed her scrambled egg and lox bagel to one side. She did not feel very hungry. This breakfast idea was not going very well.

'Why does that idiot keep smiling across at you?' asked Erik, between mouthfuls.

'I don't know who you mean.'

'Behind the counter,' snapped Erik.

'Oh, Chaviv. He's just an old friend.'

'Is he really? Old friend or old flame?'

'You really are becoming impossible, Jordan. You are far too controlling and possessive for your own good. No wonder you can't keep a girlfriend.'

'Neither can you,' he scoffed.

'That's mean.'

'Well, you can't have it both ways. One moment you are accusing me of dumping girls and the next it is my failure to keep them.'

'Fine, but I'm not about to be one of them. I *was* devastated never to see Robin again. Our relationship just *was* without trying, without games. I had found my soulmate only to lose her through the most cruel circumstances. Now I am sorry I confided in you.'

'So what? So you had a broken love affair.'

'You don't get it, do you? It was so deep, a meeting of minds. It truly messed up my life for a time. I looked wildly around for replacements with disastrous consequences.'

'You've had other gay affairs then?' he asked, taken off guard. She did not answer, did not need to answer. 'I thought you said you didn't go in for "flings".'

'I don't. I just didn't realise that was all they were at the time.'

'I suppose you consider me in the same ilk.'

'I'm not willing to make any more mistakes again,' she muttered.

'It's only because …' he began. Before he finished the sentence she got up and stormed out. 'I am here for you.' The words died on his lips.

Erik's breakfast did not taste quite so good anymore but he decided not to follow her.

* * * * *

Monday morning blues? Things did not feel the same in the office the next morning. The atmosphere was icy—not just between Erik and Celia—all the other journalists wore sullen expressions.

Celia looked across at Erik. He appeared to be studiously avoiding her, avoiding everyone else in the newsroom.

He was right to be angry with her of course. She was still obsessed with Robin. The trouble with acknowledging an obsession is that it becomes reinforced, a defence against a risky world. He had a point there too.

She plucked up courage and walked over to Erik's desk.

'What are you up to?' she asked him.

'Since Theresa May's address to the House about the two Russians involved with the poisoning of Sergei and Yulia Skripal and the English couple, Dawn Sturgess and Charlie Rowley, Nelson has had me working the case day and night. Anything to distract me from the Paxos bombing.'

'You think you've problems, he has had me covering the Thames Festival.'

'I expect he is doing his best to protect us.'

'Wouldn't it be lovely just to get away for awhile? I would love to take you wild water swimming in the Lake District,' she whispered in his ear.

'You are the most unpredictable woman I have ever met.'

'Do I take that as a compliment?'

'You can take it how you like. Anyway, isn't it a bit late in the season for anymore open water swimming?'

'How about next spring then?' she suggested. He nodded and then he laughed.

'Next spring,' he confirmed.

'What's wrong? Everyone looks so miserable' she asked him, glancing round.

'Not miserable but frightened,' he replied, lowering his voice. 'Nelson has just told them not to handle any suspicious parcels.'

'I thought we were the targets.'

'We are but they don't know that, and that doesn't stop other people carrying a parcel bomb in unknowingly.'

'Oh dear, what can we do?'

'Nothing yet.'

'Come round tonight for a vegetarian moussaka and we'll discuss it.'

* * * * *

Even without meat, Celia found a moussaka recipe that was packed full of flavour and textures. She layered a dish with eggplants, zucchinis, spinach, feta, potatoes, and tomato sauce with a hint of cinnamon and cheesy béchamel. Satisfied that they were married together to create an unforgettable experience, she placed the dish before Erik who was already quaffing a very good New Zealand Chardonnay.

They finished the meal off with lemon meringue pie.

'You have excelled yourself. That was top rate,' he told her.

Celia put a CD in her player—music she had not dared to listen to for a few years. And there she was instantly walking a paved quadrangle with barefooted Robin. Was this simply an infatuation to wallow in?—if so then the song still filled her with regret.

'*Would you hold my hand if I saw you in heaven? Would you help me stand if I saw you in heaven?*'

'I wonder what you make of this. The last present I received from Holland. It was written by another Eric,' she told him; her eyes stinging.

Was she drunk? Was he drunk? Were they both sentimentally drunk? He was forced to admit, grudgingly at first, the music was extremely haunting.

'I know it is Eric Clapton but what is it called?' he asked her.

'Tears in Heaven.'

'Oh no, not really.'

'Eric wrote it following the death of his little boy. When Robin sent me her final letter asking me to let her go, I fittingly felt part of me died too.'

'If you could speak to Robin now what would you tell her?'

Celia was taken aback by his question. Then she remembered Robin saying, *I want to be a somebody one day*.

She considered carefully before speaking. 'I would tell her if she really wants to be a somebody then she has to have the courage to think with her heart, follow her dreams.'

Erik was surprised to find that he did not mind this at all. At least he was becoming party to the obsession.

Then the phone rang.

'Miss Grey?'

'Yes.'

'Did you enjoy Sunday swim in Hyde Park?' The same metallic foreign voice.

'Yes, but how …' Erik heard the quaver in Celia's voice and saw her alarm. He indicated for her to press the speaker button.

'You've not been listening to us, heeding warning.'

'I have,' she replied with as much indignation as she could muster.

'We are serious, Miss Grey.'

'I know you are.'

'Then stop pursuing story for Intelligence Service.'

'What story?'

'You know story I mean.'

'I'm not sure that I do.'

'We also know that parents live in very nice barn conversion outside Littleborough, Lancashire. I am sure you're very protective of them as we are of our family.'

The phone buzzed a dead line.

'Hardly a veiled threat. They have tried to frighten me off and now they are threatening my parents.' Celia was shaking. She was uncertain which was the stronger emotion, her fear or anger .

'I'll get in touch with Veronica first thing tomorrow morning.' Erik did his best to calm her down.

'What about David Williams? I thought he was our handler.'

'There might be a mole in the hole.'

'Mole? Hole?'

'A double agent at Vauxhall Cross. It wouldn't be the first time. I mentioned before that there could be a leak.' Erik paused, carefully weighing up what he said next. 'I can't help thinking there was something familiar about that voice on the phone.'

'I thought so too,' admitted Celia.

'He or she is obviously distorting their voice.'

'You think it could be a "she"?'

'Voice changer apps, even megaphone toys are very sophisticated nowadays,' pointed out Erik.

'Strange, don't you think, you are writing numerous articles on those two Russians involved with the Salisbury poisonings and yet you are receiving no threats.'

'What are you saying?'

'I am merely implying that the G.U. doesn't seem to operate in that way.'

'You mean once the deed is done, it's done?'

'Exactly that. Russia has little fear of a bad Western press.'

'So who does?'

'The Paxos bombers.'

And all the while the final lyrics of 'Tears in Heaven' were playing in the background.

'Would you know my name if I saw you in heaven? Would it be the same if I saw you in heaven?'

CHAPTER NINETEEN

'Have you heard that the Russian Defence Ministry has blamed Israel for downing one of their planes, or at least accused them of allowing it to be in the path of Syrian air defence systems during an Israeli strike on Hezbollah targets in Syria?' Erik asked Celia the next office morning.

'Sounds a ridiculous argument,' she retorted, peering over Erik's right shoulder to see his screen.

'Their objection seems to be that they were only given a minute's warning, prior to the attack, to get their plane out of the way. Although Putin initially absolved Israel, his Defence Ministry has subsequently upgraded Syrian surface-to-air missile systems despite Israeli objections. They have refused Israeli offers to send a delegation to Moscow to resolve the dispute, and ignored attempts by the Israeli Prime Minister to set up a meeting with Putin.'

'So all is not well between Russia and Israel.'

'Has it ever been really healthy?' asked Erik, getting to his feet and making his way to the water cooler. 'Like one?' he asked, pointing to his plastic cup. She shook her head. 'No, because you don't want any water or, no, because the cups are plastic?'

'Both really. We criticised the Greeks for not reducing their use of plastic bags and bin liners, when we are still using plastic for drink cups.'

Celia and Erik circled each other with the sly shyness of people who have slept together. They had slept together the previous night but more out of a need for reassurance than passion. A bond of friendship was deepening between the two of them which made Celia feel safe, more protected than she had ever felt before. And today, she needed that support more than at any other time in her life.

Veronica Bruce was the first visitor that morning for a meeting in Nelson's office.

'Good morning, one and all.' Veronica cleared her throat. 'I heard about last night from Erik, Celia, and I am extremely sorry. Nevertheless, Uncle has come up with a plan.'

'"Uncle"?' Celia looked askance.

'Headquarters,' translated Erik.

Veronica continued as if uninterrupted. 'We have found out that the crew member who replaced Anna Parker on the *Bettina* was an Irish national called Caitriona Lynch.'

Celia nodded knowingly. Williams had already told her about the Irish victim's DNA results. She immediately blanked her expression. Maybe Williams should not have furnished her with such detailed information. In the event Veronica did not seem to pick up on it. Then again, it was difficult to tell what poker playing Veronica registered or failed to register.

'Caitriona hadn't much actual experience on boats,' Veronica pressed on. 'However she was a very fit young woman, a gymnast, I believe. She was regarded locally as an excellent cook, who occasionally worked in a bar near the Gouvia Marina on Corfu.'

Erik glanced across at Celia. The gesture was picked up this time by Veronica with questioning eyebrows.

'We went there for dinner only the other night.' Celia, for reasons best known to herself, kept back that prior to this they had found Jacob Simmons ensconced in rooms in the same area.

Another of Veronica's 'hmms' whose meaning was unclear. Was 'hmm' a pondering or a disapproving interjection?

'Dublin is now in the picture,' she told them. 'However, we think it is best the *London Evening Record* publishes an article announcing that the resolution of the Paxos bombing is now entirely in the hands of the Greek authorities who are conducting an intense inquiry.'

'Are they?' asked Celia, doubt imbuing the question.

'That doesn't matter,' piped up Nelson. 'Don't you see it takes the focus off both of you and the paper.'

'Indeed it does,' agreed Veronica. 'I've already had a word with our friends across the Thames. Tomorrow they are sending round a technical operations officer to secure your Maida Vale flat.'

'What do you mean by "secure"?' asked Celia.

'She means cameras, bugs etcetera.' Nelson was becoming very visible in this conversation.

'In addition,' continued Veronica. 'An officer will be assigned to follow you to and from work. We will always have someone stationed outside your flat during the night. At weekends, we will need an hour or two to arrange further surveillance for longer journeys.' Veronica took a cell phone out of her bag and passed it to Celia. 'Use this mobile encryption app only to call me. Memorise my number.' She drew a phone number with a felt tipped pen on the back of Celia's hand.

'Am I in that much danger?' Celia asked the seasoned department head.

'You could be but we won't let anything happen.'

* * * * *

'I see your birdwatcher is in place down the street,' said Erik, dumping a newspaper wrap of fish and chips on the kitchen table.

'My what?' asked Celia.

'Your friendly surveillance officer.'

'You are very familiar with all this intelligence jargon, aren't you?'

'Anyway, Superman is stationed in a car across the street.'

'I expect I should ask him in for a cup of tea.'

'Wouldn't do that if I were you.'

'All this must be costing the British taxpayer a fortune. It wouldn't surprise me if the government doesn't send me a bill,' laughed Celia.

'Makes me think not all the action is in Greece. Makes me think there is some interest nearer to home with possible connections abroad. Veronica seems especially keen to find the perpetrators of the Paxos bombing.'

'Do you think MI5 is involved as well?'

'God knows. It is difficult to tell where one starts and the other one finishes.'

'Is David Williams an MI5 or MI6 officer then?'

'He could be MI5, but more probably he is part of Veronica's team.'

'Have you noticed how he's faded from the picture?'

'Yes, it seems Veronica is taking a personal interest in our situation now.'

'Drink?' offered Celia.

'A brandy would be lovely.'

'On the hard stuff now.'

'It's Friday night. No work tomorrow. Don't you think we deserve it?'

'Does brandy really go with fish and chips though?'

'The perfect accompaniment.'

'So it proved to be—the perfect aphrodisiac too. Erik was not banished to lie beneath Anna Politkovskaya but was invited into Celia's bed once more. Not hot but a warm melting bed.

Their lie-in was rudely interrupted the next morning by a knocking on the door. The postman had a parcel for Celia that would not go through the letterbox.

'Pressie love?' he announced with a cheeky wink.

'I wasn't expecting anything.'

'A secret admirer perhaps.'

Hearing that, a half-dressed Erik appeared at her shoulder. The postman surprised by the additional audience nodded and was gone.

Celia put the packet on the table. It was fairly small and the hand written address neat. The stamps were English and the postmark London.

'Do you recognise the writing?' asked Erik.

Celia shook her head. 'Shall I open it?'

Erik examined it in situ on the table. Finally he lifted it up and passed it across to her.

'It's not ticking anyway,' he laughed

'Neither was the other one.' She carefully began to undo the Sellotape. Her heart was thumping with fear and anticipation. Inside the packing was a miniature wooden box that she did not recognise at first.

'Perhaps we are getting paranoid,' suggested Erik, until he saw her facial expression.

'Oh my God!' she screamed. 'It's a dead rat. A dead rat in a coffin.' She flung the box onto the ground. The long tailed rodent skidded out of its cist across the kitchen floor. Erik wrapped his arms around her. 'Get rid of it, throw it away,' she told him, growing hysterical. 'It's horrible.'

'I can't do that,' he replied firmly. 'It's evidence.'

'Bin it, I tell you.'

'I will take it away right now.'

* * * * *

Over the weekend Celia realised that for all the surveillance she enjoyed she was still vulnerable, these people could still get to her.

'I've been seriously mulling over your idea of taking a short break. I can't wait for next spring,' Erik told her during two quickly grabbed on-the-job machine coffees. 'We both need and are owed some leave. I am sure Nelson will be agreeable, glad to see the back of us for a while I suspect. I think we should take that trip to the Lake District before winter sets in.'

'To swim, you mean?' asked Celia, sipping gently out of her politically correct porcelain cup.

'Of course.'

'But the water will be too cold in Cumbria by now.'

'I have thought of that. We'll get wetsuits.'

'I already have one.'

'There you are. Our swim vacation is fixed then.'

Celia rang Veronica Bruce's number with her encryption phone. A cool Scottish accented voice answered instantly.

Veronica surprisingly agreed that it was a good idea for them to disappear for a few days, while pointing out that taxpayers' money could not be used to fund security for a jolly.

'As long as Erik is with you,' she stressed. 'And please, please, do not disclose your destination to anyone.'

The following Monday morning they set off in Erik's car up the M1, cutting across on the M6 past Birmingham. The car's external thermometer showed a cool 12C°. The windscreen wipers kept swishing into action. Romantically they decided to take the car ferry at Bowness across Windermere lake. The Cumbrian roads on the far shore were frighteningly narrow—narrower than Celia remembered—this did not curb Erik's rallying spirit. Eventually Sat Nav informed them that they had reached their destination in one piece: a nineteenth century whitewashed inn that appeared to be at a crossroads in the middle of nowhere.

'The Drunken Duck, Barngates,' announced Celia jubilantly as Erik parked up. 'I often stayed here in winter with my parents. The locals used to follow the hounds on foot in the hills up there.'

Erik—still on an adrenalin rush—took it all in but said nothing.

'You've booked a room with a patio for three nights, is that right?' enquired the cheery receptionist. Erik raised an eyebrow at room in the singular. 'I'll take you to your room if you like.'

She escorted them to a yard behind the inn not unpleasantly smelling of hops. Their ensuite—The Lodge—was next to the famous Barngates Micro-brewery. Barrels were being rolled out by the brewer as if in greeting.

Erik's initial optimism dissolved as the receptionist opened the bedroom door.

'I hope this is all right for you?' she asked, doubt clouding her otherwise positive demeanour. Erik nodded sullenly and she was gone.

'Yes, I managed to get us a superior twin-bedded room. As we are both more used to sleeping alone, I thought we would get a better night's sleep this way,' justified Celia.

'Fight you for the left side,' he told her, heroically discarding his disappointment.

Celia said she was happy to sleep on the right, bouncing like a child beneath a picture of white geese rummaging in green foliage.

'Very appropriate,' he announced, scanning the room.

'How do you mean?'

'Duck egg blue. The decor is duck egg blue.'

She watched him as he opened the patio door. She could hear his feet crunching on the gravel outside. He sucked in the fresh if damp air, took in the view of the fells beyond. A small wall separated each apartment.

'There's a table and two chairs out here. Come and see,' he shouted.

'I'm more interested in examining the ensuite at the moment.'

'How on earth did the inn get its name?' he asked her later over dinner.

'It comes from the story of the Victorian landlady finding her ducks lying at the crossroads, dead. When she started to pluck them, she realised they were alive, but intoxicated by the strong local brew which had seeped into their feeding ditch.'

* * * * *

Tuesday came in cloudy and cool again and they went for a quick walk round Tarn Hows.

'What's that?' asked Erik, stopping at a fallen tree which appeared to have peculiar bark running up and down its trunk.

'The money tree,' Celia told him. 'Or if you like, the wishing tree. It's an old ritual dating back to at least the seventeen hundreds and is peculiar to certain parts of Britain. You beat a coin into the bark to bring you good luck.'

'But there's thousands of coins embedded here.'

'There you are. Everyone from down the centuries is in need of a little luck.'

Erik picked up a nearby stone and immediately began striking a two pence piece into the bark.

'What about me?' asked Celia.

'I thought you weren't superstitious.'

'All the same,' she objected.

Erik passed her the stone and another two pence piece.

'Our ancestors used to believe that divine spirits lived in trees and they would festoon them with gifts,' she told him as she knocked in her coin.

'Like Christmas.'

'Yes, exactly. But I suspect these wishing trees have developed from much older customs.'

'You're fascinated by them, aren't you?'

'Yes, since childhood.'

'So, who says money doesn't grow on trees,' laughed Erik. 'Make a wish.'

'OK.'

'What did you wish for?'

'Tell and the magic dies.'

'I think I might guess.'

'How about we go to Ambleside and fix you up with a wetsuit?' she suggested.

Erik was forced to accept that the wetsuit idea was originally his. He half-heartedly turned and they started making for the car.

They found a parking space, almost outside the Swim the Lakes shop, along Ambleside's Compston Road. Pete Kelly, the owner and swim expert, could not have been more helpful and informative. He even enthused Erik. Erik making his appearance—as if on stage or more accurately in panto—in a hired figure-hugging suit.

'We're all set then, possibly to take the plunge for tomorrow,' declared Celia on their way back to the Drunken Duck.

Resting on his bed back in The Lodge, Erik was not so sure as yet another duck appraised him from the opposite wall. A small table lamp beneath brought its white plumage to life.

'Bet you don't have any qualms about taking to the water,' he sneered at the duck.

He could hear Celia moaning with pleasure as she soaked in the Victorian roll top bath. Indeed everything about their bathroom was styled antiquè, even the taps. Erik lay there entertaining serious misgivings about this relationship. It had become like a marriage with none of the benefits.

And as if to substantiate all his preconceptions of married life, further evidence was provided in the dining room that night—a room of white painted beams, bare plastered walls and mahogany. The tables were packed closely together and at first Erik thought the guests were being exceptionally loud, until he realised the couple at the window table were having a blazing row. Celia began to look uncomfortable as the F word was being bandied between the middle-aged couple. She stared with embarrassment at the out-of-commission grandfather clock in the corner and wished she was somewhere else. Other couples, surrounding them at adjacent tables, hardly seemed to register what was going on. Then they were the absorbed young who would not ever think, under normal circumstances, of venturing so much as a 'good morning, good afternoon or good evening'. Anyone who went in for these niceties had to be old or off their trolley.

Celia and Erik's first courses arrived. The red-faced man in the window seat, who was by this stage emotionally reeling from being severely savaged by the woman (presumably his wife), knocked over his wine glass showering Erik's cheese soufflé. Erik accepted his flustered apology frostily.

Shortly after that the woman stormed out followed by the man. Still no reaction from those little human islets around them. Celia and Erik relaxed back into their chairs.

'Thank goodness, they've gone,' sighed Celia.

'Poor bastard,' said Erik, sympathising with the beleaguered male.

'We can't know what was involved,' objected Celia.

'All the same you don't air your grievances in public.'

'You don't?'

'No, I don't. Never would.'

'Glad to hear it. I hope those two aren't staying here for breakfast.'

CHAPTER TWENTY

The next day, Wednesday 26th September, was a surprisingly six degrees warmer.

The argumentative couple of the previous night were in fact guests of the hotel and did appear for breakfast. Thankfully the sobering night seemed to have brought a rapprochement.

'Let's go for it,' Celia told Erik, slicing into her berry pancake.

'Go for what?' he asked, feigning ignorance. He knew exactly what she meant and, with the reality nigh, his whole being had begun to dread it.

'Wild water swimming of course.'

'Where?'

'A secret location.'

'Can't we just go for a walk instead?' he suggested.

'Not after I've gone to the trouble of bringing my wetsuit and you've hired one.'

From Barngates they took the road to Coniston then on to Torver. They turned left for the A5084 which ran along Coniston Water past Peel Island—the inspiration for Arthur Ransome's children's book, *Swallows and Amazons*. Celia again felt the Audi was far too big for the narrow Lake District roads, and Erik repeatedly failed to reduce his speed round blind corners. She looked down at her hands, they were running with sweat.

'Thank goodness for seatbelts,' she told him.

'Sorry?'

'Please slow down, Erik.'

'I thought we were swimming in Coniston Water,' he queried, ignoring the censure.

'Better than that,' she stressed. 'That's if we arrive in one piece.'

Turning right up a single metalled track at Water Yeat, matters got even worse. He bounced the Audi up the track as if it were a Defender. It was a relief to Celia when the track ran out, forcing them to park on a sloping square of rough land, by a stream, opposite a farm. Leaving the car, with a prayer for its security, they began hoofing it up a steep unmade path carrying their wetsuits. Sentinels of ferns guarded most of the way.

After another three quarters of a mile or so they finally came out on a rise.

'Gosh!' exclaimed Erik. 'Are we really going to swim in there?'

'Beacon Tarn,' proclaimed Celia. 'The site of your first ever wild water swim.'

Erik eyed the tarn and the surrounding hills for any sign of humanity. 'It's so isolated.'

She was not sure if this was uttered in complaint or as a statement of fact.

'So bleak,' he moaned and she knew.

'Come on, let's get changed,' she told him; determined to ride over any opposition after all the effort of getting there.

They helped each other zip up their wetsuits.

Taking to the water at the nearest end, they trod carefully to avoid stones on the spongy moss floor. Erik immediately felt the rubberised suit was like a floatation aid. He laughed, feeling like Michelin Man as he began a slow crawl down the tarn. Celia, accompanying him with breaststroke, never once taking her eyes off him for the four hundred metres or so. Taking a rest at the far end, looking back down the lake, he saw there was a tiny island to his right with reeds and white water lilies still in flower close by.

'This is amazing,' he told her. 'The water is so clear.'

'Wild but beautiful.'

'Exactly that.' *Isolated* and *bleak* had been put on the back burner.

'You've done very well,' she reassured him.

'Can we swim back?'

'Of course but we have to keep to this side of the tarn. We are in a deep trough here. The water is too shallow over there by the reeds.'

They set off at the same steady pace. Celia was encouraged enough by Erik's performance to swim alongside him doing front crawl.

'Can we do there and back one more time?' he asked.

She nodded, unwilling to curb his enthusiasm.

'There's a man over there been watching us during our entire swim. Can you see him?' she asked.

'I've been too concentrated on keeping my head above water,' he laughed. 'Expect he's just a walker.'

When they had completed the final two lengths and were wading out, she glanced across to the rock where the man had been standing. He had gone.

The Drunken Duck had made them up a flask and a packed lunch. As they sat on the bank enjoying a warming cup of tea and pickled cheese sandwiches, they saw that Beacon

Tarn was no longer secluded. Two divers were slithering along on the opposite shore exploring the shallower depths. And slowly people, some who sounded like locals, began to appear from all directions. It was as if everyone had suddenly appreciated that this might be the last day of summer, the last chance to bathe.

'Look,' said Erik. 'The divers have put out a red marker buoy.'

'Wonder what they are up to.'

A few people had taken to the water, most were happy to sit back and enjoy the sunshine. An hour of relaxation ensued before all hell broke out.

'Clear the area! Clear the area!' Male shouts, whistles. The surrounding hills were not only running with water but streaming with police.

'Oh God! Not again!' exclaimed Celia.

'Easy. Wait.' Erik put a hand on her arm as she began packing their things away.

'Not up here. They've not followed us to the Lake District.'

'We don't know what this is about yet.' Erik did his best to sound reassuring.

'I was so certain we would be safe up here.'

'Maybe it has nothing to do with us. Maybe it has something to do with those two divers. Let's see if we can find out.'

Although they were experienced London journalists, they could not break down the tight-lipped resolve of the Cumbrian Force. All appeals for information fell on deaf ears. Seeing their attempts at engagement with the lower ranks—their refusal to quit the scene—a police sergeant, who looked as if he was due to be put out to graze imminently, shambled over to them.

'Please evacuate the area immediately,' he told them.

'But what's going on?' asked Eric.

'Evacuate the area, sir, now,' repeated the sergeant.

'But we are journalists.'

'I don't care what you are. Please leave right now or I'll arrest you.'

Nobody at the Drunken Duck had any idea what the incident could have been about either. Not until an old timer at the bar offered his opinion.

'During t' war, returning aircrews were known to ditch any unused bombs in t' tarns before making a risky landing,' he explained.

'Aye, I've heard summat o' sort as yous, William,' agreed his drinking companion.

''appen it is, 'appen it isn't such. I canna swear to it, mind.'

'''appen it is, 'appen it isn't such",' mimicked Erik, writhing hysterically on his bed back in their room.

'Shush, don't be so unkind,' rebuked Celia.

''appen we'll have to keep our eyes on the Cumbrian Press once we get back to London.'

'London, I'm not sure I feel safe there anymore. I'm not sure I feel safe anywhere anymore. Still, I would willingly give it all up and stay here. Safer here.'

'That's not what you were saying a few hours ago, when it looked like the whole Cumbrian Force had descended on Beacon Tarn.'

'I can breathe up here,' she told him.

'Once a northern lass, always a northern lass.'

'Maybe.'

'Tempting though it might be, we have a job of work to do. We will not solve the Paxos bombing by staying in Cumbria.'

'But will we solve it in London, or even Paxos come to think of it?'

'My gut feeling is the seeds of this atrocity were sown in London. If you recall, the Service was showing an interest in us before the parcel bomb was sent to the *Record*. The sending of that parcel bomb must have been additional confirmation that we really had pressed a button somewhere.'

'Are you saying that somehow the intelligence community had prior knowledge that we had stimulated interest in certain quarters?'

'That is my belief. I'm starving,' he said. 'Let's brush up, go to that lovely bar, and forget our troubles for one evening.'

'It's difficult to forget what we are going back to but I'll try.'

'I'll pass on the starter and save myself for dessert. Chana masala, brinjal, raita, aloo paratha and pickles, for me,' announced Erik, appraising the menu, a pint of Tag Lag already in his hand.

'What's your beer like?'

'Excellent and brewed on site. Sure you won't try some.'

She shook her head vigorously. 'The suet pudding with shin of beef and a glass of red will suit me fine.'

'We'd prefer to eat here in the bar tonight by the fire, if that's all right,' Erik told the hovering waitress with an indistinct foreign accent.

'Yes, that would be lovely,' agreed Celia. 'Old inn atmospheric.'

The waitress nodded while regarding them as if they were mad. 'But this table is so small.'

'The table is just fine,' Celia assured her.

'This is all very different to Erimitis,' laughed Erik, appraising the waitress' rump shimmying away in tight denim.

'One so Greek the other so English. I love them both though,' admitted Celia.

'Me too.'

'I thought we were going to die today,' she told him later, dipping her spoon into a consoling Victoria plum frangipane with almond ice cream.'

With his mouth full of figgy toffee pudding, ice cream and caramel sauce, Erik struggled out, 'Incredible how quickly the police cleared that tarn.'

'Those two divers must have seen something suspicious.'

'And for once it doesn't look as if we were the targets.'

CHAPTER TWENTY-ONE

Veronica Bruce sat waiting for them in Gatsby's office first thing Monday morning, an untouched Royal Doulton bone china coffee cup before her. Only bone china and the plush Editor's office would do following her promotion.

'You don't mind if David here sits in on this? He has been fundamental in setting this discussion up.'

Williams merely nodded at Veronica's introduction.

So Mackintosh Man was MI6 after all. He was a Vauxhall man all along. No surprises there, conceded Erik privately to himself.

'Have a good holiday in the Lake District?' Veronica asked. They nodded. 'I'll not beat about the bush. The Cousins are getting extremely worried about the lack of progress in Greece regarding the *Bettina* bombing.'

'Aren't we all,' groaned Erik. Gatsby flashed him a furious look.

'"The Cousins"?' asked Celia. Veronica's look was scathing, as if Celia was someone who did not understand English.

'Our American cousins,' she explained with clipped impatience. 'They are eager for a resolution as am I. They feel you must have touched a nerve, someone you've met, someone you've come across during your investigation into this story. They want to know if you would be willing to take part in a covert operation.'

'As a lure for their fishing trip, you mean?' asked Erik.

'Put it this way,' said Veronica, now on full autocontrol. 'Until we find the perpetrators of this atrocity neither MI5 at home nor MI6 abroad can guarantee your safety. Your research has upset some powerful and dangerous people and we cannot detail protection for the rest of your lives.'

'Are we talking about the Russians?' Gatsby put in his pennyworth for the first time during the interview.

'We don't know that yet. What we do know is some of these people are cruel and relentless. How do you feel about bringing these people to book?' Veronica bounced the question between Erik and Celia.

'It doesn't look as if we have a choice, does it?' sighed Erik.

'Not if we are going to have to look over our shoulders for the rest of our lives,' agreed Celia.

'Might I have a word with these two alone, Robert?' Veronica asked Gatsby. Gatsby left looking slightly aggrieved at having to vacate his own office. 'I have run this past C and he is agreeable,' resumed Veronica.

'This is the same C who signs his name in green ink.' Erik began a humorous explanation to a bemused Celia.

'Yes, yes, our Chief,' snapped Veronica, irritated at being interrupted again. 'Now the plan is this, the Americans will fly you out of RAF Mildenhall in two day's time.'

'To where?' asked Celia.

'I'm getting to that,' said Veronica coolly.

'Your destination will be Souda Bay on Crete,' piped up Williams for the first time.

'Just so,' agreed Veronica.

'And then back up to Paxos.' Erik's less than educated guess.

'Paxos again?' Celia could no longer conceal her growing alarm. 'Isn't that extremely dangerous for us?'

'Not as much as getting there by public transport. You'll be guests of the CIA, the US Air Force and Navy. You will be under their protection at all times. Please pack stout shoes and casual clothing. Your route will be clandestine for a purpose.'

'I can't believe this is happening,' said Celia.

'Think of Beacon Tarn,' Erik reminded her. 'How anything out of the ordinary sends the alarm bells ringing. We can no longer live on the edge like this.'

'Quite so,' agreed Veronica. 'What is this about Beacon Tarn?'

'We don't actually know for sure. After we'd swum there, the area was cleared by the police,' explained Celia.

'Is Beacon Tarn in Cumbria?'

'It is,' confirmed Celia.

Veronica tapped into an app on her iPhone. 'There is a report here that says two divers found what they thought was an unexploded bomb dropped from a Second World War plane. It turned out to be a false alarm—some sort of agricultural cylinder used for spraying, weeding and the like, somehow found its way into the water.' She smiled smugly at their ingenuousness.

'What sort of app has Veronica to get that report on the cylinder in Beacon Tarn?' Celia asked Erik on the way back to their desks. 'I've tried to get info through every source I know to no avail.'

'Uncle knows everything,' replied Erik. 'And Williams knows more than most. I suspect it is he who has set this entire operation up with the Americans.'

'It is as if Veronica knew about that Beacon Tarn incident all along and used it as a put-down.'

'Don't be so paranoid, Celia. Everything is a game to Veronica.'

'Is she one of your conquests too? Is that why she is always trying to humiliate me?' asked Celia flushing up.

Erik did not answer at first. 'It was all such a long time ago,' he finally admitted.

'But she's old enough to be your mother.'

'A very fine, intelligent, handsome mother you have to admit,' he pointed out to her disgust.

* * * * *

They flew out of RAF Mildenhall over a patchwork of Suffolk fields in autumn colours. Their fellow passengers consisted of four CIA officers, who had already introduced themselves by their codenames, and some replacement personnel for the naval base at Souda Bay, Chania.

Celia was delighted to see that they had reached the Channel and then the Low Countries in no time. She was not the world's most patient traveller.

'Why Triton One, Two, Three and Four?' she asked one of the CIA men.

'Don't you know your Greek mythology, ma'am?' he asked. With a shake of her head, Celia admitted ignorance. 'Poseidon, god of the sea, cut off a piece of Corfu with his trident to indulge in a secret love nest on Paxos with Amphitrite. The result was their son Triton.'

'Why didn't you use the cryptonym Poseidon?' asked Erik.

'Too obvious,' laughed Triton Two. 'And there was another reason that you will find out in due course.'

Celia liked the look of Triton Two. He was less intense than the other three. He had a beaming smile beneath his blond hair—a clean-cut Langley lad—no tattoos, no horn-rimmed glasses and from solid Caucasian American stock she guessed. A good old boy with all the right credentials to qualify for the CIA.

However not even he seemed willing to expand on the operation they were about to embark on. All Erik's enquiries were met with a friendly shake of head or 'everything is taken care of, sir.' The older round-faced Triton One, who actually did wear horn-rimmed glasses, offered the information that they would eventually be staying just outside Gaios on Paxos.

Early October and as they stepped off the plane the Cretan heat still hit them as if they were walking into a Chinese laundry. They were taken from the airstrip by jeep for refreshments.

'What a lovely cafeteria.' Celia's hand guarded her cup of tea. 'So clean.'

'We call it the Galley, ma'am,' corrected Triton Four, who looked as if he had just stepped off a US destroyer.

Celia had not realised their importance until Souda Bay's Commanding Officer, with more stars and stripes than she could easily count, presented himself at their table with a salute.

'Settling in, sir?' asked Triton One.

'Sure am, already a week into the job,' said the officer confidentially. 'Came to inform you that your transport is ready when you are.'

They taxied out of Souda Bay on a King Air 350 twin-engine turboprop fixed wing aircraft—which meant more to Erik than Celia.

'Otherwise known as a special operation spy plane,' he explained. Causing the Tritons some repressed amusement.

'We in the Service find the word "spy", or "spying" inappropriate …' shouted Triton One, above the din of the plane's rattling airframe as they lifted higher.

'You and SIS both,' shouted back Celia.

'Nevertheless, Erik is right, our mission is really under way at last.' Another dental advertisement, cheek to cheek beam from Triton Two.

This stage of their journey was relatively short, and their landing careful on the Preveza airstrip in north western Greece. Although they knew they were heading for Paxos, what the Cousins had failed to explain was that their accommodation would be on a luxury catamaran flying under a flag of convenience, the Greek flag of course.

'*Poseidon's Secret*, very apt,' acknowledged Erik.

'Would you expect anything else from Langley?' muttered Triton Two.

'Never regarded the Company as being famed for having a classical bent,' retorted Erik drily.

'Consider us your crew,' said Triton One, after he had paid off the taxi driver and they began to board the big cat at the Cleopatra Marina. 'Indeed two of us do have extensive sailing experience.'

'Reassuring,' moaned Erik, who was beginning to feel exhausted.

'What about provisions?' asked Celia, looking through to the open plan galley.

'I am a fluent Greek speaker,' announced the otherwise self-contained Triton Four. 'It is my job to buy supplies for the boat although we are already well stocked.'

'You look Greek,' said Erik, suddenly aware of Triton Four's thick eyebrows and dark curly hair.

'I'm an American,' Triton Four proclaimed proudly before admitting, 'of Greek extraction.'

'And I am half American like Churchill,' jibed Erik.

'We know,' said Triton One. 'Your dad is a bright chap, was a Rhodes scholar.'

For once Erik looked taken aback. 'The question is what you people don't know about us.'

'Oh, we know everything,' Triton One assured him, striding off down the deck.

The sixty-five foot multihull had five cabins. Celia was gallantly allotted the best. She saw that her guest stateroom had a queen sized bed and even a two-seater couch by the door. Erik's cabin was a lot smaller but functional.

'This boat is perfect,' he told her. 'Self-contained and ideal for debriefing meetings.'

On cue they heard the anchor chain grating like an instrument of torture.

'Are we underway?' asked Celia.

'Finally,' sighed Erik.

* * * * *

The night was fair. Safely berthed along Gaios' long harbour, they relaxed over Triton Four's beautifully prepared salad with pasta under a canopy in the catamaran's cockpit area. As the wine flowed, light conversation took on a more serious note.

'We want you to seek out everyone you did before,' said Triton One. 'Just paying them a visit for old times' sake. Easier for you to find out what you can at a local level than for us, less resistance.'

'But what if they are no longer here. Surely the Russians have left, mission completed.' Celia made no effort to hide her scepticism. This was a wild goose chase if ever she had seen one.

'Yes, you are right, expect our friends from GRU, Boris Fedorov and Trofim Kozlov, will have departed back to Mother Russia and the Aquarium.' Triton One was always ahead of the game. 'We would like confirmation, nevertheless.'

'I thought the GRU had become the G.U.,' queried Erik.

'It has but they are still commonly referred to as GRU officers.'

'All very confusing,' said Erik.

'And "the Aquarium"?' asked Celia.

'The GRU headquarters located at Khodynka Airfield in Moscow,' explained Triton One.

'You know exactly who Boris and Trofim are then, their surnames.' Celia was impressed.

'Of course.' Triton One paused to allow this piece of information to sink in before taking a photograph out of his portfolio. 'I would like your first visit to be to Adras Christakos tomorrow morning. I want you to ask him if he has ever seen this man.' He handed them a photograph of a bespectacled middle-aged man.

'Smiley!' exclaimed Celia. She remembered now Adras had made the same connection.

'I must agree he does look like Alec Guinness' portrayal of the master spy. So innocuous, a man who blends into the background. But then most spies I know look like that,' smiled Triton One.

'I thought you didn't like using the name "spy",' chided Erik.

'Well, it's allowed occasionally.' Triton One was rarely knocked off his equilibrium.

'Few look like James Bond,' laughed Triton Three. 'Only this man here,' he said, pointing across the table to Triton Two who lapped up the accolade.

'So Boris and Trofim definitely weren't everyday G.U. agents then?' asked Erik, keen on clarification.

'No, they were high-ranking Spetsnaz operatives,' replied Triton One.

'So who is Smiley?' Erik asked him.

'Let's see if Adras can identify him first. However, if it is any consolation, we do not believe he is British.'

'Patience is bitter, but its fruit is sweet,' put in Triton Four as he delivered their Americanos.

'Aristotle, very fitting,' acknowledged Celia, redeeming herself after her Triton mythology gaffe.

'Your obvious renewed interest in the *Bettina* story might stir up some mud, flush the bombers out, help us get the bad men.' Triton One was determined to keep on script.

'You're using a lot of clichés there,' retorted Erik; rudely, Celia thought. Triton One finally scowled a little and fell silent.

Of the four CIA officers, Celia felt Triton One was the senior. His mind was mathematical, factual, rather than creative. Not a man easily diverted from a chosen course of action—the project in hand. As if to confirm this Triton One looked at his Apple watch.

'Better we turn in for the night. A big day lies ahead for you two,' he told them.

* * * * *

'Yes, that's him!' exclaimed Adras Christakos. 'I'm sure that's him.'

Luckily they had found the waiter sitting in his yard, in a wicker chair, outside his Loggos home without having to ask around. After pleasantries about the still sunny weather, Erik had passed Adras the photograph of Smiley.

'You are certain? Absolutely no doubts?' Erik needed to be sure.

'Yes, that is the pretend Englishman who was sitting outside the bar just before the bomb went off,' Adras confirmed a second time.

'We've been unable to establish his identity or what nationality he actually is,' Celia told him.

'But it is him. He is one of the few things I do remember around that time. Although I cannot remember the explosion itself or anything immediately afterwards.'

'Anyway how have you been, Adras?' asked Erik.

'I'm back working for my uncle a few hours a week. It is not the same though. The builders have done a great job restoring the bar but no one can repair this leg back to what it was.' He struggled out of the wicker chair and limped up and down by way of demonstration. Erik and Celia watched on, lost for words. 'See what I mean?' he asked them. 'My left leg suffered multiple fractures.'

'Kek …kek…kek.' They looked up to see half-a-dozen birds of prey gathering and swirling high above them.

'Eleonora's Falcons again.' Celia delighted in her recognition—a welcoming focus away from Adras' disability.

'Yes,' he sighed. 'They gather this time of year on their way to Africa.'

That isn't all that is gathering, reflected Erik quietly to himself.

'We will find the people who killed your nephew and did this to you,' he told Adras; his colour rising with repressed anger.

'It is such a surprise and so good of you to visit me again,' said Adras.

Erik looked away ashamed. Celia sighed, looking up to the circling falcons and remembered their harvested prey. She could identify with those tiny birds trapped in the rocks and rendered flightless. She and Erik had been forced by Veronica Bruce into compliance with the CIA. They were completely servile to their dictate.

'How embarrassing. Poor boy. I am not comfortable in this situation,' she told Erik as they made for their Chevrolet Orlando MPV 7 Seater. They had asked the Americans for a small hire car—this was apparently small by US standards—and who knows they might need extra power for a quick getaway. 'I never signed up to be an SIS agent.'

'Think of it like this, it's much better than being in London and having to cover every nuance of Theresa May's Brexit,' reconciled Erik.

'But I have never covered Brexit.'

'You did. I seem to remember a wonderful piece on the effect of the backstop on Northern Ireland's agriculture.'

'Exactly. And it happened to include the impact on the Republican side of the border too.'

Their next CIA directed visit was to the Villa Elina. The bougainvillea was making a valiant last stand. However the smell of flowers had been mainly replaced by rotting vegetation. Clearing a patch in the building's now smeared and almost opaque windows, they could see that the interior space was empty, lifeless, as Erik had already established a month before. According to Triton One, the Russians had taken the villa on a six month rental. It was apparent that they had not returned. Next Erik and Celia decided to visit Villa Astraea, this time on their own volition, in the hope of seeing Maria again. Dried autumn leaves floated in the swimming pool. The unfiltered water had begun to turn brown. Villa Astraea too was starting its own bleak winter hibernation.

Celia felt sad as if it was the end of a love affair. Was it though? Her relationship with Erik had begun here, could it endure into a future beyond here?

Erik, sensing her melancholic mood, took her hand in his. 'You all right?' he asked.

CHAPTER TWENTY-TWO

They drove back down the valley to Loggos for lunch—down the once green spring valley now autumn orange and gold—back to Adras' uncle's bar where the story had begun. There were still patches of wet plaster on the undecorated walls, paradoxically surrounding an eye-catching new bar and counter. Demos Christakos was up and running.

They ordered coffees and a Greek salad to share. They told Demos that they were English journalists and friends of Adras.

'On the house then,' he insisted.

'No, no, we couldn't possibly …' began Celia.

'I insist.' Demos was assertive if nothing else. 'You help find who killed my boy, coffees and salad is nothing. Mother is broken.'

A difficult pause followed. Celia could think of nothing to say to alleviate this family's grief. And she knew any further objection regarding payment would be futile.

'It's amazing how quickly you've got the bar back in business. Just under six months by my reckoning. If this had happened in England it would have taken over two years,' said Erik.

'Family, friends, whole village has helped.' Demos' eyes filled with pride; his mood lifting. 'Shutting in January for painting walls.'

'We are sorry to see Adras has been left so lame,' Erik told him as their coffees and salad arrived.

'At least he can walk.' Demos sounded dismissive. 'At least is here.'

Erik and Celia decided not to pursue the Adras line any further.

'You will have been insured of course.' Erik spoke up first.

'Insurance money will not bring boy back,' objected Demos.

'No, no, of course not.'

'Mystery donor paid thousands of euros into fund to rebuild cafe,' he finally confided.

'Mystery, you say?' Celia perked up.

'Yes,' said Demos. 'That is another reason we have been able to repair so quickly.'

'And you've no idea where this money came from?' asked Erik.

'No, came from Credit Suisse numbered account.'

'Have you tried to trace this anonymous benefactor?' asked Erik.

Demos shook his head. 'Money is good, that's all I know.'

Erik and Celia stared at each other with raised eyebrows. Demos began exhibiting increasing discomfiture.

'Good, this salad,' said Erik, in a latent attempt to de-escalate the situation.

They gave Demos a cheery wave on leaving and left a €20 note hidden under a plate on the table.

'Captain Vasilakis, really good to see you,' Erik was saying three quarters of an hour later at Gaios police station.

'So, you are working with Americans now.' Vasilakis as usual did not go in for small talk through his cloud of cigar smoke.

'How do you know that?'

'This is a small island, Erik,' he laughed. 'However Athens says I have to give you full cooperation. Greek politics change, how you say, *tout de suite.*'

'That is a French idiom,' pointed out Celia.

'In blink of eyelid then,' sniffed Vasilakis. Neither Celia nor Erik had the heart to correct him a second time. 'So to business. Athens has informed me that they have extracted DNA of two different individuals from cigarette butts you gave me. It seems filter paper is good for such collection. They also suspect cigarettes might be English.' Vasilakis smirked over this piece of information. Erik and Celia refused to rise to the provocation.

'Why English?' asked Erik expressionless.

'Owing to low tar levels.' Vasilakis smirked again at Greek forensic expertise. 'There was another partial print found with yours and two Russians on lighter. Again print has not been able to be identified to any individual.'

'Have you got any further with the murder of Aleixo Xenakis?' asked Celia.

'No. But I doubt men who pushed him off the Tripitos Arch were diamond smugglers as claimed by Russians. We believe Smirnov's gang might have been smuggling something far more lethal.'

'What?' pressed Erik.

'This I cannot say.'

'But to Israel?'

'This I cannot say.'

'What a way to die,' shuddered Celia, remembering the twenty metres or so down to the sea from the Tripitos Arch. 'It's terrible if that poor man doesn't get justice too.'

'Do you think Smirnov and all those killed or affected by bomb will get justice then?' asked Vasilakis with undisguised sarcasm.

'We can only hope,' cut in Erik, wondering if he should tell Vasilakis about the anonymous donation to rebuild the Loggos bar—if he did not know already—or save it for the Cousins. He decided on neither. He would ring Veronica on Celia's special cell phone that night. Not from the catamaran though. Every instinct told him he did not want the Cousins to be privy to this conversation.

* * * * *

'I thought it was Celia.' Veronica's clipped tone cut through the ether.

'We are sitting on a bench together by Gaios harbour. The weather is still lovely and warm here,' Erik told Veronica maliciously.

'Fog in London, what else?' Even Veronica's sigh was short lived. 'Anyway good to hear from you, Erik, how are things going?'

'Fine. We are just fine.' He told her about the Greek forensic scientists' findings and the secret Demos' donation via the Credit Suisse Bank. 'Any chance we can trace the donor?' he asked.

'Hmm, Credit Suisse, that might be a difficult one unless we can connect this person with criminal activities. Money laundering and the like.'

'Isn't the murder of four people and a child reason enough?'

'And then there's that Greek Interpol chappy. Everyone seems to forget about him.'

'Aleixo Xenakis.'

'Yes, that's him. The two incidents must be connected surely.'

'Murders not incidents,' reaffirmed Erik.

'You really think the Credit Suisse donation could have been made by the bombers?' asked Veronica dispassionately, neutralising Erik's emotional response.

'Why not?'

'Bombers with a conscience?'

'I am sure Dmitry Smirnov was the target. The rest were simply collateral damage.'

'Terrible two words those, "collateral damage",' groaned Veronica with disapproval.

Two-faced bitch, thought Erik, knowing full well that Veronica would have been personally responsible for plenty of innocent casualties in pursuit of a main objective.

'Nevertheless, I'll see what we can do,' he heard her saying. 'Might have to bring the Doughnut in on this.'

'Bring in GCHQ Cheltenham if you like. Bring in anyone who might help resolve this story.'

'Before I forget,' said Veronica, who he knew forgot nothing. 'Nelson contacted me. It seems a woman from the Association of Ukrainians in Notting Hill Gate wishes to speak to you. She says it is rather important. We weren't sure if it is OK to give her your mobile number. She's seen an article on the bombing and substantiates the possibility that Anna Parker might still be alive.'

Buzz! Buzz! Never one for wasting time, Veronica rang off.

It can only have been a matter of minutes later that Erik's personal mobile began vibrating in his jacket pocket.

'Mr Jordan?'

'Yes.'

'My name is Galina Bondar. I don't suppose you remember me but I work in the archives at the Association of Ukrainians.'

'Yes, of course I remember. I had the pleasure of meeting you a week or two back. You were very helpful.'

'A lady from your newspaper just rang and said it was all right for me to phone you like this.'

Not exactly from my newspaper, thought Erik caustically.

'How can I help you, Galina?' he asked.

'Someone showed me a newspaper cutting of Anna Parker the other day. The paper said she might still be alive. I think I recognised her.'

'Really? From where?'

'I think one of our members brought her to see the Holodomor archives about April time, the same archives you came to see.'

'Jacob Simmons?' offered Erik.

'No, I don't know that name.'

'His Ukrainian name is Yakiv Balanchuk.'

'Yes, I know Yakiv quite well,' she admitted. 'It wasn't him. The young woman was accompanied by a much older man.'

'Did you recognise this older man?' asked Erik. Galina hesitated for so long it became embarrassing. 'Well, did you?' he persisted.

'I believe him to be Yakiv's father.'

'George Simmons,' murmured Erik. 'Perhaps better known to you as Yegor Balanchuk.' The same Yegor Balanchuk who had wrongly given him the AUGB's address as being in Holland Park Avenue, maybe in the hope he would not follow it through.

'Yes, Yegor Balanchuk.' There was still a reluctance in Galina's admission. 'Mr Balanchuk is a lovely old man.'

'I know, I've met him,' agreed Erik. Galina seemed to relax a little at this.

'His family suffered greatly in the Holodomor.'

'Yes, I know that too. Nonetheless you have to report this visit to the police.'

'The police,' exclaimed Galina in horror.

'Yes, the police,' confirmed Erik. 'This must have been one of the final sightings of Anna Parker.'

'Well, I'm not a hundred per cent sure it was her.' Galina began backtracking.

'Report it to the police, Galina,' asserted Erik before ringing off.

After a quick return update to Veronica on the special phone, Erik asked Celia to ring Anna's parents and check with them if their daughter had visited them in London last April.

'Has Anna been found?' was Mr Parker's first question.

'No, no,' conceded Celia. 'We are just checking a few more details.'

Celia was still shaking her head as she switched off her phone. 'They've not seen Anna for almost two years,' she told Erik.

'Let's walk awhile,' suggested Erik.

'Anna was in London and she didn't bother to visit her parents?' asked Celia in amazement.

'There must have been a good reason for that.'

'However, she is very involved with the Balanchuks.'

'Very.'

'With Jacob especially, I presume.'

'Presumably. They sailed together and were of an age.'

'Could it be that they are all involved with the bombing of the *Bettina*?'

'It is beginning to look that way.' Erik finally allowed a suspicion he had been reluctant to voice.

'But why?'

'The Holodomor.'

'But that was eighty-six years ago,' exclaimed Celia.

'Some things are never forgotten.'

'But Anna wasn't with Simmons in his rooms at Gouvia Marina,' pointed out Celia.

'No, he will have secreted her elsewhere. He must have given her the Russian thimble before he arranged for her to disappear. No doubt the intention was to send it to her mother in compensation for the loss of her daughter.'

'But how could she have done such a thing to her own mother, hurt the Parkers so much?'

'Infatuation can cause people to do all sorts of things. Infatuation is a dangerous thing,' said Erik pointedly.

'Is that message intended for me?'

'Not at all. It is a statement of fact.'

'Are you saying Anna Parker couldn't help herself?'

'No, I am trying to explain how she possibly became involved. No doubt she was swept away by Jacob and his ideology. People do strange things once they are caught up in a fanatical stream. And you yourself found him charming, charismatic.'

'Not to the point of murdering innocent people.'

'Maybe they weren't regarded as innocent by the Balanchuks.'

'What? A young Greek boy?'

'Collateral damage.' Erik bit back on the words for a second time.

'I hate that expression.'

'You and Veronica both.'

'God help me if I share any sentiments with her.'

'She articulates accepted norms, you really feel them.'

'"Norms", me?'

'Yes, essentially you are a very moral person.'

'Let's walk back to the boat,' she told him, waving off the compliment. 'And, whatever you say, I hate to think the Parkers' daughter was involved in any of this. They are such decent people.'

'Fancy a sail trip back to Corfu?' Triton One asked them as soon as they stepped aboard the catamaran. 'We've had a sighting back there on the island.'

'A sighting of whom?' asked Erik.

'Now that would be telling. Let's keep it a surprise.'

'Whom?' Erik insisted.

'Two old friends of yours.'

'Not Boris and Trofim?' moaned Celia.

'The very same,' laughed Triton One.

'But why are you still so interested in them?' asked Erik. 'I thought they had gone back home.'

Triton's strong American jaw clamped tight. He obviously was not going to reveal anymore information.

Erik slumped back into a canvas boat chair. Now it made sense why the Cousins had them check out the Villa Elina.

They had sent them for final confirmation of what they suspected all along. They must have had tabs on Boris and Trofim, lost them, and guessed they had gone AWOL but not actually returned to Russia.

'But you led us to believe ...' began Celia.

'Supper is almost ready and you can tell us about your day,' announced Triton Two.

'I guess we are in your hands,' conceded Erik. 'By the way, Adras Christakos recognised your photograph as the man he served at the bar just before the bomb blast.'

CHAPTER TWENTY-THREE

Under the cover of darkness *Poseidon's Secret* slipped out of Gaios harbour bound for Corfu. The crossing must have been calm because Celia slept soundly until dawn the next morning. Sunshine shone through the porthole warm on her face. She washed and dressed in shorts, a cotton shirt and her walking shoes, and went up on deck to find they had anchored—where? Somewhere totally unfamiliar to her.

'Where are we?' She asked the only other person seemingly awake.

'Just off Agni in north eastern Corfu,' explained Triton Four.

'It's lovely, so peaceful.'

'Especially at this time of year,' he agreed. 'See, that's Albania across there on the right.'

'But what are we actually doing here?'

'I'd better leave that to my colleague to explain.' Guarded again. 'How about some breakfast?'

'Just a cup of coffee and a croissant for me.'

It was not long before the others surfaced, one by one, sleepwalking to join them in the cockpit area. Only Triton One looked fully awake.

'So what is the order of the day?' yawned Erik, pouring himself a large cup of orange juice from the communal jug.

'Well,' paused Triton One, 'I can tell you now that we have received intelligence that Boris and Trofim have been seen in this area.'

'Doing what?' asked Erik.

'Our informant was unable to be specific but anything those two guys are involved in can be regarded as suspicious and up-to-no-good.'

'Are they still on the island?' asked Celia in trepidation. There was not much she was afraid of in life but after the Russians had kidnapped her, forced her to go with them to Villa Elina, made her feel totally small and vulnerable, she had developed something akin to post traumatic stress disorder at the mention of their names.

'You'll need to change into trousers for this expedition,' Triton One told her.

'What expedition?' asked Erik.

'All will be revealed soon enough.' A tight Triton One attempted a reassuring smile.

All six of them helped launch and piled into a large inflatable. It was early morning, late in the season, as they crunched across the pebble beach at Agni. No one was about until a man emerged from a coppice of cypress trees. He was wearing a dark T-shirt, trousers and a Greek fisherman's cap pulled low over his eyes. A blue handkerchief hung from the side of his haversack, which at first Celia thought strange before realising it must be for identification purposes.

Triton One rushed forward to greet him.

'Do you want help with translation?' Erik's offer trailed after him.

Triton One turned briefly. 'That won't be necessary. Draco is fluent in English and is our guide for the day.'

'We are heading for the area of Palea Peritheia or Old Peritheia if you prefer. Unfortunately it involves a bit of a mountain hike. We can drive so far but we don't want to be too obvious,' explained Draco with an American accent.

They waved to Triton Four who had remained in the inflatable and was setting off back to the catamaran.

Draco's SUV was parked behind a taverna. He opened the boot of the Mitsubishi Outlander for Triton One's inspection. Celia was horrified to see four assault rifles and plenty of ammunition stacked inside.

Triton Two saw her alarm. 'Just for extra security,' he assured her.

Erik had seen the weaponry too but said nothing.

They drove on a winding road to Porta, and parked the Outlander at the hamlet of Mengoulas outside a large Venetian manor house. At the back of the vehicle all three Tritons and the guide equipped themselves with the rifles. After a careful examination of each gun, they zipped them into camouflaged cases and slung them over their shoulders.

'We are on an authorised hunting trip should anyone ask,' Draco told them.

'Hunting for what?' asked Erik.

'Wild boar, partridge, thrush, quail, you name it,' shrugged Draco.

Celia screwed up her face in disapproval.

Unfazed, Draco turned to lead the way.

A sweating Celia and Erik struggled up some stone steps behind him, the others seemed to take the steep steps in their stride.

'Come on,' cajoled Triton One.

'We're doing our best,' complained Erik, wishing he had done more workouts at the gym.

From there on the party joined the Corfu trail. Soon they came out on a faint track. They continued up a crest beneath the flanks of Mount Pantokrator—the highest mountain on

Corfu—hardly a word had been spoken since the steps. The only noise came from the occasional scrabble of goats on the rubbly unforgiving ground. The goats caused the Cousins to occasionally twitch on their ever ready weapons.

'Nearly there,' announced Draco, as a mist descended on them blocking views of the Kerkyra Gulf and straits to Albania.

'This cover is perfect for our mission,' Triton One told Draco.

'We have almost reached Palea Peritheia. At one time a lush pastoral location for farming, and a safe hideaway from pirate attacks.' Draco had suddenly transformed himself from Green Beret into tourist guide.

'Yes, looks like a good place for concealment,' replied Triton One, surveying the landscape. 'Water anyone?' he offered. They all shook their heads.

As they carefully made their way down a deep gully, they were surrounded by the ringing bells of flocks of unseen sheep and more goats among the rocks—a sure sign they were nearing human habitation. Just as the houses of Palea Peritheia began to appear through the fog like apparitions from the past, they pulled off to the left and started making their way through a densely wooded area. As they closed in on what looked to be a deserted farmhouse, Draco signalled with a finger across his lips. The Cousins began arranging themselves in a semicircle round the building, crouching behind trees and shrubs.

'What do you want *us* to do?' whispered Erik to Triton One.

'Walk up and knock on the door of course.'

'You are joking?'

'No, I'm absolutely serious. We have no wish to kill the young people who, we believe, are inside that building. If Jacob Simmons is there he knows you, knows you've been looking for him to finish your story. Maybe you and Celia can draw him out into the open safely.'

'Celia? You're not involving her in this?'

'Keep calm and keep you're bloody voice down,' drawled Triton One. 'If you don't want to witness a bloodbath, do as I say. These people are more valuable to us alive than dead.'

That's the real reason, realised Erik. 'And what about us?' he asked.

'We don't consider them a danger to you.'

'But aren't they murderers?'

'They are professional assassins, only concerned with carefully selected targets.'

Erik pulled Celia to one side and quickly explained the situation.

'Are the Russians in there?' Was her first question.

'No, I don't think so. But I suspect Boris and Trofim are the ones who have led the CIA here.'

'Let's get it over with then,' she said. She never failed to surprise him.

Celia was sure she could hear her heart beating in the muffling miasma of rotting vegetation round the farmstead. She and Erik slowly crept from the trees towards the door. Erik gave three hard raps. No response. They could sense the tension of the gunmen behind them. He knocked again. Silence. He looked back charily to the scrubland for support. An expressionless Triton One waved them on.

Erik turned the door handle and pushed.

A rich stench like no other hit Celia and Erik, jerking them backwards in shock. Rotten eggs, rotting cabbage, rotting meat all rolled into one. Erik was familiar with this odour, Celia was not but she guessed what it was all the same. She stepped away as Erik beckoned the Americans forward, flinging the door back on its hinges a swarm of flies bounced off his face.

Four bodies were found, each in a bed. The three young men on the ground floor looked asleep apart from the smell and bright red discoloration of their faces. The Simmonses, aka the Balanchuk brothers, looked as if they must have succumbed to something a few days before. No obvious stab marks or bullets appeared to have penetrated them.

In an upstairs bedroom of the isolated farmhouse, Triton Three found more flies and the body of a young woman with twisted russet braids. There was something almost religious about her pose—a reclining Burne-Jones beauty even in death.

'This one is still alive,' Triton Two shouted across from an adjacent bedroom. 'Barely!' Barely believing his own pronouncement.

A window above the bed had been left slightly ajar. A cool breeze had whipped up and was channelling into the room. Triton Two easily picked up the flopping limp body of the petite girl. He rushed downstairs with her and out into the open yard, where he checked her airway before performing mouth-to-mouth resuscitation.

'Clear the house,' yelled Triton One, as Two and Three worked on the girl. 'Erik, ring one-six-six for the ambulance helicopter. Tell them you have found four deceased people and a young girl in a serious condition. Tell them the police are needed here too as it is a possible crime scene.'

Celia guessed the girl might be Anna Parker from her photograph, from her hair colouring, but she could not be sure. She had never seen anyone so unresponsive—the girl looked shockingly ill.

Triton One began to examine the outside of the farmhouse with Erik and Draco. 'See these flues have been blocked with rags. My bet is those poor bastards have been poisoned with carbon monoxide.'

'The bad guys have done this.' Draco liked stating the obvious, perhaps his linguistic acumen had deserted him owing to a long assignment in Greece. However, laying his rifle down on the ground without further ado, he began shinning up the drainpipe like a Barbary macaque. 'This chimney is stuffed up with garbage too,' he confirmed, peeking down on them over the eaves of the roof.

'The damn Russians,' swore Triton One.

'How can you be so sure it's them?' asked Erik.

'Russian revenge.'

'Revenge for what?'

'The demise of Dmitry Smirnov of course.'

'Are you saying the Russians believed that Jacob, the Balanchuk family, were responsible for the bombing of the *Bettina*?' asked Erik.

Triton One nodded. 'Don't tell me you haven't thought the same?'

'Of course, but without any conclusive proof that would hold up in a court of law.'

'The Russians don't do "conclusive proof" or "courts of law".'

'But why would the Balanchuks do such a thing?'

'Now that is the sixty-four thousand dollar question. The probable reasons are complex, overly complicated to explain here,' replied Triton One, marching back to the yard to report his findings to Triton Two and Three.

Celia placed her own sweatshirt under the stricken girl's head, as the Tritons manoeuvred her into the recovery position. The girl began to vomit. Celia saw this as a good sign. Triton Two was not so sure. He knew only too well that, irrespective of recovery, carbon monoxide poisoning could leave the victim with permanent brain damage.

They heard the thrumming of an approaching helicopter.

'Come on boys, make yourselves scarce,' yelled Triton One. 'Sorry we will have to leave you with this, Erik and Celia.'

'What?' gawped Erik in disbelief.

'Yes, surely you appreciate we cannot be found in a foreign country, armed to the teeth, with four dead bodies on our hands,' confirmed Triton Three.

'This is your story after all,' pointed out Triton Two.

'See you back at the boat,' added Triton One; handing Celia a spare sweatshirt from his backpack.

The Americans disappeared down the side of the gully as the air ambulance helicopter made its descent. Luckily the farmhouse yard was just big enough for it to make a safe landing.

Erik explained that their patient was suffering from carbon monoxide poisoning, and that there were four dead bodies in the house. One of the medics immediately started trying to stabilise the critically ill girl out in the yard, the other went across to the house to check for signs of life. He soon emerged shaking his head.

'Was it you, sir, who requested our helicopter and the police?' he asked Erik in perfect English. Erik nodded confirmation. 'Is this sick young woman known to you?'

Erik shook his head. 'We must get her to hospital straight away. Please stay where you are. The police are on their way.'

The girl, whom Celia still presumed to be Anna Parker or maybe she was just hoping it was Anna, was stretchered up into the helicopter. Her condition remained critical.

As she and Erik mooched around outside waiting for the police to come, Erik picked up a filtered cigarette butt near the farmhouse door. He showed it to Celia.

'I'm sure this is like the ones we found in the soap factory of Anemogiannis at Loggos.'

'What a tragedy this has turned out to be. By the way, what's our story for the police?' she asked.

'The truth. That we are two London journalists who had arranged a meeting with Jacob Simmons to discuss the Paxos bombing, only to discover this,' said Erik, pointing to the house.

'But that isn't strictly true,' objected Celia.

'It is near enough the truth,' said Erik dismissively.

Celia could feel goose bumps forming up and down her arms. 'To think four young lives have been extinguished so easily.'

'Don't forget that the Ukrainians, in turn, possibly took people's lives. Some very innocent lives.'

'I can't get my head round the fact that we all finish up like this. All our senses, smells and the images we absorb over the years, all our unique life experiences come to this, to naught. We finish up as merely empty husks.'

'Unless, you write about them for posterity,' whispered Erik.

The police helicopter whirled above before landing. More police came along the rough tracks in their four by fours in a flurry of dust. They could be heard through the farmhouse open door tut-tutting over the dead bodies, before re-emerging to regard Erik and Celia with both interest and suspicion.

'Those inside appear dead for a few days,' one of the older officers with pips told them. 'How long have you both been here?'

Erik looked at his watch. 'Just under an hour now,' he told him.

'Please leave name, mobile phone number and address where you stay here on Corfu with one of my colleagues.'

Celia left her encrypted cell phone number, Eric the fictitious address of an apartment in Kalami Bay.

The police helicopter crew kindly dropped them off at a boat and car park near the beach. Kalami was only a bay or two along from Agni.

'Do not to leave the island as you might be needed for further questioning at the police station in Corfu Town,' an officer shouted after them above the noise of the rotor blades.

They sat on the beach, still in a state of shock. Erik rang Triton One for rescue.

'You OK?' asked Triton One.

'Yes, yes, we are OK,' muttered Erik with little enthusiasm. 'You really set us up there.'

'We needed you to lure the Ukrainians out. In the event …' Triton One did not finish the sentence. 'We're sending the rib round to get you both straight away,' he announced instead.

'So why did the Russians hold the Ukrainians responsible for Smirnov's death?' Erik asked Triton One as soon as he was on board *Poseidon's Secret*. 'What proof did they have?'

'As I told you before, Russians don't need proof, suspicion will do.'

'I think you at least owe us a full explanation,' complained Erik. 'I don't buy that you knew the Balanchuks were hiding out in that remote farmhouse by monitoring the movements of Boris and Trofim. Those two men were far too professional to allow that to happen. So who told you? How did you get to know?'

'There is no doubt that the Balanchuks *were* responsible for the Paxos bombing,' established Triton One. 'However they were not alone, someone else was pulling their strings.'

'Who?' demanded Erik.

'You must ask your Miss Bruce that.'

'Veronica?' groaned Celia.

'Yes, Veronica Bruce,' confirmed Triton One. 'She is your handler. Now I believe Triton Four has the coffee on. Please sit back and relax. We are about to set sail back to Crete.'

'Why can't Celia and I just get a plane back to England from Corfu?' asked Erik.

'As you well know, as material witnesses, the chances are you would be arrested before you set foot on the plane.'

'Yes,' agreed Erik resentfully, 'I see that.'

'Ultimately we are responsible for you.'

'"Responsible"?' exploded Celia. 'We could have been killed back there.'

'You wanted the story.' *Was that a sneer on the American's mouth?* 'Anyway we were covering you.'

'What about the murderers of Aleixo Xenakis, the Interpol man?' she asked.

'An interesting question. Draco told me that the Greeks have arrested three Athenians for that in the last few days. They were part of Smirnov's smuggling racket.'

Suddenly they heard a familiar rumble—the anchor was being lifted.

'What if the police decide to chase us?' Celia could not get over the idea that things had turned out badly and they could get even worse.

'For one thing the police don't know you are on this big cat, and for another I don't give a damn.' Triton One gave Celia one of his rare and smoothest Clark Gable smiles.

CHAPTER TWENTY-FOUR

6 December 2018. Back to the daily grind. Back to the *click, click,* of roaming mice. Back to flashing computer screens, insistent information flooding in from Reuters and sources around the world.

There were riots in Thessaloniki and the anarchic Athens' district of Exarchia on the ten year anniversary of the police shooting of a 15 year old boy, Alexis Grigoropoulos. A police patrol man and his partner claimed Grigoropoulos threw a bottle at their car. The two officers returned on foot to the scene, one of them saying he merely fired warning shots— warning shots that killed the teenager—despite the culpable officer being given a life sentence, for numerous Athenians this was just another example of never-to-be-forgotten police brutality.

Celia smiled at the thought that perhaps Captain Vasilakis' posting on Paxos was not too bad.

The next day Erik alerted her to another news item: the Greek prime minister, Alexis Tsipras, had gone to Russia on a working visit, his first visit to Russia in three years. After talks held with Vladimir Putin, both leaders expressed hope that the spat between the two countries was in the past. Bilateral agreements were signed, international issues such as the Cyprus dispute were discussed. Alexis expressed to Putin his concern at Turkey buying advanced weapons, such as the S-400 missile system from Russia. Experts noted that

Greek and Russian relations were not as they had been prior to their quarrel. They pointed to the growing importance of Greece's strategic military ties with the U.S. in a situation where military cooperation between Russia and Turkey was in the ascendant.

'It is hard to know these days who is allied to whom,' said Celia.

'Be sure I am firmly allied to you now like a limpet,' replied Erik, holding her gaze.

* * * * *

'We've got her back,' cooed Mrs Parker, sitting by her daughter's bedside in the Royal London Hospital. Celia's eyes welled with tears. They had got her back but at what cost, in what condition? Since her repatriation Anna had failed to regain full consciousness and looked to be in a vegetative state. Her empty stare fixed on the white ceiling.

Still, Mrs Parker was simply glad that they had got her back.

Everything about the room was spotless and soothing, even the cream bed curtains were intended not to upset the patient's equilibrium. The only colour Celia saw in the room was arranged on the top of Anna's locker. Someone had sent a huge winter bouquet of flowers: large headed roses, white chrysanthemums, blue eryngiums, white tracheliums and white antirrhinums with pine, gold asparagus fern, olea europaea and birch. She shot an enquiring glance over at Erik who was sitting opposite. He shook his head.

'Beautiful, aren't they?' Mrs Parker was smiling like a born-again Christian.

'From you?' asked Celia.

'Alas no. I'm not exactly sure who they are from, dear, but there is a note.'

Wishing you a speedy recovery,
From us all at the AUGB

'AUGB—The Association of Ukrainians In Great Britain,' deciphered Celia.

'They'll be from Galina Bondar,' confirmed Erik.

'Well, I don't know who these people are,' beamed Mrs Parker. 'But what a kind thought.'

'Indeed,' agreed Celia.

'Winter can be beautiful,' said Mr Parker ambiguously. Erik and Celia were uncertain if his comment was intended to be profound or not. After all it did look as if their daughter was in the winter of her life.

Erik reached forward and squeezed Mrs Parker's hand.

* * * * *

Following their hospital visit, Erik and Celia had been invited to Veronica's castle in the sky—85 Vauxhall Cross—Erik said it should be renamed Veronica's Cross.

After a brief body search and being forced to relinquish their satchels, they were escorted to the higher echelons by burly security. Erik already knew that the building covered 295,000 square feet and was constructed from very tough bombproof man-made ochre granite. There were approximately ten to eleven floors above ground and reputedly at least five floors underground housing a command centre, labs, workshops and so on. The green-tinted windows were triple glazed to safeguard against laser and radio frequency flooding techniques, and there were many more preventions in place which he was not privy to. Nevertheless, he whispered to Celia, as they rode the lift, the Real IRA had attempted to breach LEGOLAND with a Russian rocket back in 2000. There had been no deaths and little success.

'I don't think the police will press charges against Anna Parker,' shrugged Veronica dismissively. 'Any barrister worth their salt would argue she is unfit to plead, and that she was coerced into an act of terrorism by Jacob Simmons.'

'And she is in the winter of her life not yet twenty-four,' muttered Erik.

'Well, she did rather bring all this onto herself,' replied Veronica, her expression attempting a brief flash of commiseration. 'Coffee, tea?' she snapped. Erik and Celia shook their heads. 'I understand you have had a rather trying time with the Cousins in Greece.'

'You could say that,' retorted Erik.

'So Boris and Trofim were assassins all along,' interrupted Celia. Celia who was never too willing to engage with Veronica.

'Indeed, Fedorov and Kozlov are just that. Although I doubt we will ever bring them to justice.'

'I asked the Cousins how the Russians knew that the Balanchuks had bombed the *Bettina*, and killed several other innocent people just to get at Dmitry Smirnov. They said I should ask you,' said Erik.

'Did they indeed,' sniffed Veronica. 'It is an extremely complicated story.'

'That's what they said.'

Veronica carefully lifted a large photograph out of her top draw and held it up. Celia recognised it as a copy of the same photograph the Americans had showed them.

'I believe you and the Cousins have seen a resemblance between Alec Guinness and this man.' The side of Veronica's mouth almost twitched into a smile. 'Well, I can tell you that your Smiley is in fact Alon Rubin, one of Mossad's senior operatives. Rubin is a strange Ukrainian hybrid having a Jewish maternal grandmother and a Kulak grandfather. As a young man he decided to settle in Israel. Fluent in Ukrainian, he was sent by Mossad to investigate the rise of the neo-fascist Right Wing Sector there. A history buff, Rubin became fascinated by Stalin and the Holodomor. This is when he made the connection between Dmitry Smirnov and Agavva Bychkov. Like the Balanchuks he identified Smirnov as being a descendent of Commandant Bychkov, a man responsible for committing many atrocities against his relatives in the early 1930s,' explained Veronica. 'But more significantly Mossad had had their eyes on Smirnov for several years. They suspected him of running arms to both the Sunni backed Hamas and Shiite Hezbollah. Here was an opportunity. However they didn't want Israel to be directly implicated in the death of a Russian national and friend of Putin's, so they looked around for someone else to do their dirty work.'

'The Balanchuks,' sighed Celia. 'Mossad coerced the Balanchuks into bombing the *Bettina*.'

'Yes, with the help of Rubin, father George, sister Alexandra, Jacob and his two brothers had an old score to settle with Bychkov and his descents. The people of Kharkiv have long memories and traditions of honour.'

'And Anna Parker?'

'Anna got sucked into the group because of her relationship with Jacob.'

'The group? What exactly is their ideology?' asked Erik.

'An overwhelming hatred of Russia,' explained Veronica. 'The Balanchuks always belonged to a pro-western clan back in the Ukraine, no doubt owing to their history.'

'So this Rubin character gets away with it.'

'Yes, I guess he is hiding in a kibbutz somewhere,' Veronica snorted contemptuously.

'So it must have been Mossad that alerted the Americans to the Ukrainian hideout in Palea Peritheia,' reasoned Eric. Veronica nodded. 'The Balanchuks had served their purpose,' he concluded in disgust.

'True, but it is fair to say that the Cousins—and perhaps not even Mossad—had any idea that the Russians had got to them first,' pointed out Veronica.

'And the Greek Interpol officer, Aleixo Xenakis?' asked Celia. 'The Russians told me they had witnessed him being thrown off the Tripitos Arch by the Smirnov smuggling gang.'

'That could well be so. But without Fedorov and Kozlov to testify it will be difficult to bring a charge of murder against the three Athenian men. However, I understand the Greeks have enough evidence against them to indict them for international smuggling.'

'So what were the Smirnov gang smuggling?' asked Erik. 'Fedorov and Kozlov led us to believe diamonds; Greek sources suggested something more sinister was being shipped to Palestine.'

'Your Greek friends were nearer the mark. Smirnov was in fact smuggling sophisticated mining drills and equipment to Hezbollah to dig tunnels under the Lebanese and Israeli border.'

'Not on the *Bettina*?'

'No, no, of course not. They were using container ships ostensibly carrying wheat into the Port of Beirut.'

'So Hezbollah not Hamas were the beneficiaries.' Erik was surprised.

'Correct.'

'No doubt a worthwhile operation.'

'Correct again. These tunnels would allow weapons and Hezbollah fighters into northern Israel unopposed. By the way, Celia ...' Celia nearly jumped out of her skin: this was one of the few occasions Veronica had chosen to address her directly. 'We've got to the bottom of your threatening phone calls. My people found out that George Balanchuk made them. We found a simple voice changer toy hidden in his house.'

'"Mr Balanchuk is a lovely old man",' murmured Erik.

'Well, lovely old men don't always do lovely things,' said Veronica with characteristic cynicism, her hearing as sharp as ever. 'Mr Balanchuk is in custody at the moment for threatening behaviour, making nuisance calls and possibly for an act of terrorism.'

'The parcel bomb,' acknowledged Erik.

'Yes, but we might not be able to make that stick. No doubt he sent you that rat in the box too, Celia. We are undecided how to proceed with him. He and his wife have lost their entire family. In the end it might depend on whether or not either of you wish to press charges.'

Celia shook her head. She could not get the image of a bereft Julia Balanchuk out of her mind.

'Husbands do horrible things but it's always their wives who suffer most,' she told Veronica.

'I'm with you there.'

'I'm more interested in writing up our article at the moment,' said Celia.

'Me too,' cut in Erik. 'How much can we use of what you've just told us?'

'Some,' replied Veronica. 'Your reward for helping us.'

'Great!' exclaimed the journalists with one voice.

'Subject to my approval of course,' stipulated Veronica.

'Of course, your approval,' moaned Erik.

Veronica ignored him. 'Strange, don't you think, ultimately it looks as if only one homegrown English national is an innocent victim in all this?'

'The *Bettina's* crewman, Robert Perceval,' filled in Celia.

Veronica nodded a glance of admiration in Celia's direction; her one and only indication of esteem. 'Exactly, Robert Perceval. Perhaps you could approach the story from a Perceval perspective.'

'Speaking of tunnels,' said Erik.

'No, the answer is no. I know what you are going to ask me, Erik. You ask me the same question every time.'

'Well, is there a tunnel between here and Whitehall?' persisted Erik.

'If I knew I wouldn't tell you. Is he always like this?' Veronica asked Celia.

'Always,' chuckled Celia. Finally Veronica had acceded proprietorship.

Now they had got the conditional go ahead for the Paxos story. After collecting their satchels at reception, they skipped out of Vauxhall Cross like schoolchildren freed for the day.

'So Gorgias the Nihilist, who knew nothing according to his friend Nicos, had been right about the involvement of Israel's Institute for Intelligence and Special Operations in the bombing of the *Bettina*,' Erik told Celia as they waited for a taxi.

'But he was wrong about the details of the smuggling operation.'

'How could anyone have known? We were all wrong about that.'

They took a taxi along the south bank of the Thames. They asked the driver to put them down near London Bridge. It cannot have taken them much longer than six minutes but cost Erik twelve pounds. He gave no tip.

Crossing the bridge and looking down into the ponderous murky water, a thought suddenly struck Celia. 'Why is she letting us go ahead with this article?'

'Who, Veronica?'

'Of course Veronica.'

'Because of this,' he said, waving at the security barriers on either side of them. 'Since the June 2017 attack on here, the Service has been at pains to show the public they are ahead of the game whenever they can.'

* * * * *

Scoop, scoop, scoop, was playing on Nelson's smirking lips the next morning. Sales figures for the *London Evening Record* had taken a hit lately. A story of spies, terrorists and bombs was just what was needed.

The newsroom itself was humming over the vague possibility that something big was afoot.

'Veronica has insisted on passing the article before we go to print,' Erik explained to Nelson and Gatsby.

'Take your time,' instructed Gatsby magnanimously. 'Too much jolly holly stuff at the moment. The article will be perfect for the New Year editions.'

'Approach it from the personal, the human angle,' said Nelson.

'You sound just like Veronica,' Erik could not resist saying.

Ignoring Erik's barbed observation, Nelson continued beaming, continued wishing the article was his to write. 'Above all, make a thorough job of it,' he told him.

Erik remained locked onto the political side of the story like a heat-seeking missile. It had already been in the news that Russia had backed Israel's security concerns over Hezbollah tunnels dug under the Israel-Lebanon border, urging Lebanon to resolve the issue. Erik learnt later, from a Lebanese source, that Russia had secretly told Lebanon 'to keep the border quiet'. Hezbollah's support of Bashar al-Assad's regime, along with Russia, politically and physically collided with Hamas soldiers fighting against the Syrian leader's regime. Hezbollah had expelled Hamas out of Lebanon in 2013. But in the complex changing allegiances in the Middle East both Hezbollah and Hamas were now paying lip service to—surprise, surprise—the Iranian giant.

Erik had drawn the short straw for Boxing Day and had been chosen to man the news desk. As Celia had decided to visit her parents in Lancashire for a family Christmas, Erik did not mind too much.

Whether by fate or choice, it was during this western holiday period that Russia chose to openly condemn Israel a second time in less than four months—this time for an airstrike on a Syrian arms depot—claiming that the 'provocative actions of the Israeli air force directly threatened two (civilian) airliners'.

Simultaneously Erik's and Celia's mobile phones buzzed with a simple text message at 10 a.m. that morning.

Please go ahead with article unabridged.

Shortly after, Erik's phone rang.

'I am on my way back to London,' Celia told him.

Background to the Terrible Events in 20ᵗʰ Century Ukraine

Before researching this novel I had never heard of the Holodomor—in Ukrainian *holod* means hunger and *moryty* extermination—neither had I fully grasped the terrible deprivations in the Ukraine caused by Stalin's agricultural collectivisation programme, started in 1929.

That changed as I waded through horrific images of starvation and even cannibalism. Robotic town's folk walked past dead bodies on the streets of Kharkiv. Corpses of farm labourers lay sprawled across fields. But the main target of Stalin was the Kulaks—wealthier peasants who might own 24 acres of land or more—as well as any farm workers in rural communities who resisted collectivisation. Above everything else, Stalin feared Ukrainian nationalism. He feared rebellion led by the Kulaks and declared them 'enemies of the people'. They were made homeless, every possession taken from them, even their pots and pans. It was forbidden by law to help dispossessed Kulak families. Many were deported by rail in cattle trucks to slave camps. Arrests, expropriation of property, deportations and executions spread to all peasants who resisted orders to join collective farms. By 1931, 75% of Ukrainian peasants were working in collective farms, where productivity fell and wastage increased, at the same time as grain quotas for state use were being increased. Draconian quotas set by the Russians led to famine on an unimaginable scale. When those workers left behind were denied even their own grain to eat, they took to eating each other. A Ukrainian female doctor wrote that she too was so hungry and desperate she was on the point of cannibalism herself. I have seen photographs of peasants standing behind tables with severed heads and other body parts for sale. I have seen starving children standing in line with stomachs the size of women in the latter stages of pregnancy. I have seen mass grave mounds in the Kharkiv district photographed by an Austrian chemical engineer, Alexander Wienerberger, working there during the Holodomor.

Estimates of the number of dead vary: partly because records were falsified or destroyed or simply stopped being kept, and partly because of uncertainty about how many deaths were directly attributable to starvation. But according to the Association of Ukrainians in Great Britain, at the height of the famine in the spring of 1933, 17 people died each minute, 1,020 people died each hour, 24,480 people died each day.

I can quote various statistics incessantly but it is the personal images that are left to haunt the mind.

OTHER TITLES BY THE SAME AUTHOR

ARAM

ARAM is a true story of class and religious bigotry, incest and murder. The story unfolds through the investigative eyes of Felix Kendle.

R v Houseman, Aram and Terry was the sensational cause célèbre of eighteenth century England. After his co-defendants had turned King's evidence, Eugene – a brilliant linguistic scholar – conducted his own defence, attacking the doctrine of circumstantial evidence and so making legal history. The nineteenth century saw Thomas Hood's poem, *The Dream of Eugene Aram*, in print and Lord Lytton produced an imaginative work based on the same subject. In the early twentieth century, Aram was the subject of three melodramatic silent films.

What exactly did happen when a young shoemaker, and a historically ignored travelling Jewish servant-boy, simply vanished on that snowy night back in 1745? With the help of extensive research and a lot of luck, the writer has done her best to solve a cracking mystery that has intrigued generations.

Brilliant book, fantastic read.

A readers review

This award-nominated Dales author hopes not only to entertain but solve a real-life murder mystery from the 18th century.

Graham Chalmers,
Weekend Editor of the Harrogate Advertiser

THE FALCON WITH A VIRGIN'S FACE

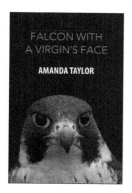

Fifteenth century England is in turmoil with the noble houses of York and Lancaster vying for the throne. Following one of the bloodiest battles in history, an oxcart travels east from Skipton Castle. It carries a farmer, his wife and a seven year old boy. The boy is Henry, Lord Clifford, son of the man who has recently slain the new king's favourite younger brother. Henry is fleeing for his life and will be pursued for the next twenty-four years by Edward IV and Richard III. This is the stuff of legend.

I read this book in just two days; it is impossible to put down, especially for someone so familiar with the places central to the story - Barden Tower, Bolton Priory and Skipton Castle. This is a fascinating imagining of a very turbulent time in our history and I finished the story wanting more.

The Duke of Devonshire

www.amandataylorauthor.com